Fountain's Edge

Paul M. Salvatore

Published By

AM PUBLISHING

First Edition
Copyright © 2014 By Paul M. Salvatore
All Rights Reserved

ISBN: 978-0-9850514-1-9
Library of Congress Control Number: 2014936401

To:
Lynn Simon, who helped to free my mind.

And, of course, my Dear Natalie,
Who had to put up with me as I kept
Going on and on about a make believe story.

TABLE OF CONTENTS

PROLOGUE

"I can't breathe!"

The sound was more choking than speaking; she was getting worse. Julen was a normal twelve-year-old girl only three or four weeks ago. Now everything was changed as she started this downward spiral into the darkness of ever decreasing health.

"Julen, darling, what can I do for you?"

He knew that this question was more to help him feel better, than for her. There was, at this point, not much he could do for her before the next healer arrived. It was becoming unbearable, watching her fade away behind curtain after curtain of sickness.

The days before she began showing symptoms were average days of childhood play. She and her girlfriend were roaming the hills and beginning to skirt the forest next to the western arm of the Akkerand Mountains. It is too hard to tell children not to go into the forest. Fairy-tale stories of dragons and goblins that live behind the wall of trees only work for a short time. The curious children had begun to displace their faith in those stories since the goblins never showed themselves. Still, the forest was dark and smelled musty. It could still be conceived that there may be something in there, lurking. Maybe they would try to take a few steps into the green barrier next week.

For now, there were miles of farmland and plenty of things to get into. There were always other people waiting for them to come around questioning how things were made and grown and reaped.

"How do you make a knife?"

"How do you grow corn?"

"Where does leather come from?"

Living in a small community was educating in itself. Everyone was part of the childhood up-bringing. Since everyone needed all the children to learn as much as they could about helping the community, there was always someone who could give interesting facts on their certain tasks of the day. These people were masters of the chores most essential for country living, farming, smithing, and building. The kingdoms were spread out enough that there was no real allegiance to anyone. This was a good thing when it came to being left in peace, but it was not a good thing when there was a need for a more artisanal creation that was not part of the regular textiles that could be fashioned within the community.

Julen and Toc were nearly inseparable. It was not uncommon for the girls to get together and spend entire days away from the circle of huts that made up the village. They would sometimes stay for a day, learning about making horseshoes with the smithy or helping with the picking of vegetables with the many farmers needed to reap the crops. But, because of their numerous interests, they were hard to keep an eye on at all times. It was never certain that they would be anywhere when expected, since they could be with any of the neighbors on any given day.

"Julen, we should try to go into the forest tomorrow."

"I don't know, do you think we'll get into trouble?"

"Not if we don't tell anyone. It isn't going to be bad. My brother told me he did it once. Now he has to work in the fields all day and doesn't have free time for exploring. We should do it before we get assigned some real chores."

"Well, putting it that way makes it seem like we would be missing something if we didn't go."

"Just meet me in the morning tomorrow and we'll go. Bring something to eat in case we stay all day. And don't tell anyone, so we don't get scolded or made to stay with someone to watch us."

So it was set, Toc and Julen would try to venture into unknown territory. The morning was cooler than the previous few days, and there was a fine layer of dew covering the earth. It was a white and green speckled carpet with tracks crisscrossing over the fields from the animals hurrying across before the men began their work for the day. The sky was light grey with some sparse clouding and a blanketing of fog over the area they called home. They set off before anyone could come asking for them to help out for the day.

"What do you think we will see in there?" Julen asked.

"Maybe we'll find some treasure," Toc said.

She was always searching for treasures everywhere she went.

It didn't take them long to get to the Glacon Forest. It was only a few miles from their homes, and the distance was over the fields they were familiar with. Their tracks were added to the tracking from the animals. Some of the tracks went into the forest; others came out of the forest.

When they got to the edge of the tree line, they found that the air was even cooler here than around the huts. The fog here was thicker and had not burned off yet. They decided to sit at the edge of the forest and have some breakfast while they waited for it to warm up and displace the fog.

After they had finished, they realized that the fog was only slightly thinner but still ominously present.

"Are you sure we should go in?" Julen asked, knowing exactly what the answer would be.

"We won't find any treasure out here. Let's go exploring!"

With that, Toc stepped into the forest and disappeared into the fog. Julen hurried right after and found that the fog was only gathered at the first few trees. Just beyond the first trees was a clearing and then bramble before more trees. Toc was waiting right there and was smiling.

"We're in the woods!" Toc said.

"That wasn't so hard," exclaimed Julen, as they both started to giggle.

They started tromping through the thistle but found it more bothersome than expected. It began to scratch their legs up, and soon they were both irritated.

"There aren't any trails through this brush," complained Toc.

"I bet these woods haven't seen any humans in a thousand years!" remarked Julen.

She was becoming enchanted with being away from the village and having an adventure like the old great explorers. They continued on and were pleased that the day was beginning to warm up. They found some water, but it did not look like the kind of water that was good for drinking. The bog was covered in mossy algae and smelled of sulfur. There were some toads sitting on the edge of it, and they all began slipping into the mire when the girls approached it. Toc was just getting to the edge when there was a splash right next to her.

"What was that?" Toc asked, reeling away.

"I found a stone and threw it in!"

"I bet I can find a bigger one!"

They each took a few turns throwing in some of the stones they could find around the swamp. Each time the splashes seemed to get bigger and the smell seemed to become a little more putrid. The mossy algae was beginning to look pocked, like the craters of the moon.

"I want to find a really big one and then we can move on," said Julen.

They moved away from the shoreline looking for a rock. And when they found a suitable one, they saw that they would both have to pry to free it from the earth. They had gotten it levered up a little when something flashed out from under the rock and darted past Julen.

"That thing scratched me!" Julen screamed.

"What? What thing?" Toc replied.

"That!" Julen pointed to the ground.

It was hard to see at first because it blended in so well. But there it was, a few feet away, sitting on guard and looking at the two intruders.

3

It was a four legged, furry animal resembling a squirrel but with four eyes and a forked tail that was shaped like a 'Y'. It was hissing and pawing the air.

"We must have upset its nest under that rock," said Julen. "It hurts."

"Let me see...It is so hard to tell, even, where it might have gotten you. Our legs already have some other scratches because of the weeds, and they are so dirty with the pond mud. I didn't realize how dirty the forest was."

"It's right there," Julen complained, pointing at her leg and beginning to show tears around her eyes. "And it burns."

"Maybe we should be getting home then to get cleaned up."

They were more careful on the way toward home. After that, it seemed more like the old forest that their fathers had told them about. They were scanning in all directions for things to jump out at them. They kept hearing all the sounds now that didn't seem so terrifying as when they had just entered the forest, full of excitement.

Toc said meekly, "We are going to get into trouble, aren't we?"

Julen was thinking the same thing, "I am going to have to tell my father where I was and what happened and how I got hurt."

She was beginning to cry now, more at the thought of being in trouble than the pain in her leg.

When they arrived at the edge of the village, Julen had gained some composure back but was feeling a little dizzy. They got to her hut and she burst through the doors and into her father's arms sobbing. She told him everything that they had done and apologized profusely.

"It's alright, Julen" he cooed.

The next day, Toc was back to visit and to ask if Julen could come out to play. She had gotten a scolding, but was not severely punished. She promised to be on better behavior and remain within eye sight of the village; no more adventures.

"Lorn, can I play with Julen today?"

"Not today, little Toc," Lorn said. "She hasn't been able to get out of bed today. You can check in again tomorrow if you'd like."

The night before, when Julen arrived home, she had washed her legs off in the basin and then gone to bed after dinner. In the morning, she was complaining of a headache and had the chills. When she rolled down the blankets from her bedding, she saw that her ankle was swollen to twice the normal size, and the scratch on her leg was beginning to ooze.

"Julen, you should stay in bed and leave the covers up to keep yourself warm. I'll make you some tea."

Lorn was a farming man. He was a hard worker, and all he had to look forward to was caring for his darling little girl. Now that she was feeling ill, his duty was to keep her comfortable. But he didn't know how he would make her feel better. The symptoms were showing for a common ailment, and rest was what was needed. The exception was that the wound on her leg was impressive and needed attention. The next day the healer of the area came around. He smelled the wound and looked at the now shivering girl. He said he needed to make a salve from some roots and other ingredients Lorn had never heard of. The healer put the salve over the wound and said he would return the next day.

Over the next few days, Julen became even worse. Her shivers were now becoming more like convulsions, and she was complaining of an aching in her stomach. The vomiting started after that. She was so weak that when she needed to purge herself she couldn't even stand. She was laying in her bed full time now. A few times she would use some of her spare energy to call out for food or water, but she could not always control herself to keep it in her belly.

The healer said that her condition was more serious than previously expected, and that she would need medicine from the apothecary in one of the towns in Sehaida or Gildesh. The distance was long and would take some time to cover. The medicine was expensive, but the community would band together to get it.

After a week of dehydration, the aching in her abdomen subsided. She was feeling happier that she wasn't constantly leaning over the side of her bed. But now when she talked, there was a deep clattering in her lungs. She began to cough violently and sometimes would bring up mucus. Her coughing was sporadic for another day and then became more consistent. She was beginning to have a headache more often, and when she coughed there was blood mixed with it. She had broken some blood vessels in her left eye, and now she looked like she was in pain.

When the apothecary arrived from Sehaida, he said that she would need the medicine, but that he had never heard of a symptom track lasting this long or including this many problems.

"The medicine is good sir, but I must say that I feel there is more at work here than just one ailment. She may have multiple things going wrong at the same time. Surely you can agree that she has something wrong with more than just her coughing. Consider her head, stomach, lungs. There may be no medicine to cure all of that."

"Is there nothing that can be done?" Lorn was looking tired and his eyes were saddened.

"You must take her to the Fountain!"

5

"The Fountain?"

"Forgive me…If you have lived in such a small community your entire life you may not have ventured past your own countryside. The Fountain is sacred and known by most of the peoples among the lands. It is a healing fountain!"

"Then we can save her!" Lorn exclaimed, nearly knocking over a chair when he stood up.

"The Fountain is sacred and has been around for as many years as history has in her books. It has the power to heal. In fact, some of our medicines have a small amount of this precious water as a base. In Julen's case, I don't think there is enough of it here to reverse her symptoms."

"But she is in worse condition every day. Can she make it there?"

"This is a chance you will have to take. The trek is over the plain and through the foothills to the base of the mountain range. There is a climb to a plateau, and then there are mountains from that base to the clouds. The Fountain starts at the summit of the higher mountains and cascades down elegantly into a basin on the plateau. You may make it there in time, but if you leave her here, she may not last long enough for you to return."

"Then we must make haste!"

** ** ** ** **

The next few hours were gone in a blink of the eye. Lorn had gathered his small collection of belongings and outfitted his cart. He borrowed a pulling horse from one of his neighbors, who was also a farmer. After that, he fashioned a cover for his cart to keep the conditions from attacking them during the haul and to give Julen a more comfortable place to ride in. She was starting to look ashen now, and he made sure that she had enough blankets for the cool nights.

He wasn't much of a hunter, so he brought along as many loaves of bread and dried fruit and meats as he had. He could always try fishing if the journey lasted longer than planned, but that would undoubtedly take him away from his goal. The ocean to the west and the river Triffin were equally far away from his path toward the Vitirral Mountains and the up to the Fountain.

Lorn and Julen traveled north for two days before they came across a caravan. They were a roving band of gypsies. The gypsies were a grouping of about thirty people with a few covered wagons and many animals. There were a plethora of dogs and many horses and cattle.

They were a moving collection of rubbish. Their dress was garish and unmatched. When they caught up to them, someone was handing out vegetables. "Not a bad crop this year. We got enough vegetables to last a few weeks and plenty of corn." "We need some meat to get us through the winter months. Maybe we can ambush a bear and salt the meat." "The foothills aren't far away and the caves there will provide us with shelter once again."

Lorn could hear the rest of the conversation, even from his cart several yards away, and was amazed at the ramshackle scavenging way of life. Living in caves and eating bear was not part of what he called routine living. His routine was sitting by the fire during winter after a long season of harvesting in the fields. As long as they harvested enough food for the community, all was well; and there was a lot of sharing to go around.

There was no way of getting around the caravan unseen, so he just waited until they spotted him.

"You there! A lonely stranger on the road?"

There was no hiding; they were the only cart for miles around. Lorn jumped off of his mount and squared himself. He was no match for all of them. His play would be friendship and bargaining if need be.

"I mean no harm. I am traveling north to the Fountain."

"We are also traveling north for the winter. You can join us if you have something to offer. If you don't want to join us, perhaps we can take a look at what you have under the cover and see if you want to change your mind."

"I have no possessions, save for the blankets that are warming my daughter. I can work for you, but please do not hurt my daughter. She is very ill."

"Very well, a bargain then…We'll offer you protection for the amount of work you put in. But you just keep your cart back and away from ours. If she is sickened, we don't want you very close to us. And you won't receive any food from us. You stick to yourselves, but you report for duties of the day at sunup."

So it went for another two days until they got to the foothills. Lorn was put through near continuous labor, and they were kept slightly separated from the caravan. When they arrived at the foothills, there was another mass of people in a camp. There were many tents set up, and there were people milling around and having friendly conversations.

"What is going on here?" asked Lorn. "Are these your people?"

"Nay, these people are believers of the Fountain, and they are

7

making the annual pilgrimage to it for prayer. They mean you no harm, but the Fountain is sacred to them."

"There are so many!"

"Aye, normally the Fountain is secluded and peaceful. Since it is free to use at any time, there are never more than a handful of people who gather here over the course of a month. You could visit it in total privacy without another person around. But this time of the year is different."

"I have to get through them. There may not be enough time for my daughter!"

"Whoa stranger…You may have a pressing need, but these people may be in the same lot as you. You will have to wait your turn, or there may be consequences. For now, we will set up camp and then you may do as you please."

They settled in and set camp in their normal fashion, with the gypsies in a tight circle and Lorn's cart off to the side. When morning came, the gypsies were gone, having struck camp in the middle of the night.

"They took my horse!" Lorn yelled at no one in particular. "Those worthless thieving gypsies and their so-called protection! They were in it the entire time for my biggest possession, and something that I didn't even think of as a bartering tool. Very sneaky of them, letting me do their work and then stealing my horse as payment." He was raving mad now and pacing around his cart.

Some of the pilgrims looked in his direction. Lorn was making a scene and disrupting their ritual. He started towards the base of the plateau and found that there was a massive staircase hewn out of the stone. The sides of the stairway were nearly perfect vertical cuts as they climbed up along with the steps. The steps were cut directly into the mountain as if a giant knife had cut down through it, leaving a perfectly square opening in the facade. The stairway was wide enough to fit an entire cart through with plenty of room to spare. When he climbed to the top step, he had the sensation of peeking over the crest of a mountain to infinity. The plateau was perfectly level; one could see for miles in each direction, with the appearance that it went on forever.

The plateau was also swarming with pilgrims who were closer to getting to the Fountain and casually forming into a waiting line. Still feeling the anger at the gypsies, Lorn decided to leave Julen down at the bottom while he tried to get to the Fountain. Most of the pilgrims were having quiet conversations amongst themselves. They seemed to know one another. Perhaps they were from the same camp, or even, that they knew each other from previous journeys to the Fountain. Lorn used this distraction to get closer to the front of the line. The Fountain was almost in reach. He could hear the falling water now. The Fountain was at the end of the plateau and was elegant, as the apothecary had put it. Lorn had not expected to see how dramatic it was. The mountain behind the Fountain's basin was sheer and stood vertically nearly twice as tall as the plateau he had just climbed. The stream was cascading between two gargantuan pillars which were also hewn from the rock. The pillars were gleaming and showed the beauty of the underlying stone, which when wet, looked flawlessly smooth. The basin was raised on a pedestal and had several concentric layers of rock carved under it. The basin was very much bowl shaped and had layer upon layer encircling the base with the smallest circle at the bottom and growing right up to the lip.

He began to move even closer to it now, mesmerized by the grandeur that he was admiring. That is when he got very forcefully bumped into.

"Hoy! Take your turn there!"

"I didn't see you there," Lorn replied, knowing full well that he was trying to get to the Fountain before the others.

"I saw what you were doing," said the pilgrim, poking his finger into Lorn's chest. "You've been sneaking to the front of this line for a few minutes. And you're getting close to making me angry. Step back now, before you do something else to get me up in arms."

"I need to get to the Fountain, and now you are in my way!" Lorn had had all that he could take at this point.

"You'll wait your turn, like the rest of us. I've got my eye on you now."

The pilgrim placed his hands on Lorn's chest and pushed him back a pace. After the last few weeks of watching his daughter diminish, combined with the gypsies and the amount of pilgrims, it was too much for him to bear. He drew his long knife and took a fighting stance. Before the pilgrim know the seriousness of his actions, he found himself on his back with a knife bearing down toward his neck.

Lorn had crouched and sprung into action, catching the pilgrim off guard. This attack came as a surprise to the pilgrim, since his warning was given and was expected to be taken into a far different manner. Lorn had the low position and caught the pilgrim off balance, knocking him over in the first thrust. Then he brought down his knife and sliced the pilgrim's neck as if slaughtering a cow. The pilgrim went limp but the slaying did not go un-noticed. Blood was all over Lorn's tunic and there were, of course, another hundred pilgrims on the plateau watching and waiting in line.

Lorn picked up the short sword of the pilgrim and brandished it in the air. That was enough of an invitation for the other pilgrims to descend on him. Soon there was a great clamoring and clanging of weapons. Lorn had the power of a boost of adrenaline and was fighting to save his daughter. He was withstanding the onslaught of eight other men. He was purposeful to mind how close he was getting to the Fountain. If he could just get there first, everything would be better. As he inched closer to the Fountain, he could see the number of angry pilgrims swelling and preparing to rush him.

When he finally got to the lip of the basin, he had managed to distance himself from the onslaught. He turned to look into the basin and could see his reflection. At that moment, he could see the sadness in his own face. That was when he felt a pinching pressure in his back.

An arrow had pierced him just under the shoulder blade. It had enough force to spin him around in time for the next two arrows to lodge into his chest. Blood was beginning to soak his shirt as he stumbled backward.

Tripping and weak, he collided into the basin, flipping over the lip and into it, motionless.

** ** ** ** **

Lorn's blood was mixing with the water and swirling like ink into intricate patterns. Then the coloring started to turn black. There was a monstrous thunderclap, and the earth trembled. The pilgrims were shaken to the ground.

The water, which was healing, was now nearly completely blackened. It was changing from life-saving to life-taking. Lorn's blood, spilled by cruel intentions, was reversing the purity of the waters. The Fountain began to ripple and surge in the basin. There was another thunderclap, and the water shot skyward in a column, taking Lorn's body with it. Its last life-sustaining act was to resurrect the man into a dark nebulous cloud.

The cloud slowly descended onto the plateau and began to take a more defined shape. The man who was Lorn was erased and a new being was taking shape. The dark power coursing through him was enlarging his body and ripping slits into the pale blue skin. Powerful energy was emitted from these slits, and they constantly were being healed and opened anew with even more powerful bursts. The mangled body was morphing, transformed by damage, scarring, and open wounds.

When the pilgrims got their bearings and turned to gaze at the

10

Fountain, he was there. Standing at over eight feet tall, he appeared to have a cloak over his shoulders. His bare chest and arms were crossed with scars and slits. Some of the slits were open and were leaking black wisps of noxious smoke. His fingers were long, and they were garnished with black clawed nails. His face was equally scarred, as was the rest of his body, and his eyes were red with fury.

He merely lifted his arm, and the pilgrims were shattered and then blown off of the plateau like seeds in the wind. Their blood sprayed over the plateau and washed over the side of it.

The shockwave from his magic reverberated down the side of the precipice and demolished every trace of the camp below. No one survived the attack.

I

"Have we received all of our responses to the invitations?" The excitement was building for the celebration in honor of the prince, Panalt Dito. It was a special time in his life. His accomplishment was getting to a full twenty years of age, and finally, to the marrying age. The time was nearing for him to pick a mate and begin the sequence of events for preparation to take over kingship of Gildesh.

King Palantine Dito had invitations sent throughout the lands a few weeks earlier for the festivities. Now the event was just on the horizon, only a week away.

"We have received most, my liege. I have been informed that nearly all of the nobles in our nation, and some of them from Caldorn, have accepted the invitation," replied Tobin.

"Has Queen Crissannah Reesh replied in kind then?"

"Indeed, as well as King and Queen Secandor of Strayos."

"What of the invitation for King and Queen Deland?"

"We have not heard from the nation of Sehaida as of yet. But having the royalty of three out of the four major nations is an honor."

"Tobin, my friend, you are always the optimist. What would I do without you?"

"Respectfully Sire, I should say the same to you…"

Palantine and Tobin had been together nearly from the start. They had been the closest of friends even as youths. It was frequent for Tobin to spend a week at a time in the palace with Palantine. Tobin's family was one of many servant houses around the palace performing tasks for the King, Palantine's father. While not objected to, their friendship was unconventional. Palantine's mother and father understood that they may not be able to control every aspect of their son's life.

Before Tobin was ten, however, there was a tragic accident in his own household. His family's cottage had burned down while he was away at the market in the center of Albinion. When he returned from the market, only the chimney was standing and the ruined foundation was smoldering. He called for his parents and searched their meager plot of land for them. It wasn't until he returned the second time that he caught a glimpse of the ring that his mother had worn. When the shock hit him, he fled through the woods running as fast as he could with no regard to his direction of flight or his personal safety. Whipped by saplings and muddied by puddles, he was blinded with guilt that he was not there. Soon he was lost and shaking with terror.

Tobin swore that he would have helped his mother and father escape if he had been there. He came to live then, with Palantine. It was during his adolescence that he made a pact with himself to become strong enough to defend the people he loved. His training sessions were long and grueling. Soon he was a master of the sword, as well as the spear, and could best even Palantine in their sparring.

As they aged, Tobin's mastery of weapons was exceedingly impressive. While Palantine was gifted with the sword and shield, Tobin could seemingly pick up any item at random and put it to deadly use. He was quite the marksmen with a bow and could wield a polearm halberd with success. His delicacy with double swords was as striking as his power to use a broad sword, even one-handed.

As they grew into adulthood, Tobin assumed the role of advisor to Palantine. When Palatine relieved his aging father of his kingly duties, Tobin was ensconced into his own wing of the palace. There, he continued his training. Even as a middle aged adult, he still looked trim and fit. He was graced with the height of six and a half feet and had worked through agonizing hours of training to achieve the physique of a titan. His seafoam green eyes had a twinkle in them that was mischievous and beguiling.

"We had better begin preparation for accommodations of the guests."

"Yes Tobin, have someone see to it that our guests are situated into the east wing. I shall make sure that there is no spillover into your wing, especially since it is beginning to be frequented by my sons."

"I do not mind their presence, Sire. It is another way for us to keep an eye on them, and they are excelling in their training. Both Dur and Tiras are becoming snipers with the bow and have begun to have competitions between themselves. Panalt is taking after you and is mastering the sword, but I have seen him try double swords, as well."

"That is something I see he is taking after you too, then, Tobin."

"He is using a hybrid technique. Starting with the sword and shield, he has modified the handle of his shield to allow for a quick release while holding a knife. This was his own idea, and when he employed it for the first time, I must say that I was caught off guard."

"It does not sound safe to sacrifice your shield for a surprise attack."

"That surprise may be deadly, but I will try to coach him then, my liege, in a manner that does not sound like it came directly from his father."

Tobin chuckled under his breath as he strode away. He did not even begin to tell the King of the twins' new form of attacking.

Maybe another conversation or even a viewing of the sparring would be necessary to exhibit the acrobatic techniques that Dur and Tiras were working on.

** ** ** ** **

The palace was set up in a traditional 'T' formation with east, west and south wings. Its shining white stone walls were balanced by a dark grey crown. To the north was set a garden with high hedges to either side of a majestic pathway, laid with crushed shells. There was a fountain mimicking its cousin of grandeur in the center. The sea was visible from the top parapets of the castle. These were the King's quarters in the rear of the south wing. The immense foyer led into a great hall with surrounding balconies that just preceded the King's southern wing.

There was a wall surrounding the perimeter; it was wide enough for a cart to be drawn along the top for replacement of armaments or ammunition. A lazy river surrounded both the outside and inside of the wall so that a double draw bridge was necessary to bring in goods. The inner moat helped with landscape and décor and made it easier to allow the wall to fade into the outer consciousness of vision.

To the south of the west wing were courts for sparring and jousting. This court was closest to Tobin's wing and was the main training ground for the King's three sons and others needed for specialty tasks in the royal army. To the south of the east wing was a large storage house for weapons and small war machines for defense of the castle. Beyond the wall to the south was a vast forest, which was beginning to show its green bloom in the early spring.

Upon waking in the morning, a collective sigh of relief was given. The sky was crisp, and the air was cool. The day was going to warm up and be a gem. There was always more merry-making if the weather was perfect. If the guests had to hurry through the rain or muddy their traveling garments, the minstrels would have to work all the harder to set the mood.

The procession of guests began in the early morning and continued throughout the day. Palatine had gathered Tobin along with Panalt, Dur, and Tiras to welcome everyone at the stairway into the main entrance.

"Your mother would have been proud today, my son," the King said to Panalt.

"Yes father…I will show her honor."

"I am sure you will. She was always enamored with the castle's appearance and the pride of our country. These events do not happen very often, but we can show the heritage of our nation and of our family. Remember, though, today is a celebration of you. There will be many a mistress ready to fill your house. The nobles have gathered, and each would be honored to give their daughters to the next King of the throne. Choose your Queen wisely."

King Palantine Dito's Queen was Lanna. Fair of skin and short of stature, her brown eyes were attractively inviting. She was the King's sweetheart and had been from even before Palantine's twenty-year-old celebration. Theirs was a secret relationship for years before the marrying age. It was an easy decision for Palantine to choose, when the time came for selecting a mate.

Their first child, Panalt, was born only three years after their matrimony. From then, it was another three years before she became pregnant again, this time with twins. She was so much bigger this time than before, and it was said that she was blessed for the glory she was giving to the kingdom.

Her delivery of the twin boys was difficult and complicated. The baby boys were in excellent health, but she had lost much blood and her recovery was long. She succumbed in the end, only a few months before she was thirty years of age.

The King's grief lasted years and was the cause of concern. He had gained much weight and was frequent with the wine flask. His servants did most of the child rearing in the early years. Palantine had to retrain himself into the general things that were a normal part of his regimen. The thought of raising three children brought only thoughts of sadness and remorse during those first few years.

Gradually, things righted themselves, and he saw that he could take happiness from rearing children. They were a gift to him from his beloved, Lanna. He was as devoted to them as he was to his love, and he could be seen with the three youngsters throughout the kingdom. He was always bringing them to see the various regions under his rule and teaching them things they would be expected to know in adulthood.

Now, many years later, he had lost most of his weight. Only a small bump was the reminder of his weight gain. His face had aged, as all men's do, but now he was beginning to show the rosy red veins around his nose. The wine was just as sweet now as then, but now he knew what the tolerable amount was. His emerald green eyes no longer showed sadness but an appreciation of all that was surrounding him. His fine wrinkles around the eyes were distinguishing, as was the wisp of graying hair at his temples.

Panalt, as an adult, would have made Lanna very proud. He had the physical gifts from both of them. His short cropped, sandy blond hair was the same color as his mother's. His eyes were the combination of theirs, hazel. He had taken a more fair skin tone. He was trim and athletic and nearly six feet tall. There was a fire in him that was admirable to any onlooker. Inquisitive yet decisive, he would make a fine leader some day.

His brothers, Tiras and Dur, had taken more after their father, and each had green eyes with light brown hair. Their build was similar to their brother's but only a few years smaller, as they had yet to put on the muscle of their elder brother. Not as tall as Panalt, they were spry and stealthy and were comfortable using each other in games of deception and logic. They were exceedingly good at teamwork and could work together as one, for nearly any goal.

"Father, who is that approaching in the large coach?" Panalt asked.

"That is Ashlyn Reesh. She is the daughter of Queen Crissannah Reesh."

"Never-mind her, Panalt. Look over there…" Tiras was pointing in the direction of another coach. Dur was pointing at still another.

"Young men, let us try to keep our wits and manners about us!" Tobin interjected.

The King turned in his direction and gave him a wink and a grin of approval. After each coach stopped at the stairway, the occupants were announced by the squire, and they all greeted the King and his family.

"From the land of Caldorn, I present Queen Crissannah Reesh. She is accompanied by her daughter Ashlyn Reesh."

They were then quickly whisked away to their chambers in the east wing of the palace to make room for the next coach in the slow convoy.

"From the land of Strayos, I present King Vernon Secandor and Queen Merkette Secandor. They are accompanied by their son Merion Secandor."

It proceeded in this fashion until the afternoon was beginning and all the coaches were emptied. Tiras and Dur could be heard snickering behind Panalt from time to time. The entrance was deemed successful though, since Panalt, guided by King Palantine, was so respecting of each guest.

The guests found their accommodations to be luxurious and welcoming. They were to be ready for the opening ceremony within the next two hours. The festivity was opened by dancing by some of the King's servants and was followed by a light harp playing during the dinner service.

After the dinner service, the floor was opened up for dancing of the guests, and a less formal attitude was settled on for the remainder of the evening. King Palatine remained at the great head table and looked on with pleasure at Panalt, waltzing with a host of young women from around the country. There were two additional tables of honor set up for each of the other royal families. Palantine noted that the table of King Secandor was occupied by both the King and Queen. The table for Queen Reesh was deserted.

In time, Panalt could be found talking with the princess, Ashlyn Reesh. Tonight she fashioned a dark blue gown flowing to the floor with layered folds of iridescent material. Her dress reached up toward her neckline and circled it with a shining collar of white gems. She had elegant white gloves on that covered nearly her entire arm's length.

"M' lady, Ashlyn. You look stunning tonight."

"Why, Prince...I did not think you would notice me among the other guests."

"Surely you jest. With such beauty and polished dancing, you would be hard to miss. And the Princess of Caldorn is not easily over-looked."

"I thought I would be out-shown by my mother this evening."

"You mother is eye-catching indeed, but she is not on my list of people I must speak with on this evening. May I ask to have this dance with you?"

They began flirting with each other and laughing with grins that told of their attraction to one another.

Once, Panalt was stolen away from Ashlyn by another young lady, who had taken his arm and spun him around. This lasted merely half of a song before Ashlyn won him over with her smile, and Panalt took her back into his embrace.

** ** ** ** **

After some time had passed, Tiras had found the remaining prince at the gathering, Merion Secandor.

"Dur and I would like to challenge you in an archery exhibition."

"Do you mean me?" Merion asked, looking over his shoulder.

"Well, I do not see you participating in the dancing. What would be better than some sport in the training arena?"

"I shall accept, then. These gatherings tend to be long and wearying, especially when you are required to attend by your mother and father."

"Relax," said Dur, "We are not under scrutiny right now. Our presence here is secondary to our brother's. We will not be missed."

"Lead the way, then, my new friends."

Merion was only a year older than the twins. He was at the age that his festival was not far into the future, but he understood that this was not the time to be looking for his mate. And this enterprise of competition was far more alluring than being under the microscope of which actions were deemed to be worthy of royalty, and which were not. This was not his house, and he was not the center of attention. His time would come, and when it did, he would acquiesce to the formal attitude required at those functions.

Merion was not a tall young man, and he fit in well with the other two. They almost looked like brothers themselves. Merion also had brown hair, but it was long and fell almost to his shoulders. His skin was tanned, matching his family and fellow countrymen. The climate of Strayos was much warmer south of the sea and did not have the wind effect of Gildesh. Strayos' geography was mostly plains, and agriculture was the main occupation and hence, export.

The three of them slipped out of the ballroom and headed in the direction of the west wing. After several doors down the main hallway, there was a short corridor that led to a door and then the exterior courtyard. When they got outside, they were surprised by the faded light and drop in temperature.

"I did not think it would get so cold, so fast, after such a warm afternoon," Dur said.

"This was not in my plan for our escape from the banquet," said Tiras.

"You asked me to relax before, now I ask the same of you two," replied Merion. "Have we not found ourselves some amount of freedom?"

The three nodded in agreement and went looking for a proper target. When they got to the storehouse, they were greeted with a gruff voice.

"Would you care for a light?"

Startled, they jumped and looked at each other, preparing to be reprimanded. The voice materialized itself and stepped out of the shadows. Wearing a dark hooded robe, the figure reached his hands up to remove his cowl, revealing that he was an old man.

"It is much harder to strike a target in darkness," he said.

It was then that they watched him conjure a ball of fire into his hand and then light a torch.

"Kelduun!" The awe was apparent in Merion's voice.

"I see it takes a little light for you to recognize me as well," replied Kelduun, giving a slight bow.

"We have heard of you before but have never had the opportunity to meet you in the flesh," exclaimed Dur.

"What are you doing here?" asked Tiras.

"I am preparing to watch a lesson in archery, isn't that true?" asked Kelduun perceptively.

"How did you know that? We told no one what we were planning," stammered Dur. "And why are you not in the ballroom?"

"A wizard knows many things, and the best of them can detect the information needed by simple observation. I need not be in the main hall to deduce the goings-on. Part of our culture is not being in the public eye. I am quite comfortable being behind closed doors and counseling, rather than being brash and outspoken. I do not need to get too close to any one man, nor do I need their approval on what information I deem is necessary. Now carry on and let the games begin!"

The target was a barrel set on its side, on top of a hay bale, about twenty yards away. The first to take a try at it was Tiras. The arrow was well placed and only five inches to the right of the exact center. Dur then took the bow and let fly another well-placed shot, which hit its mark at just over the five inch mark to the bottom. Merion was the last to try a volley and his arrow found the target only 2 inches from the center spot.

"Merion! What a shot! I wasn't trying very hard for my first shot and I didn't want to discourage you!" Tiras cried.

"Say what you want, but I'll wager you cannot beat that mark with your next shot! It looks like you aren't the only marksman here!" Merion was beaming.

They each had another three arrows before they went to retrieve them from the battered barrel. There were two arrows within the two inch mark when they were done and it was agreed that the three of them were nearly equal in their deadly precision.

"Well done, my young friends," said Kelduun. "If you will excuse me, I must leave you for now. I would like to speak with your father before the morrow."

Dur and Tiras looked at each other perplexed, but they felt confident that Kelduun would not let the King know that they were not present during the main portion of the festival.

** ** ** ** **

"Excuse me, My Lord?"

Interrupted by the inquiry, King Palantine turned his head

to find Queen Reesh. She was extravagantly dressed in a white gown covered with accents of layered fabric and flowered embroidery with embedded gems. Her collection of jewelry was exquisite and she was sparkling from head to toe. A thin woman, her skin was pale and her black hair was a contrast to the other softer qualities of her shapeliness. She had sharp blue eyes, the color of the sky, and they were captivating when she glanced in his direction.

"Queen Crissannah! You look simply enchanting this evening."

"Thank you, My Lord. I was wondering if I might join you at your table for a moment?"

"Please, you may call me by my name and drop the kingly titles."

"Crissannah is fine with me as well."

She sat down gracefully, and they faced each other. He was grateful to have some company. He was happy to see Panalt getting on with his evening, but he was equal in noting the other royal families and their actions. King and Queen Secandor were very much in love, and they were never far from each other's side. He noted also that Merion was not in the main hall. The princess, Ashlyn seemed to be entertaining Panalt. Up to this point, the Queen was hard to find in the crowd and could be seen here and there dancing with some of the nobles from both Gildesh and Caldorn.

"Windon, would you please bring us another goblet of wine?"

"Right away, Sire."

"Crissannah, your daughter is as beautiful as you are. The two of you look nearly identical."

"I must say thank you, again. And thank you for such a lovely invitation to a fine gathering. I saw that you were sitting by yourself. I know that Tobin is watchful, and of course you are waited on by your servant. Windon was it?"

He was just returning with some goblets lined with gold and adorned with the crest of the King.

"Thank you, lad," Palantine said, turning back to the Queen. "It has been a long time since a Lady has sat at my table. I am pleased to have you here."

"I also know what you must be going through. The thought of missing someone at a great celebration. As you know it has been four years since Turg fell."

Turg Reesh was the King of Caldorn. He married Crissannah, and she had born Ashlyn before even one year had passed. Times were remembered as fond and plentiful. There was a big business of exporting the various mined goods. Caldorn was known for its mined gold, gems and ore.

King Turg Reesh was an avid hunter, and the awful day of his fall was still in the memory of the Queen and princess. He was with the captain of his army, hunting puma in the Tributary Forest and foothills of the Cysterule Mountains. They had found a den and flushed the cats out, into the forest. They were tracking the cats down when they heard a noise beside them and found the tables turned. The cats were ambushing them and turning the hunters into the prey. They ran until they came to a clearing. Behind them, there were two larger pumas and a smaller one, presumably offspring. As they raised their bows and backed away, the captain tripped over a root and partially fell. The pumas leapt forward and one caught his leg, bloodying it with one scratch. That offender was the recipient of an arrow through the snout and fell nearly instantly.

The King and captain both gathered themselves together and ran toward the sound of rushing water. The captain was limping the entire way and was leaving behind a trail that was easy to follow. When they got to the edge of the Gallendar River, they saw the waterfall as a beautiful refuge, if they could only get to the other side. The King had the captain begin his descent as he scanned the forest for the attackers.

Just as King Turg had turned and begun to breathe normally, the puma surged at him with an aerial attack. The puma had climbed the tree and hurtled itself down on Turg, driving its four paws into his back. It was clawing and tearing gouges through the skin. The force of the attack drove the King over the side of the cliff and over the path of the waterfall. The captain could only watch as Turg Reesh flew over him into the depths. When the captain finally got to the ground level, he examined the aftermath of the fall and saw that nothing could be done. The King was lying over a rocky bed that was breaking the waterfall into rapids at the bottom. The water was turned pink for yards down the gorge.

There was a great clamor then throughout the nation of Caldorn. A nation without a King would be weak. Queen Reesh stepped up and assumed the role of the leader quickly, but her time for mourning was cut short. Over time, she began to feel as though she was abandoned to lead a country that did not want her. Her difficulties, both personal and nationwide were beginning to take a toll on her overall quality of life. She grew wearisome of the blind accusations of not leading Caldorn in the right direction, even though there was not a decline in production of the mining exports.

"Yes m'lady. These gatherings were difficult in the beginning," Palantine said solemnly, "but they have been easier these last few years."

"I think we can agree to that. I now look forward to getting to these events to see how other nations are prospering and to help my own understanding of leadership. I was wondering if a visit to your kingdom in the future would be agreeable."

"My dear Crissannah, you may visit anytime you wish. If not for counsel, our country has many pleasurable areas to visit that your country may not. We have the sea, and you have the sky and the mountains. I must admit it has been a long time since I have visited Caldorn as well."

"Palantine, we may have to remedy that, and soon," she snickered. "I was wondering if we may talk a while on exports and alliances. Perhaps we can get to know each other better and even join our trades?"

"What are you proposing?"

"My mining enterprise is in need of counsel, and I see that the shipyards you have are succeeding mightily. I want your help. I can make it worth your efforts."

"You may not be aware, but Tobin has a fair amount of control in the ship-building industry."

"I am not interested in Tobin, my Lord. I am interested in you," she moved closer to him. "I am proposing a union, not only of our exports, but of our nations."

"And how would that come to pass?"

"With me sitting at your side..."

This was a turn that Palantine was not expecting. The Queen was beauty personified, and her country was in no way inferior to his own. It was an offer which was mixed with repercussions. On one hand, it was almost too good to pass up without second thought. To gain a vast new countryside with a healthy business of mining and combine it with his rich nation and the very way to export these minerals using his own ships was exhilarating. On the other, there may be unrest within his own nation for taking a partner after such a long hiatus.

"Crissannah, you have surprised me tonight. I must take my leave and ponder this for a while."

"My good King Palantine, I hope to hear your decision soon," she smiled at him, capturing his eyes with hers as they each stood up.

** ** ** ** **

King Palantine stepped away from the table and had a curious look of youth in his eyes. He did not want to be surrounded by others at the moment. He told Tobin that he was going to retire to his chambers. With Windon trailing him, he made his way down the corridor to the great staircase leading to his palatial suite. He dismissed his servant shortly before climbing the steps and bade him to attend to Tobin if he had any needs for the evening.

He redressed into his night garments and sat in his chair for a long time. The candles had all but burned to their holders. The sky was as black as pitch, and the room was dimming further with the candles beginning to sputter on their last breaths.

Presently, there was a knock at the door. Almost imperceptible at first, he had to question if he even heard anything. He looked toward the door to his chambers when he heard a second more authoritative knock.

When he opened the door, he was surprised for the second time that night.

"Would you care to entertain a visitor?"

"Crissannah!"

He smiled and gestured his arm into the room with a welcoming motion and then closed the door behind them.

II

King Palantine awoke to find that his bed had emptied itself during the night. There was still a fragrant scent in the air, and this made him smile in spite of himself. His guest was not about to make either of them look disreputable by over-staying and thus being cornered in the King's chambers if another visitor came calling.

His bed was facing to the north, toward the sea, and he could just see some light between a small gap in the curtains. After some effort of dragging himself out of his warm bed, he dressed in comfortable and warming robes. Walking a small distance across the room, he opened the thick draperies and began to squint slightly in the morning light. He then stepped out onto the balcony and gazed over his country and past it into the horizon, where the blue sea reached up to meet the graying skies.

The morning's weather brought on a change, as the spring continued to be unpredictable. The ceremonial celebration had taken place on the best day of the new year, but today looked overcast with low clouds, and there was a chill to the air.

Tobin was already dressed and helping to direct the guests around their quarters. They were each welcome to spend the week at the palace, and some guests took up the offer to do so. They were still trying to sway Palantine to talk Panalt into courting their daughters or some other agreement. Their requests to speak with the King were to be taken in turn, as Tobin had said. They would get their time with him throughout the week. What they did not count on was that Palantine had made a commitment to his son that he would not interfere with him picking a partner. He had seen how some predetermined marriages had gone and would not subject his son to a life of heartache without the woman he loved.

Some of the women were clamoring to be around Panalt. He had gone into the garden area around the fountain and had a host of women around him. They were trying to best each other and be noticed for this attribute or that trait.

Panalt was pleased with himself. He was not acclimated to being the center of attention. He felt almost like a king, even right now. Though he had already narrowed his choices down, this exhibition was fun and could be interesting to see what each of these suitors would say to him.

Conspicuous in her absence was Ashlyn Reesh. She had made her impression the night before, and Panalt did not mind that she ignored playing the game that the others were. She had caught his eye, and he was thinking of her even while in midst of the others.

King Palantine looked down on this scene and thought of his own happy times in his life. He was happy even now, but his happiness was mixed because he was missing a mate. To share those memories with a partner seemed so tempting that he was beginning to be intoxicated with the thought of it. He was daydreaming and relaxing on the balcony when he heard knocking at his chamber door.

He was thinking of his encounter the night before as he opened the door.

"Kelduun! I did not expect you at this hour. These last two days have been full of surprises. How have you been keeping yourself my old friend?"

"Our fifty years of history can attest that I am the same now, as then. I am pulled in many directions at once, but I am still young enough to find a way to enjoy a party."

"When you live for six hundred years, the days must seem so short," Palantine jested with him.

"It is not the length of the days that seem short but the time for sleeping. I have been able to push myself for nearly a full week before sparing a precious moment on sleepy recovery," Kelduun returned.

"Well spoken, my friend. I have seen your dedication to the people and nations who need your services. I may even need to bend your ear with a decision I have to make of my own."

"I will listen to your dilemma, but first I must ask…How long has it been since you sent anyone to the Fountain?"

"My, my…it has been at least a half of a year now."

"Was that before or after the pilgrim's ritual?"

"I believe it was before that. They are always there for so long, and it is hard to get the amount of water that we would like to use for our medicines and such. But, why do you ask?"

"That area is changing. I can't be sure what is going on. There seems to be an odor permeating the land, and there is a darkness surrounding the mountainside. There is magic spilling over the plateau and into the valley. I can feel it."

"As you know, commoners cannot feel magic."

"This is no joking matter, King. And you are a commoner by no means. Some magic caresses you as would a down feather. This magic is grating, as is a bone saw. Dark, foreboding, and menacing, it is screaming to retreat."

"Forgive me, comrade. I did not mean to insult. Merely that we are not in tune with such anomalies. What can be done?"

"I must speak with King Deland at once. It will take me half of a fortnight to arrive at his gate on foot. I do not expect a long stay, but I must warn him of the impending danger to his lands. His kingdom is the closest to the Fountain, and as you know, they have acted as its keeper for hundreds of years. Send no one to the Fountain until my return."

"Aye. We will wait for you then. You may take a horse if you would like. Take care on your journey."

"With gratitude, King. That will nearly cut my travel time in half. Until we meet again, then."

** ** ** ** **

Sehaida was situated in a vast peninsula with the ocean to its west and the sea's inlet to the north and east of it. It was naturally protected on three of its four borders. The south was nearly closed in with the mighty West Vitirral Mountain range where the Fountain had sprung. Given its size and geography, it was host to nearly an equal amount of shipping, as well as farming.

Not long after the Fountain made its change, the cascading effect of darkness began taking hold of the countryside. Spreading outward in all directions, the neighboring mountains began to be surrounded by graying, low clouds. The very air seemed to be a noxious gas, not welcoming to any visitor. The skyline over the plateau and mount of the falls was nearly lost in the murkiness. The billowing clouds resembled that which was spewed forth from a volcano. The near acidic atmosphere appeared to show destructive power as the mountainsides began looking pock-marked and unnatural. With the continued descent of the dark magic, the slopes looked cracked and broken, leaving large crumbling areas of crag. The shell of the mountain was shedding its dead skin in layers.

The foothills were next, and thereafter, the fertile plains. The plains began looking dried and arid. The wind was picking up and blowing dust at high velocity. The earth itself was beginning to blacken over, as ink would stain a tapestry. The threatening magic groped over the ground and advanced to conquer the area with creeping tentacles of foul and filth.

The few months it took for the sinister shadow to capture the mountain was hidden by the gloom of any natural occurring winter. It wasn't until the plains were affected that humans became aware of the changes.

There were several farmers who lived among the foothills. It was they who noticed a changing of the weather. This was not crop sowing weather; the ground was dry and rock hard. The very plain itself seemed to be decaying and dying, looking as if soot was strewn about. The closest fields to the mountain were plainly different from their land the previous season and would have to be sacrificed and given up. The crop fields further away from the mountains seemed undisturbed though, and they would try to manage with less possible area of harvesting.

When they began noticing that their livestock were going missing, there was a call for action. A messenger was sent to Brondin, the capital of Sehaida, to report to the King. The land change was a challenging matter of experience; they had had poor growing seasons in the past. Having livestock disappear was more insidious. Where the cattle were going was a question on each of their minds. They knew these lands better than anyone else, and there were no caravans in the area for the possibility of thievery.

After the messenger was received by King Mata Deland, a royal scout was sent back to the borderland plains to investigate the situation. The two young men travelled back together, the farmer's messenger and the King's scout. When they arrived at the small settlement of houses near the foothills that belonged to the farmers, they found it deserted. There was no sign of any livestock or that of people.

After an exhaustive search, they heard the lowing of a heifer near the foothills. They had all but given up on the search for any living creature. The closer the two men got to the animal though, the more it ran toward the hillock. When they had nearly caught up to it, it darted into an opening between a thicket and a large boulder. Inward they followed, and at once, they noted that the air quality was different than out in the open plain. The air was dryer in here; the very moisture in the mouths and eyes was beginning to be leached away. They could barely breathe as they looked around, and the lighting was dimmed significantly.

The lowing was still continuing, but seemed much farther off than was expected for the time it took them to dive into the thicket. Climbing now, the two persisted on, so that they may find out what was going on in the hills. Just as they cleared a slight rise, they caught a glimpse of a black tower rising from the area around where the Fountain was. This startling new addition stood out from its background, an eyesore in a once pristine setting. The sounds of construction could be heard, even from their considerable distance to the site.

Slowly, they crept up the slope and peered over the edge to find the farmers and livestock working in unison toward finishing the substructure and main hall of the black tower. The tower was huge, and the hall was as large as the palace of Sehaida. There was no sign of the Fountain to be found. The tower was enclosing the entire waterfall that had fed the precious waters to the plateau, and the Fountain must have been covered by the main hall. Smog permeated the area, and not even the sparse rays of the sun reflected on the tower's parapets. There was a dimness to everything, and the feeling in the air was one of dread and death. The farmers were acting as if possessed and trudged along as they toiled at their tasks. Something was changed about them, the way they moved and acted. Soon it was apparent that they were no longer the mere mortal beings that they were only a few weeks prior. They each possessed the power to lift huge sections of stone and timber beams, and they were beginning to have a hulking look to them. The livestock looked absolutely rabid as they sputtered and bucked, drooling and flashing their opaque white eyes.

This was the answer to the disappearance of everyone. It was time to report to the King of this new danger breeding within their own country. They did not know when it came, or what its nature was, but there must have been magic afoot. The sudden appearance of a black tower could not have happened without magic. Their ghastly looking fellow countrymen were enough to make them quiver as they backed away. There was a dark purpose at work here, and it would take more than just the two of them to absolve it.

The two men managed to find their way back down the slope and beyond, into the plain. The journey back to Brondin would take just over a week. During that time, they noted a small change in each other as well. They were rasping and wheezing, and they had begun to think the toxic air must have stirred up something in their lungs. There was no doubt, they were lucky to escape with only a mild cough, but there must have been some irritant in the air. Their only mission right now was letting the King know what was happening.

King Mata Deland was waiting for them as they dragged their weary bodies up the steps to the entryway. He was beginning to become worried about the clouds that were advancing slowly across the nation. They had advanced far enough over the country that he could see them from the palace.

"What is this madness?"

"My Lord, there is a tower!" "Sire, we are in danger!" they both blurted, wheezing and panting.

They were looking homely, and their travel did not improve their appearance. Each was dirtied by the ride, and their garb was wholly unclean. Their posture was drooping; they looked beaten and frail. These men were ailing and could find nothing more rewarding than rest.

"One at a time, if you please. Let us start from the beginning."

They told of the ghost town farming community and of the lost cattle. Then came the short climb upward and the tower, which was of peak interest. The weather patterns were proof that they had not fabricated the story, even though much of it was fantastical in nature.

"And you have seen all of this?" King Mata Deland had to ask even after hearing firsthand of their account.

"Everything we have said is the truth, as our very eyes have seen it."

"This is troubling…"

The King bade them to get indoors and to rest themselves, but only after having a proper bath. He needed to think about what his course of action would be. First there was the initial messenger's report, then this second more terrorizing recap of the wicked changing of the mountain's climate. It was possible that this was going on for far longer than anyone anticipated or could guess.

After speaking with them, the King himself felt soiled. The grime of their bodies seemed to saturate the air, as would grease in a hot kitchen. He could almost feel it sticking to him. He headed straight to the baths to soak and brood. When he was finished he lifted his portly body up and out of the bath.

King Mata was a large man. He could be considered jolly, even, partaking in the festivities of his kingdom. He was a lover of food and would imbibe in the wine. His demeanor was not of overbearing optimism but merely hopeful of all things. This led him to be labeled as imprudent at times. Though he would naturally consult with his Queen before making a decision, he could be easily strayed with thoughts of grandeur. There had been many subjects over the years who tried to put one over on him with a new invention or better way of producing agriculture. Each had shown their prowess in their field, and some really had a good product. Lucky for the King, his counsel was equal to the task of picking the advantageous solutions and not the frivolous.

The Deland palace was set up in a square pattern that surrounded a courtyard. The outer protective wall was hollow, in that you could move freely about the enclosure around the perimeter. The double square wall system was implemented for the ability to move guards around and ambush attackers by exiting via different outer doors. Just inside the second wall were the living quarters. The main hall was first among rooms to enter and did double duty with a foyer. The King could sit on his throne and see all that could be seen of visitors without them having to enter too far into his private mansion. The main hall was surrounded by guest quarters to the left and right, and they each had an extension by another hallway to the rear of the castle. There were great oak doors that blocked the guest's access into the royal sleeping quarters and baths.

The courtyard was not expansive, since it was surrounded, but it had the privacy the King had grown fond of. Though he was seen in nearly every corner of his country, this courtyard was where he was truly comfortable. It was lined with great trees butted up to either side, where the hallways connected the front to the back areas. There was a small pond with numerous varieties of fish in it featuring exotic colors.

Dressed only in a robe, he sauntered down the corridor toward his sleeping chambers where his Queen already laid. She was not as large as he was, but she had her size spoken for by way of her first pregnancy. They were expecting her to birth a child within the next month.

"My dear, Kitara."

"My King…Have you come in to bed me?"

Mata had to clear his throat before speaking, "I am sorry, I have not. Not tonight my darling, there are many things requiring my attention."

He recounted for her, then, the scout's tale of the mountains. He found that he needed to pause a few times to continue clearing his throat. He was beginning to be uncomfortable with the build-up of phlegm in his sinuses and finished with a cough.

"Are you quite alright?"

"Yes Kitara, I must have stayed too long in the baths. The humidity is getting to my head. Let me rest for a bit and we will continue devising a plan."

He kissed her forehead and lay beside her. He was sweating mildly, but this was not uncommon. His breath was slightly labored, but this too was not uncommon when lying on his back. Presently, he began snoring, but the raucous sound seemed even more intense than usual.

** ** ** ** **

The next day was met with trouble as the King continued to have a chilled sweat. Combining that with a headache, he was uncomfortable and getting irritated quickly. This was not part of his usual attitude toward things. He also had begun to have some visitors from around the city complaining about the water seeming foul. Between his symptoms and those of the people around him, there was no doubt that there was a bug going around. It did not take long to realize that he was not equipped to deal with these problems at the moment. His Kingly duties were to oversee the overall quality of life of the city and nation, but this would have to wait. He finally decided that he would go to bed again and rest until the fever broke.

On the second day, Queen Kitara Deland awoke to find her bed sheets moist with her husband's sweat. He was still sleeping, but fitfully. The King was making moaning sounds and his dreams had brought on thrashing through nearly the entire night. He seemed gripped in a fever and was clammy.

She quickly roused herself and thought of going to the bath. Before this though, she decided to open the curtains and allow some light into the room, which was feeling decidedly steamy. When she did this, Mata covered his glassy eyes and yelled at her, delirious with a sleepy mind and a fevered body.

"Why would you do that?"

"The morning light isn't even that bright. It is odd though, the hourglass is nearly empty. It should be much brighter at this hour. It is approaching noon."

"Noon or not, why don't you come back to bed?"

"You have made it stink in here. You are sweating so profusely, I could not stay in that mire we call a bed for another instant." She turned from him and gazed out the window.

"All I asked for is rest and you…"

"Mata!" she interrupted him

"WHAT!" he bellowed, clearly out of his mind.

"There is a man in the field outside of the city borders."

"Don't be ridiculous woman. That is over two miles from here. If there was a man out there he would have to be a giant."

King Mata was grumbling and feeling an ache in his back and knees as he slowly dragged himself out of bed to have a look at what she was seeing. Though his vision was poorer than hers, he could still make out a silhouette of a man in the distance. More concerning to him though, was the cloud formation over the mountain range. Additionally an arm of cloud cover seemed to trail toward the city in a thick line that gathered over the black shape in the field.

"Another messenger, perhaps. I will ride out to meet him."

"Take your royal guard with you at least. Stop acting like such an ass. You have not been in your right mind since those messengers returned. Any other time you would have them brought into the city walls or even here to your throne room."

"Very well, then. I will do as you say."

The King gathered some of his guard about him but had not told them what they were to do. They questioned the need for his presence at all, given his haggard appearance. He assured them that he

31

was going out to the field, and that he was giving the orders, not the other way around.

Disembarking from the outskirts of the city, they saw the figure in the field appeared framed in by several boulders situated into a semicircle. They did not seem to have previously been there when he cast his gaze down at the field from his chambers. The distance was far, though, and was passed off as an oversight from his diminished vision. When they finally got within speaking range, they found that he was mammoth in size, at least eight feet tall. Men like this did not go unnoticed in the kingdom. This stranger was not like them. His cloak was black with some red coursing threads through it, and it was closed tightly about him. The hood covered his face in shadow; there was only blackness under it. When the King jumped off of his mount, the stranger remained motionless. The King's guard followed him in turn, dismounting.

"Who are you?"

"I have no name. But plague and pestilence shall precede me."

His deep voice was thunderous, his tone, almost growling. The cloak shifted itself to his shoulders, and the cowl folded backward, without his arms even moving. The cloak slid open very smoothly, almost organically. His bluish skin was visible then, and there was a curl of blackened smoke released. He was a formidable creature and looked as evil as death itself. He lifted his arms then and pointed to the sky.

"Do you see my power for destruction? I could crush you where you stand without a second thought or any effort. The transformation of the landscape has been my doing, and I am only getting started."

"Why are you here?" Mata asked, noting his guard was teetering in the balance of nervousness.

"To collect my soldiers and begin my war."

"I do not see anyone around to help you."

"Look around you and then look at yourself. I am now your leader and you are all my pawns."

Mata then cast his gaze furtively toward his guard around him but saw that they were beginning to cower in the presence of the stranger's voice.

"I am King in this country," he said, though not boldly.

"You were King. Now prepare yourself to bow down before a God."

The rocky shapes behind him stirred then, brought to life. In their previous existence, they were the farmers of the foothills. Grotesquely altered, their hulking bodies were plagued by disease. Their sullied forms had decayed flesh dripping from them, revealing a harder, shell like, scaly appearance underneath. Their skin appeared in constant motion of dying and rebuilding. Their heads were a combined form of a bat with a more reptilian snout of a gator; their canine teeth were flashing in the dim lighting. There were two rows of them around the necromancer. The ogre's in the center of the formation stayed in placed while the rear row flanked the royal guard and formed a tight perimeter around Mata and his men. There seemed to be a doubling effect as some stayed still while others moved. This stealthy maneuver went unnoticed by Mata. He was locked in place with terror by the sight of the blue devil before him. The rolls of smoke coming from under his cloak and the constant morphing of his skin sickened him, but he could not look away.

"I will make your pain disappear but replace it with disease."

At these words, the rocky giants quickly closed in on the group and grabbed each man in a tight grip. There was a frenzy as the monsters opened their gaping mouths and bared their razor sharp teeth. The guttural sound and fetid stench from the brute's throats was overwhelming, but short lived, as they buried their teeth into the fleshy skin of their captives' necks.

There was no cry from the men. The attack was too swift to deflect. Even if they had their full faculties and were not quaking in fear, they had no chance of escape. They simply sank down to their knees and then collapsed onto the ground.

Mata watched in horror as he stood alone in the midst of the chaos. The dark conjurer looked down at him and then strode to stand directly before him.

"You are mine!"

He clenched his grip into Mata's shoulder and spun him around to face to carnage.

"Watch!"

That touch was the catalyst for a metamorphosis. The talons on the necromancer's hand were digging and slashing into the soft skin. Mata was beginning to lose the very fiber of his being as the transformation began to overtake him. The disease was ravaging his flesh, and his body was in an utter breakdown. Through his deadened eyes, he saw that his men did not perish. They were beginning to stand and file into a formation. They were transformed into the very same beasts who had accosted them, already showing signs of damage over their carcasses. They were growing and looking as terrible as the previous batch of scaly fiends that resembled the crumbling rocks around them.

Mata, who was a large man to begin with, increased in his size to seven feet, and his girth was tremendous. He was a juggernaut of sizable proportion and looked as if nothing would be able to penetrate his skin or stop him in his path.

The blue devil did not have to clap his hand down on his shoulder a second time. The animal turned to him of his own accord.

"Who are you?" the warlock asked.

"I have no name. But there is death in my path. I shall wreak havoc for you, my master."

"Assemble your army, then. Fly to the city. Finish the task of transformation, and let us breed a new civilization of dominance and despair."

III

Kelduun was only a mile away to the east of Brondin when he saw King Mata Deland open the gate. To his surprise, the King and his company did not ride in his direction to greet him but rode directly into the southern field. He had noticed the darkening clouds over the southern field and the utter wall of cloud formation to the south, over the West Vitirrals.

There was the feeling of an electric vibe of magic in the air. When he cast his gaze to the King's target, a grouping of boulders could be seen with a dark statue situated in the center of them.

His instinct was to drop to the ground for cover and observe the situation before deciding on his course of action. He had no choice but to let the horse he borrowed from the royal stable in Albinion to run free. His irritation with this was mixed simultaneously with the hope that the horse would not draw attention in his direction.

He surveyed the scene before him. Even at great distance, he could see that the King was in distress. The statue revealed itself to be a man of sizable proportions. When the boulders started moving, his mind was made up to get to the gate of the city as fast as he could. He was scurrying as low as he could while covering the distance to the city's entrance.

As Kelduun got to the archway, he looked back and saw the royal guard sinking to the ground after an attack. He quickly ducked inside and made his way to the palace. He was seeking the Queen.

When he found her, she was pacing to and fro and muttering to herself. She was in a daze.

"Queen Kitara?"

"Kelduun, how did you get in here?"

"I have my ways, but that is of no consequence right now. I fear something terrible has befallen your King."

"What do you mean? And why should I believe you, coming in here unannounced and gossiping bad news?"

"I am merely saying that something has happened. What has you up in arms? You seem ready to pounce."

"I am fine, am I not? What is the meaning of your intrusion into my home?"

"You can trust me. I have been guiding you and your family for many years now."

The Queen was not as she had spoken. She was not acting in

her normal, level-headed manner. She was beginning to look crazed. Her untrusting nature exposed in these last few minutes was a departure from her usual benevolent attitude.

"Has something happened in here?" asked Kelduun.

"You are not welcome here."

She was delirious with fever, looking sweaty and uncomfortable.

"If I may, I am trying to help you. Perhaps I should get the healer in to attend to your needs. You look as though you have caught a bug. But we have no time. I fear that evil is coming your way."

"I need my husband."

"You must come with me. We can look for him on our way down to the city's gate."

"I will go no place with you. I need my husband."

She was beginning to shut down and close herself off to everything around her. She turned toward him and sheepishly smiled. Before he interpreted this, she ran from the room and disappeared into the labyrinth of corridors in the palace.

Kelduun was dumbfounded as to what he had just witnessed. He was not only welcomed in the past but invited to be privy to some of the deepest problems of the country. He was enemy to no one, and yet not exactly an ally. His gift was being able to stay nonjudgmental and keep the problems of one nation separate from that of another's. His mediation of the land's issues was why most of the peoples had good international relationships and alliances.

Not being able to comfort the Queen was going to weigh on his conscience. But the fact that she retreated from him as if he were a threat to her was altogether baffling.

He began descending to the foyer of the palace when he heard screaming from outside the protective wall. The citizens of Brondin were awestruck at the sight of the molting skinned men issuing from the entrance to the city and dispersing, with blood on their minds. There was panic in their voices, but it left them trembling in place, not running away. This confusing scene before Kelduun made him stop and study them momentarily.

When he realized his scrutiny had cost him precious seconds for plotting his escape, he found himself confronted with the biggest brute in the company. This was the former king, returning to raze his own home. Though he was concealed inside the double wall, he could see that the monster was approaching with vengeance. There was no thought of confronting him right now, before a weakness could be detected. He was trapped in the castle.

** ** ** ** **

Strayos was a beautiful country. It was the farthest travelling distance from Albinion, capital of Gildesh, than any of the other countries. King Vernon Secandor had no reason to stay an extra week after the Dito festival. He had no daughter for courting, and thus, felt that his needs would be greater served by returning to his homeland.

The route home led King Secandor's caravan south around the Cysterule Mountains and then curved along the western edge of the vast Lake Proseccan. The fertile plains leading to the south were the signature of his land. Agriculture was the main source of export, and there were many aqueducts running throughout the kingdom. The criss-crossing of watering lines was expertly planned and the pride of the King. The amount and sizes of the crops were a marvel to visitors and pulled in top prices as a valued commodity.

Crute, the nation's capital, was situated on a small peninsula that pushed into Lake Proseccan. Surrounded by water on three sides, it almost gave the appearance of being on an island. Its coastal partner, Albinion, may have the sea before it, but the lake was large enough to command its own spectacular view. The difference was in the waters' behavior. The lake system was calm, and there were no tidal periods and thus no large weather swings.

The great lake was nearly one hundred miles across, and the Cysterule Mountain range, tall as it was, could not be seen over the horizon. The outlet to the sea was the Gallendar River, but no ships would pass that way. The Gallendar had rapids along its path and many tributaries reaching into the mountain range with waterfalls and gullies.

Reaching Crute from Albinion was an arduous trip that lasted almost half of a fortnight. Even though the caravan had many horses, the pace was purposefully slow. The distance did not need to be accomplished with hastiness. The trip was meant to have the luxury of a comfortable ride, and many stops were made. This gave the royal family time to enjoy each other and talk about the celebration.

King Vernon Secandor was a powerfully built man, standing at six feet tall. His short dark hair was beginning to show signs of thinning, and a small balding spot could be imagined. He was in good shape for a man of fifty-five years of age and could still lift great weights when called upon. He regularly worked out his muscles and tried to stay limber. He was constantly looking for advancement, but his life already had so much happiness that you could practically read it in his hazel eyes. One of his hobbies was deep meditation. He felt that clearing the mind helped with decision making.

His Queen, Merkette Secandor, was of like mind. Her first thought on many of life's outcomes was that things would come to pass as they are destined to. Life did not give itself over to torture when you knew that things all would happen for a reason. The reason is sometimes hard to find, she would remind her husband, but once you found it, you could learn from it. She was diminutive compared to her husband only in stature; they shared power equally over the country. They would naturally come to decisions together and rarely had to quarrel over anything.

When they arrived at the city, there was a small banquet set up for the royal family. The palace of Crute was circular in shape and had many layers stacked upon one another. The outside wall was purely for guarding the keep and was mirrored interiorly by another wall. This ensured that even if intruders breached the first rampart, they would find themselves facing another equally tall and smooth wall. Protectors of the castle could retreat layer by layer, redoubling their efforts and changing defense tactics for an additional two layers before take-over was even a forethought.

The aesthetic appearance of each of the layers was to give the entire structure the look of impressive massiveness. In the interior, the lowest circlet was the main hall and was overlooked directly by balconies of the higher circlet. The guest quarters were located in the layer just above the main hall, and their vantage point was one of splendor, as they could look down over a guest-filled area of merriment. Each layer was joined by great spiraled staircases to each side of the circle, so as not to take away space from the room with a large sprawling stairway. Each of these bottom two circles was lined with a marble colonnade, giving a temple-like appearance. The two layers just above the main area were sectioned off and did not have the view below. These served as a private library and the King's quarters at the very top. There was a separate staircase leading down to a wine cellar beneath the structure and then out to the sea via a secret passageway. The King maintained a watchful state of readiness and could escape over Lake Proseccan by boat if the need should arise.

After the short dinner session, the King retired with his family to the top of the palace. The top layer was divided nearly equally in half. The King's area was the northern half and overlooking the lake, and had the benefit of a nightly breeze. His son, Merion, had his quarters occupying the southern portion, which overlooked the vast plains below.

When King Vernon arrived at his room, he was surprised by a small jingling sound by the window. There was a carrier pigeon perched on a rod and pecking hungrily at some seed. The small cylinder attached to its leg had a message in it.

GILDESH AND CALDORN UNION POSSIBLE
QUEEN C. R. HAS STAYED WITH KING P. D.
FOR OVER THE STANDARD WEEK OF COURTING
ADVISE

The message was dated from three days ago. It must have been written just after the Gildesh celebration. Taking into account the distance in line of sight, as the bird flies, versus the caravan's travel time across land, this message could already be four days old.

The message was cryptic. There were a few possibilities that could be deciphered from this. Was Queen Reesh staying in Gildesh for the purpose of having her daughter Ashlyn have more time with King Dito's son, Panalt? Could it be that Panalt was planning on marrying Ashlyn? Would Panalt marry Ashlyn and then take over Caldorn instead of Gildesh? Would the alliances be changed based on Palatine and Panalt each having rule over their own countries? Would Queen Reesh be unseated in Caldorn if Panalt marries Ashlyn? But, the message had not stated anything to answer this and had not even mentioned the names of the prince and princess. More information was needed.

King Vernon was a patient man. He devoted much time to thinking and did not come to decisions lightly. Though he was tired from the journey and was being called into bed by his lovely Queen, he needed to give some time to the task at hand.

He wrote quickly on a new piece of parchment and then read it silently to double check what he had written.

CONFIRM THE RELATIONSHIP
PRINCE TO PRINCESS?
KING TO QUEEN?
REPORT ON PLAN FOR UNION

He knew it would only take another day for his message to be received. It may take longer to receive another note depending on how events played themselves out. This new drama was such an interesting prospect. King Secandor could not wait until he knew how things would go. It was late the next day when he heard another jingle at his window.

QUEEN C. R. STAYING IN KING P. D.'S CHAMBERS
UNION OF KING TO QUEEN
JOIN THE COUNTRIES INTO ONE

PRINCE P. INTERESTED IN PRINCESS A.
NOTHING MORE, YET

This was a turn, and the change was wholly unexpected. King Secandor thought it interesting that Queen Reesh of Caldorn had taken a liking to King Dito of Gildesh. It made sense on a small scale. They were both in the same position. Widow and widower brought together by tragic events. They would have some of the same feelings as one another.

Even more interesting was the fact that the festival was planned with the intention of the prince finding a mate, not the King. He had seen the prince of Gildesh dancing with the princess of Caldorn. At first glance, he could have mistaken the note's meaning. He quickly looked at it again to confirm what he read.

This required some time for thinking. If the two countries were to turn into one, undoubtedly then, Panalt would be given an extended section of the land to rule over. It was very cunning of the Queen to use her beauty, intelligence, and emotional past to sway the King. Also impressive, though, was the thought process of King Dito. His rule would extend to nearly the entire civilized region of the seaboard. Even though Panalt may be a king of an adjacent land, he is still King Dito's son. A son would still be ruled over in many ways; it would be hard to consider them as equals.

But this union would not come without some backlash. There would be some unrest in each populous. He scrawled another note out.

HOW SECRETIVE IS THE RELATIONSHIP?

He waited another day and a half for the response. The wheels in his head were turning now.

FEW KNOW
RUMORS COULD BE SPREAD
ADVISE

He sat back in his chair. When he read through the note again, he realized that in a small way, he could take some amount of power in this situation by divulging information. He wrote yet another response.

STAY QUIET FOR NOW
OBSERVE AND REPORT A CHANGE
THE RUMOR WILL SPREAD REGARDLESS

These events presented an opportunity for teaching. It was time for him to call upon his son, Merion, for a lesson on kingship. He made his way down to the library level and got comfortable in a large armchair. The King called a servant to him and requested a glass of wine and then to have his son shown in.

"Father?"

"Ah, Merion. Please sit down with me for a while."

Merion did as he was told. The room was dimly lit but had a cozy feel. This was his favorite room to be in. There was no end to the knowledge that could be gained by devoting time reading the tomes and scrolls of history and theory.

"My boy, if the timing were only slightly different, we might have found ourselves in a powerful position."

"What do you mean? Are we not in power now?"

"Yes, Merion. But power can be extended through many circumstances. If you were only slightly older, or perhaps even if I were slightly older myself…" Vernon trailed off for just a second.

"What are you getting at?"

"The countries of Gildesh and Caldorn will be fused into one, in a short matter of time."

"What? How can this be?"

"The Queen of Caldorn, Crissannah Reesh, has slipped into the highest regard of the King of Gildesh, Palantine Dito."

"What manner of joking do you propose to me? That is not what I saw at the banquet in Panalt's honor. It is the prince and princess that looked to be together."

"Appearances…merely ripples in the surface of the water. I know that this is not entirely true. The King and Queen are the highlighted partnership here. When they make their union known publicly, the countries will join. I am sure that Panalt will have rule over some portion of it, but the bulk will remain with the elders. We have grown comfortable with our nation's borders, and now I see that we may have been beaten to the punch. It would have been a sweeter ending to the story if I had put you on a path to court the princess, Ashlyn Reesh."

"How do you know all of this?"

"Therein lies the reason I brought you here today, Merion. Information. That is the key to making decisions that will form history. Information is how battles are won and how to gain an edge over your adversaries. A secret is private only if it is not shared with someone else. You would be surprised, though, that when you do share a secret, the listener you have told may have ulterior plans. Or worse, they may not have been the only one to hear it. If you are not careful, an eavesdropper may foil your plans. That eavesdropper is my source in the palace of the King of Gildesh."

"What? I had no knowledge of this before."

"You had no need to know of this before. Did I not just tell you how secrets are kept? They are private until shared. As I said, information is the key to many advances."

"How did you obtain this mole in the system? This cog in the wheel?"

"Merion, that is the question you needed to ask. We will now begin your conversion from a boy into a man, and a man into a King. Strategy was the key in the beginning. Many years ago, before even my father's rule, the lands were unsettled. King's were trying to establish their power and there were many battles fought over where the land would be divided. These were times of nations being regarded for the power of the King's army and less of the boundaries that separated them. The ebb and flow of military advances and retreats set a stage for espionage. A wise man made a suggestion that having a mole inside the counsel of another nation could be beneficial to knowing when a garrison was moved around the countryside, and then when and where it was preparing to attack.

"This was especially dangerous, but the plan was not merely to send in a sacrificial pawn. The first infiltrator would do nothing except gain trust of the leader. Then, as time passed, his child would be granted the same rights and accepted into the counsel of the King. This is when the information began flowing. It was hard to doubt the allegiance of a council member when they had been born into this role. The double agent, though, was never fully in the service of the King. The generations carried on, and new spies continued the tradition of advising while remaining undercover.

"Some of the battles started to be won before the advancing army was even prepared to mount an attack. Before anyone was ready for it, the warring stopped, and borders were established just as they were when the militia halted. Each army had camps along their borders for quite some time, but no one attacked the other. Things uncomplicated themselves, and then a fairly certain truce was signed into a treaty.

"The role of the insider was not as important then. But information is always valuable. We have had the same borders for many years, but if a King wished to test the strength of our resolve and invade, information would allow the victor to prevail with as minimal damage as is necessary. I have maintained a low level relationship with my insider for many things over the years. It is mostly for petty information, but you can never count out the possibility of an assault."

"This is beyond what I had expected. There are layers upon layers of deception," Merion said.

He had to collect himself. He was stunned.

"Do you have questions about this?"

"No, I think I understand it. But where does it leave us for now?"

"My source has given me the information I have told you. The King has taken the Queen into his bed. King Palantine has played an interesting move. This union is bold, but also straight forward. No battles will be fought this time to gain the land needed to expand his empire."

"Will you stop him?"

"It is not only Palantine we would have to deal with. I'm afraid that Crissannah has a country of her own to deal with. We would be going one against two, should we instigate conflict. The fact is, I was a tight ally to King Turg Reesh before his demise, and we remain close with Caldorn. There will be no battle with her. I have no intentions of invading Gildesh either. Their land is spread out over too far a distance to continue to hold control over it. The distance, from here alone, would mean a second ruler would need to control the western half.

"You see, this is how deep it goes. With Panalt already interested in Ashlyn, the second command seems plausible. Had things worked differently, you may have courted Ashlyn, and then the tables would be turned in our favor. Secondly, there is nothing for me to offer Queen Crissannah, unfortunately. I am very happily married to your mother, and I would not entertain a second suitor. She may have manipulated the situation and seduced Palantine. It is easy to see her wanting to attach herself to a strong man and also get what she wants. She'll get to stay in power, and her needs will be met as well as Palantine's. They would gain a greater area of land with a higher export trade. Her position is interesting. Caldorn is the smallest country in comparison to the others. Their army is proportionately small as well. Why not make everyone around you an ally, thus preventing attack from anyone. But to go so far as to give up her country is unexpected."

"What is your plan then, father?"

"We will congratulate the Queen upon her return from Gildesh. We need to be certain that our alliance is still strong. If the two countries form a union, we may not have the strength to fight both at the same time. I shall send you to see Queen Reesh as soon as I have word that she has left Albinion and is en route to Creyason."

"What if she is suspicious of our knowledge of the situation?"

"There are two answers to give her. You must decide which is more pertinent to your conversation. You could either say you are talking about congratulations of her daughter's relationship with the prince, or you can deflect the entire conversation and fall back on maintaining the strength in the bond we have had with her nation. Either way, information will be gained."

IV

Kelduun reevaluated his position. He was behind the threshold of the castle's gate. He could see out into the flat entry area, but he was fairly certain that his position was concealed from the outside. He needed another moment of observation before turning to flee. And he also needed a moment to recollect the strange occurrences that had happened in the last few minutes.

He was not far behind the Queen when she darted away from him earlier. Though he had no idea what her intentions were or where she had gone in the palace, his plan was to try to find a squire in the estate to help him find her. He was sure that reason would prevail and that he could help her to see that what was going on was highly irregular. That was how he arrived in the foyer.

He was taken completely off guard, though, when he heard the chaotic screaming outside the castle's gate. This caused him to give pause. He would have to delay his search for Queen Kitara. The sun's rays had cast a sharp diagonal line demarcating the shadows from the light. His cloak camouflaged him in the shadows, and he inched closer to the gate's opening, venturing to gain a better vantage point.

The citizens of Brondin were beginning to reacquire their wits about them, and they began uprooting themselves from the earth's grip of terror. The commotion dulled momentarily, and something seemed to catch the crowd's attention. When Kelduun looked in the direction they were, he saw the Queen. She was swaying as if drunk but making her way to the gargantuan beast standing just outside. She must have used another exit in the outside wall and avoided him altogether.

To his dismay, she was not running away but seemed calm and docile. She was not hasty in her speed to the animal, but not wavering either. When she got within an arms distance to it, she stopped and stood upright. The juggernaut's mass dwarfed her; he towered almost two feet above her full height. He then scooped her up as if she were nothing more than a doll and sunk his teeth into her chest. She went limp, and he dropped his arm to his side holding her in a one-handed grasp.

Surprisingly, this did not cause the stirring that Kelduun would have expected of a terrorized people. Rather, they became hushed. There were other smaller fiends joining the giant, who was holding his prize. They looked just as gruesome, baring their teeth in elongated snouts and flexing their pointed, fleshy ears. The dead skin was beginning to fall away revealing a hide of scales and fur between, poking out at erratic angles.

Kelduun had a feeling of dread wash over him as he anticipated what would happen next. The band of mutants began to overrun the citizens, and there was mass carnage. There was blood splattered everywhere. He turned away, having witnessed a massacre, and headed for the upper area along the wall.

He needed a plan of escape, but he wanted to stay and obtain as much information about this new threat as was possible. He would need to maintain extreme vigilance in order not to be captured and possibly killed.

When he reached the top of the rampart, he looked over the side and into the city's gathering area before the castle. He was shocked at what he saw. The Queen's body suddenly coiled around her would-be murderer's hand and sprung away, coming to life. He turned to see the townsfolk morph, as well, into monsters. Instead of thirty enemies, there was now twice that amount.

His escape was made even more improbable with the gathering of adversaries. Even if he used his magic, the best he could do would only eliminate half of them. They would be on him before he had the time to conjure another strike. Patience and caution was now required by him. His capture would spell doom for the rest of the lands. He needed to find a way to escape and warn the other nations.

The transformation of the people was fast. Over the course of the next two weeks, nearly everyone left within the city's walls was infected and then succumbed to the poisonous bite delivered from the ever growing horde. The city was turned into a writhing mass of bodies scrambling over one another to try to get to the very last sources of fresh blood.

With the completion of the takeover, the drones were split into several groups. The bulk of them were mobilized over the remaining portion of Sehaida to terminate even more people and bring them under the same curse. Some of them stayed behind in Brondin to begin fashioning war machines and armor. Others were ushered back to the Vitirral Mountains to finish the black tower that was the altar of their master, the dark conjurer.

The turmoil and chaos was spreading around the region. The wave of disease was gaining power. There could be no doubt that time was waning before imminent attack. The predatory creatures seemed not able to be controlled. Their forces were continually growing and started to gather out on the plain. The number of transformed victims was staggering.

** ** ** ** **

Clang.

Wish.

Ping.

Bang.

Whoosh.

Gong.

Thud.

"Do you yield?"

Panalt was standing over Dur, pointing down at him with his sword.

"I'm not finished yet," Dur said, smacking away Panalt's sword with his own and rolling to his knee.

"Let's try this again," Dur invited him.

He smiled and looked over his shoulder at Tiras who was standing at the ready. They both took to arms and prepared an offensive stance.

"Two against one?" Panalt asked.

He turned to confirm this with Tobin. Tobin bowed his head slightly in agreement and then said, "Do you think that all fights will be one on one? Even if they were, you cannot even expect your opponent to fight a fair battle. They will try to use any number of ways to beat you in any way that they can. Remember, in battle, the fight is to the death. A weakened or cornered opponent will do whatever it takes to remain alive."

"Very well then, let us see how this pans out," said Panalt. He turned toward his brothers and then added, "Let's go!"

The very instant Panalt finished his challenge, Dur dropped his sword and crouched in a powerful base, with his hands on his knees. Tiras was already in motion and took a small jump. He planted foot on Dur's back to jettison himself even further upward in an aerial assault on Panalt. His motion paid off with a clearance of seven feet. Tiras had his sword high above his head; his descent was met by Panalt lunging up to block him with a clashing of their swords. The force of the blow knocked Panalt's sword downward, and he could feel a tingling in his shoulder. When Panalt gained his defensive position back, he saw that Dur had already scooped up his weapon and barrel rolled to his flank. He had an attacker on either side of him.

The feeling was returning to his hand, but he did not let on that he had any weakness. Panalt quickly turned toward Dur while Tiras was steadying himself after his leap. There was a small melee with the swords, but then he had to turn to guard his side with his shield from a second strike from Tiras. Panalt easily deflected the blow by Tiras. He swiped his sword once more across the path of Dur and then turned full on to Tiras and swung his shield at him. The blunt force knocked Tiras' shield out of his hand, and he found that he had a slight gain with this side of attack. He then turned back to Dur who was already advancing eagerly and gave him a straight kick to the stomach. Having the wind knocked out of him, Dur coughed a few times and raised his hand to halt the action.

Tiras was ready for yet another onslaught but no longer had a shield. Panalt allowed his attack to jab through the air to his left after making a quick dodge. He then grabbed hold of Tiras' arm before he could draw it back and swung his fist to punch him in the face. Stopping inches short of contact he smiled and said, "Do you yield?"

"He beat us both that time!" yelled Dur.

"You gave up too quickly, Dur!" Tiras argued with him.

"I did not. He got in a lucky hit."

"You were too forward in your attack. He saw it coming and you didn't have any guard. He could have run you through if you weren't his brother."

"He could have hurt you too," Dur said meekly.

He had taken the worst of the melee and was starting to feel embarrassed. Tiras did not do much better than him, but it didn't feel that way. Tiras' small edge over him would probably lead to some gloating that evening.

"Young men. That is not the way of the warrior. Do not give in to emotional distress when on the battlefield. You must continue until you cannot lift yourself even one more time. You must push your opponent until they break, not you," Tobin was instructing.

"Tobin is right," Panalt agreed. "If you are not mortally wounded, the fight must continue. We cannot back down."

"We are just training right now, Panalt," Tiras complained.

"Yes, but do not forget these words when the time comes, my friends," Tobin interjected. "You may be fighting for your lives, or for someone whom you love. These can be very tough circumstances. You will have to make hard decisions quickly and under a great amount of stress. Part of the training is not just physical prowess and stamina, but a focusing of the mind."

"Do you think we will ever need these skills?" Dur asked.

"I hope not, but there is no telling what path the future will lead us down," Tobin smiled at him. "Come, let us have another exhibition."

"How about a challenge?" Panalt asked, looking in Tobin's

direction.

Tobin pointed at himself and was answered by way of Panalt nodding. He was sitting on a stump casually, but now stood and stretched his back. He looked back at Panalt, raised his hand, and then folded it in, beckoning him to advance on him.

Panalt was ready, and quickly covered the short distance between them. Tobin was standing loosely and did not have a weapon readied, yet. A little too hastily, Panalt rushed in and jabbed with his sword straight on. Tobin turned quickly to dodge and then came down across Panalt's shoulder blades with his elbow, nearly knocking him flat. Stumbling, but not completely losing his balance, Panalt took a few extra steps, turned and exhaled a big breath.

"Challenge accepted," said Tobin.

He still stood without a weapon in hand. Panalt advanced again, this time with a diagonally downward swinging motion. He sliced only through the air again as he missed a second time. Tobin had already ducked to the right and turned his torso, allowing the blade to pass. Then he stepped into his stance and rammed Panalt shoulder to shoulder. He had the upper hand due to Panalt already being slightly turned from his attack, and Panalt tripped and staggered backward.

"Are you going to fight me?" Panalt asked.

"Are we not having an exhibition, right now? Am I getting under your skin?"

"Fight like a man and arm yourself with a weapon!"

"Perhaps I need no weapon to overcome this attack. But if it is a weapon you want, you will have your fill."

Tobin drew out both of his swords, one in each hand. Now standing with the swords crossed over his chest, he looked menacing. Panalt grew wary of his competition and began to circle him.

Panalt swung again and again, another right slash diagonally downward, then a left slash horizontally. Each time was met with an equal parry to his attack. Tobin seemed to not even be using much energy in neutralizing him. The double sword technique seemed the most optimal for this foray.

Tobin then went on an attack of his own, which Panalt blocked with his shielded left arm and then had to parry against the other sword coming from his right. Tobin continued attacking from both sides in an unending, rhythmic assault. Bang, bang, bang, bang. This was not giving Panalt any time for countering or thinking. Panalt was inundated with swinging metal and blinded to the nature of his rival's advancement. Tobin was playing with him. Tobin's rhythmic swinging was in an effort to lull Panalt into the false sense of security, that his opponent was not gaining an advantage.

Finally Panalt used a move that he felt would pull him out of his situation and leave him to be on the offensive. He dropped his shield and ducked to the left under Tobin's blade. He had his long knife in his left hand now to complement the sword in his other. His move was to even the playing field and take on the double swords with a pair of his own.

Tobin was waiting for this maneuver and allowed Panalt to duck to the left while spinning simultaneously along Panalt's right side. They were standing almost back to back. Then Tobin used his right handed sword in a reverse grip and touched the tip of it into Panalt's left side.

"Do you yield?" Tobin asked, allowing the irony of these words to sink in. Panalt had said this twice already today to his brothers

"How did you do that? How did you know I would try that?"

"My dear young man…that was the second time you used that tactic. A master in the arts of combat would not be fooled again."

"I did not think you would remember."

"Panalt, there is not much that would give me pause. I have studied nearly all of the forms of combat, with practically every weapon. If there was a maneuver to be learned, I would want it in my repertoire. The first time you used that move, it surprised me. Had I given you the wrong look, you may have been able to take me. But a strong warrior would never show his adversary weakness, nor give an edge. Only the strongest of minds can detect that his enemy is showing a weakness inwardly. The best defense can sometimes be showing strength and grit. Perhaps a lesser man would even give up his attack knowing he cannot beat an enemy without outward weaknesses. Even a strong opponent can sometimes be beaten by a weaker fighter, if he employs the proper wisdom to the situation. That is why we train the mind, as well as the body."

"Do you mean that Panalt could have beaten you that day?" Tiras asked inquisitively.

"Maybe, but maybe not. Surprise is but one way to gain control of a match. You must have knowledge of your skills and your opponents. You need to predict sequences and probabilities of events. Thinking one or two moves ahead is how to ensure your advantage is not erased. The moment you have your enemy questioning himself is the moment to capitalize on the situation and take command."

"That is what you were trying to tell us before when we could not beat Panalt," Dur said.

"Yes, and no. Understand that the message of the day is knowledge and planning, not merely brute strength and reaction. But you two were beaten not only because of Panalt's defenses, but also because your attack was headstrong and not calculated. You two were too hasty. The two of you working together may take down nearly any foe, no matter how large. But you need to think it through and plan it out. I can see that you have begun working well with each other and playing off of one another. This will become instinctual, and you will know what the other is doing. You must work to develop this though. No matter the strength of your natural bond of being twins, you must harbor these thoughts at all times."

"Thank you, Tobin," Tiras and Dur said, in unison.

"That is all for now then gentlemen," Tobin said. "Take a break and let it sink in. You will be better fighters tomorrow than even today. Mark my words. You are all excelling in your training and are getting better. Take this lesson with you but do not dwell on it. Use it to your benefit and integrate it into yourself."

They placed their weapons on a rack designed to hold them before walking a short distance back toward the castle wall and into a shady area under a stand of trees. There they sat and waited a short time to be served a light lunch. There were several fruits and a few loaves of bread, along with a platter of cheeses, and a pint of ale for Tobin.

"Panalt, I saw you with all the girls, dancing at the party. Did you pick one yet?" Tiras asked of him.

"Tell us, big brother, do you have a favorite?" Dur said, before tearing off a piece of bread from a loaf on the table.

"No one has stayed longer than Ashlyn Reesh, with her mother, the Queen. I have had a nice time with her, and I have to say that she is the front runner. There was another that caught my fancy, but her family has already left. Since Ashlyn has been around so much, I can see her being the easy favorite."

"She is the prettiest of them. I'll say that. If you don't want her, then maybe I can step in. I wonder if she likes younger men," Dur jested with him.

"I don't think that will be happening," Panalt shot back quickly, giving him a sharp look.

"When are they going home, anyway?" Tiras asked.

"I don't know, Ashlyn thinks very soon. Do you know, Tobin?" Panalt looked at his mentor.

"They are royalty, and they will do as they please," Tobin started. "Keep in mind how it might be for you to visit their land. You would not wish to be escorted out before you were ready. Your father has determined that they do not interfere with his daily activities. However, I believe the Queen has a matter to attend to in Caldorn. They will be leaving in the morning."

"I didn't expect it to be that soon. I knew our time was short, but I am betting Ashlyn did not have full knowledge of their departure plans."

"Time? Short? Come now, Panalt. It has been over two weeks," Dur held up his first two fingers.

"Sounds to me like lover boy has indeed made his pick, and now she is going home," Tiras joked with him, pointing at him with an apple core.

"That is enough, both of you," Tobin interjected. "Your time will come soon enough, and we shall see how you handle it."

Tobin sat back and leaned against the wall with his cup in hand. They were all finishing up their lunch. The twins both stood, again in near unison; they turned to head toward the door leading inside. Panalt grabbed another portion of bread, then stood up himself.

"I am going to see her tonight then, before they return to Caldorn. Thank you, Tobin, for letting me know."

"Panalt, would you stay for just another moment," Tobin asked.

He sat back down then and waved to his brothers. The twins entered the palace and went to their quarters to relax. Tobin and Panalt were left alone under the shade of the trees.

"Panalt, do not let them get under your skin. If you have indeed made a choice, then it is a day worthy of praise. You will be a King some day, and you will make her a very happy Queen."

"Thank you Tobin. They don't bother me, though. We each give one another a hard time for anything we can get a rise out of. It was my turn to be the underdog that time. I'll get them back, you'll see."

"I trust that you will," Tobin replied with a chuckle. "I wanted to talk to you a moment about our sparring session. Your skills have grown so much. I hope you did not see your loss to me today as a regression, and certainly not as an insult. It was not my plan to make you look poorly in front of your brothers."

"I did not feel that. It makes me want to try harder."

"There is a special lesson for you in today's sparring. I do not wish to see you fall to defeat because you rely on one creative movement. Study the forms. Use your skill set. Attack and counter. You will see that you already have what you need. You only need refinement. Use your mind, my friend. That is what truly wins the battle," Tobin said, tapping his finger to his head.

** ** ** ** **

Panalt left Tobin to relax out in the shade for the afternoon.

He was thinking of how he would overcome his tutor the next time. Tobin was right; study was needed, and mental discipline. He needed to sharpen his mind.

He went directly to the baths and freshened himself. Strangely, he did not see his brothers in his passage through the hallways, but they were likely to deter him from his true goal at the moment. He wanted to go to see Ashlyn. If he ran into his brothers along the way to the baths or even in the guest wing, they would start a conversation or ask him to join them in doing some task they felt was important. He did not want that to delay him.

He finished dressing and decided to see her before dinner was served. When he arrived in the guest wing, he found that all the doors were closed. He knocked on the door to the room that Ashlyn was staying in and got no response. He tried a second time and stood in silence in the hallway. Just as he decided he would try again later, he heard muted voices behind the door to another chamber.

If it wasn't so quiet during his wait for Ashlyn to answer the door, he may not have heard the voices at all. He walked up to the room, but then had second thoughts of knocking on the door. Clearly the door was closed for a reason, and he saw this as a request for privacy. He could tell that there were two women talking but could not make out the words through the thick wooden door. Presumably, Ashlyn was conversing with her mother, the Queen. They must have had some of their guards with them because he felt he could sense movement behind the door.

When dinner was served, he was surprised that neither Ashlyn, nor the Queen was present. It did not go unnoticed, and his father, the King, seemed to be a bit less jovial than he had been over the last three weeks. He felt that his father had an equally good time entertaining his guests and seeing that every one of their needs was met. It was strange that he would take it so personally that the Queen and her daughter were not at the dinner. They were becoming nearly a fixture around the palace. It seemed odd that they would be leaving, almost as if this was unexpected that they would ever return to their homeland.

He tried again after the dinner service and was met by silence for the second time that evening. There were no voices to be heard from behind any door now. The entire hallway seemed dark and quiet.

In the morning, he was awake and alert at dawn. He resolved to be present, at least, when the caravan got underway. He ate a meager breakfast and then sat on the steps outside of the palace. The garden was beginning to bloom in the mid spring, and the air was still crisp. The sun was over the horizon to his left and rising.

After a short time, he heard some stirring behind him and saw

53

that the Queen's guard was readying the assortment of baggage to load into the carts. The Queen's coach was driven right up to the steps where he was sitting.

He stood up and walked over to the entrance, and saw Ashlyn coming toward him. He almost wanted to run to her but remained where he was and waited for her. She came up to him and smiled as they looked each other in the eye.

"I came to see you last night, but your door was closed."

"Oh, my mother required me. She wanted to have a talk about how things were shaping up. I am sorry I missed you."

She turned away slightly and blushed.

"I heard you were leaving today, and now I see it confirmed," Panalt said, gesturing to the baggage.

"Panalt, I didn't know we were leaving today. I would have told you if I did."

"I know that Ashlyn. We have grown close since you arrived here a few weeks ago. I don't want you to go. Can you stay here with me and let your mother return home?"

"I would like that very much. But I cannot, right at the moment. My mother would like me to return with her to Caldorn. There are things she needs to settle, and I need to know those things. If I am to be her heir, I need to know how she makes her decisions. Maybe I can come back in a week and stay for a little longer."

She had sadness in her eyes but also a twinkle. Panalt read her eyes; they did have a connection after all. She did not want to leave him. Panalt was excited to see this, and he began to feel happy enough to last him a week.

He understood that there were things that needed proper planning and orchestration so that order would overcome chaos in the kingdom. Even he, himself, knew that there were things that his father did that he would need to know.

He also knew that Ashlyn was strikingly different from her mother in terms of how they saw their country. Ashlyn would not back down to anyone and told herself that strength was needed. Whereas the Queen would play mind games and try to manipulate a scenario, Ashlyn would stay on course and continue in a time honored traditional way.

She also had physical training. Though her mother would probably say it was dangerous for a princess to be training with weapons, Ashlyn made it a point to know how to defend herself. She did not take for granted that there would always be a guard to protect her. There were many things that Panalt had learned about the princess in the time they spent together. She was intelligent, beautiful, and knew her way around a weapon. Combining it was as attractive of a package as any there was.

"I would like it very much if you returned, Ashlyn."

She reached around him and held him in a warm embrace.

"Thank you Panalt. I will send word soon."

Panalt felt as if he would float away as he disengaged from her. He kept her hands in his own. He knew she would return and could barely think of it any other way. When he stood back, he realized that there were other people all around them preparing for the trip to Caldorn. He had not even noticed their presence there; he was so focused on her. Then he looked to his left a few paces and saw that his father was also in an embrace with the Queen of Caldorn.

Though this was odd for two leaders to embrace, he put it out of his mind. His emotions were racing and he could think of nothing except what was in front of him. They climbed into the coach and disembarked for their journey home.

** ** ** ** **

Nearly five years ago, the urge to explore the region outside of the city overwhelmed Panalt, and he decided to venture out. He travelled south and into the forest and hiked for a few miles. Immediately he felt that he could be at peace here. The natural feel to everything and the earthy smell was so different from what he was accustomed to.

After almost half of a day of hiking and observing, he sat down on a stump to rest. After only a minute, he heard a low whistle and looked in its direction. He almost fell off of his perch when he saw another man standing only three yards away and looking at him. He was dirtied and almost blended into the background with the rest of the forest.

"Look at you," he said.

"What do you mean?" Panalt asked him.

"Well first off, look at what you are wearing. If your crashing through the woods with no regard to how loud you are doesn't scare off the wildlife, then your fancy clothing might."

"These are my clothes. I have no others."

"City folk. They always say they don't have this or that. If you really didn't have this or that you would make do anyway. Look at these clothes…"

He raised his arms, and his cloak hung loosely from his shoulders. It had some minor holes under the arm and a dark stain on the front left side. The color was tough to tell with all the muddied clumps ground into it.

Though he was an older man, he stood fully erect and did not have a bend in his back. His gray hair did not match the fire in his eyes.

"Who are you?"

"My name is Alden. And what are you doing in my woods?"

"My name is Panalt. I come from the castle. I am just walking and exploring."

"Walking like an elephant maybe. I cannot hunt with you traipsing through here. You have to be quiet."

"I'll be quiet. What are you hunting?"

"Nothing right now. Maybe city folk..." Alden said, facing Panalt.

"I have training in grappling," Panalt said, raising his hands.

"Relax, young one. You are just a boy. I have no need to overpower you. How old are you anyway?"

"I am fifteen years of age, and I am the oldest of three."

"Oh, that is all well and good. But you don't need training in wrestling out here. You need training in hunting.

"Can you teach me?"

"I could teach you, but first, you need new clothes. Come with me. It is a few miles to my cabin, but we can begin a lesson with you staying as quiet as you can."

Over the next five years, Alden taught Panalt as much as he knew about hunting and trapping. There were various ways to create a fire and different types of snares that one could employ. The lessons were always informative and had a reward of being used right on the spot. Most were techniques that were perfected by time or by trial and error. Alden had been hunting in the woods since he left his family as an adolescent. He felt the call of nature and wanted to live off of the land.

They made a deal with each other. Panalt would bring a wineskin and thus, the shelter was his to use and the lessons would continue to come. Sometimes Alden would not be around for weeks at a time. Panalt knew he would go on longer hunting expeditions. Alden was such an outdoorsman that even having his shelter was not challenge enough. He would constantly go on lengthy hunting trips with only what he could fit in his pack, to see if he could beat nature at its own game.

After Queen Reesh's caravan departed for Caldorn, Panalt decided that he wanted some time to himself. He was grateful that he had his brothers, but happy that they did not come to the morning's send off. Not only did he get to see Ashlyn before she left, but they were not around to give him a hard time about it.

He gathered some loaves of bread and fruits and stowed them into a pack. He also packed a full wineskin. He hadn't been to the cabin for a long time; he was sure that it needed restocked. This was his refuge. Though he enjoyed the lifestyle of royalty, he found that he sought equally after the freedom from being so formal.

After he left the city's perimeter, he quickly changed his clothing into his forest garb and transformed into a woodsman. The appearance of prince was dropped, and the mind-set of the range took over. It did not take him long to find his markers to lead him to the cabin. When he got there, he found it deserted. Alden must have been on another of his excursions.

The first time he arrived in the cabin to find it empty, he thought Alden may have met his demise. He was thoroughly surprised when the gruff old man barged in the door later in the evening. But it was his house, and he could come and go as he wished. From then on, Panalt did not give attention to the cabin's look of emptiness. It was always the same whether Alden was there or not. It was frugal and dirty, and sometimes vacant.

Panalt sat down in a stiff wooden chair that creaked and groaned with his presence. It was always an adjustment coming here. There was no plush seating or comfortable bedding. It was drafty, and the air seemed moist. That was part of the fun for him. If he wanted opulence, he would have stayed home.

Since it was still early in the day, he decided to get moving and do some hunting. Before he left, he lit a small fire in the hearth and laid out knives on the table. The fire would be hot enough for cooking by the time he returned. He could spend the evening skinning and preparing his catch.

It took him several hours to justify quitting. He set snares in various positions hoping for rabbits. The rabbit snares each seemed to take a while before they yielded anything. He also set a trap that caught a small wild pig before the day was through. This was highly unusual for a catch to be made so quickly. It must have been the right place and time. Normally he had nothing to show for his first day here. The pig triggered its trap within three hours. He just happened to see it from a distance hanging upside down from a sapling and squirming into fatigue.

After cleanly and quickly silencing it, he grabbed both front and both rear legs and slung it over his head, allowing the body to rest on his shoulders. He would retrieve the rabbit snares the next day. Trudging home, he noted that the small chimney had some smoke coming from it and was satisfied. He would have meat tonight, not only bread and fruit.

Panalt entered the cabin and laid the pig down on the table for butchering. Since Alden was not around, he helped himself to some of the wine. It took just under an hour to clean the meat, and he roasted a small amount for himself. There was more than enough to last the few days he would be here.

After his dinner, he relaxed by the fire. He thought about how the last few weeks of his life had gone. He never felt lonely in the cabin before. He had made his decision about his future Queen. That was as pleasant of a thought as any, as he dozed lightly in his chair.

Panalt was startled awake by a knock at the door. The fire had died down, and the lighting was very dim. Groggily, he made his way to the entrance thinking it was odd that Alden was knocking on the door to his own shelter.

He had only gotten the door opened a few inches when it was barreled into by an unseen force from the outside. The door struck him in the forehead, and he saw stars. He was knocked backward to the ground. The jolt surprised him; his sleepy mind was not ready for a physical onslaught. Trying to focus after the blow to his head, he blinked his bleary eyes just long enough to see a canvas sack go over his head.

V

"I can't believe they are finally gone. Did you think that they would ever leave?" Dur asked Tiras.

"Can you imagine staying in another palace for three weeks? I am surprised they did not run out of clothing to wear."

"I'm not sad to see them go, but I bet Panalt is. He probably cried himself to sleep last night after being by himself all day."

"Hey, give him some credit. She is a beauty. But he didn't ever actually say that she was his pick," Tiras defended Panalt.

"She is...I know it. He is going to have the prettiest girl in all the lands at his side. Lucky dog, he is. Have you seen him today?"

"No, I have not. Let's try to find him and see what kind of shape he is in."

They searched the usual spots for their brother, the dining hall, the King's chambers, and Tobin's wing. No one had seen him since the caravan left the day before.

"It is no surprise that no one knows his whereabouts. He must have gone to his cabin in the woods," Tiras explained.

"That is probably the answer. It is funny when you think about it. He doesn't think we know about it."

"It is hard not to miss the fact that he can be gone for a day or two."

"We must have noticed it what? About two years ago?" Dur asked.

"He is always so sneaky when he leaves! I never had a chance to follow him. If I knew where it was, I would pay him a visit there. I bet the look on his face would be priceless. Secret no more!" Tiras was smiling mischievously.

They went back and forth a little longer before tiring of the conversation.

"Panalt has had the attention now for the last few weeks. Maybe it is time for us to step up and earn some praises."

"What do you have in mind, Dur?"

"We need to do something that our father would appreciate. Something that he would recognize us for."

"Go on..."

"I want to make him proud of us."

"Will you come to the point already!" Tiras begged him.

"I want to run the gypsies out of our kingdom!"

"You cannot be serious. There are some thirty of them. What will we do to them anyway?"

"Just send them a message. Father does not think they are a nuisance enough to send the army down there. But we constantly hear folks from the border coming to him to complain about how there are crops that are damaged or stolen."

"I know. One can never guess what one will hear while eavesdropping in the throne room. But he always tells the farmers that there is enough food to go around and that they will continue to earn their wages."

"But they are not part of our people! And they are stealing!" Dur started to get angry.

"I see your point and understand your patriotism. Let's do it."

"Alright, then. It is agreed. And we can hone our skills in ambush tactics while we are at it. Tobin said that we could use some practice."

"I hardly think that is what he meant. But he isn't around to stop us either, now is he. This could get..." Tiras paused. "Exciting!"

"You meant to say dangerous, didn't you?"

"Maybe, but then it wouldn't be as worthy of praise, afterward."

** ** ** ** **

Someone roughly braced themselves with a knee in his back, bound his hands, and then hauled him up. The attack was swift, but not elegant. The intruders were loud and obnoxious. Panalt could hear them complaining that there was nothing of value to steal or even to break. He hoped he would have a chance for revenge and knew he would fight the rogues to the very end, if given a chance. But he knew they would have killed him outright earlier if that was their motive. They were kidnappers, and he would have time to think of a way out of his predicament.

Nightfall was creeping in when the kidnappers drug him out of the shelter. Blindfolded and bound, he had little control over the situation. He was shoved in the back and rammed into a cart. Had he been able to see, he may have avoided smacking his head again off of the tail board. His captors spun him around rigorously and then hoisted him into the wagon. Dazed again from a second shot to the head, he remained laying down. He felt the world spinning even through his blindfold. The headshots and spinning made him feel like he would vomit. It was not long before he passed out on the floor of the cart.

When he came to, he could see a sliver of light coming from

under his chin. The kidnappers must not have tied the canvas bag tight to his neck. He thought about trying to squirm out of it, but he did not want to act too hastily. He may have given his captors an easy catch before, but now he could feel his wits returning to him. He could not gauge how long he had slept, but he did not even have a headache or other after effect from his ordeal.

Panalt could feel that his position had not changed, from what he could remember. He was still lying on a flat surface and his hands were still bound behind his back. The rear axle of this wagon must have had a slight bow in it because the right side of this cargo space was slightly rising and lowering in rhythm with the speed they were going. This also caused the wheel to squeak. He wondered if there would be a wobble in the wheel's tracks. Not that it would help anyone find him, but it may help him return along the same path.

Panalt stayed quiet for a long time. He kept his breathing very low. He was trying to give the impression that he was still sleeping while observing if he was alone or not. He could hear the driver speaking with a companion. There were other sounds too. It seemed as if they were surrounded by other wagons. The wheels were sucking at the muddied ground, and the cart next to him on the right was creaking.

He stayed quiet for the entire day, or what was remaining of it. When he saw the fading light under his chin, he made his mind up that he would try to wriggle out of the blindfolding canvas. He made a low moaning sound and rolled to his side. As he expected, no one was there to check on him, and the cart did not slow. He remained quiet, then, for another bit of time.

He began to stretch his fingers and test the bindings at his wrists. It was a very thick rope and seemed as if it was for towing carts around. This was not a rope that would typically be used to make small knots. Though it was tight now, he felt that he could loosen the knot by continually moving. This rope would not hold forever. Maybe his captors knew this, but he doubted it based on their behavior when they nabbed him. These were not refined woodsmen, and they probably did not know any better when they used this rope on him.

He worked on the rope for a few minutes and felt it grating against his skin. It was loosening enough for him to twist his arm. He felt warmth in his palm and knew that the rope had begun tearing at his skin. He pushed through the pain, and he felt the rope get moist with his blood.

Panalt was feeling very close to escape. He took a little rest and then worked on it again. This was more intense than he had expected it to be. Perhaps his captors were not as dim-witted as he had supposed.

It was getting dark now and he was starting to get hungry. His one track mind had not allowed any thoughts other than escape until just now. He had to put that out of his mind until he was safely away. He tried putting his hands beneath his rear and under his legs but that did not give him the clearance he needed to bring his hands to the front of him. This maneuver however seemed to loosen the rope again, marginally. He gave one last pull and his left hand popped free, banging into the side of the wagon. He almost let out a yelp of pain, but caught himself; something was different. In his concentration, he had not noticed that the cart had stopped.

** ** ** ** **

The day was still in its infancy, long before the sun peaked over the horizon. The sky had only begun to show the first gray band of light that marked the dawn of a new day. Even in this early twilight, visibility was good. The air was crisp and clear and had the smell of newness, fresh and invigorating. The days were beginning to grow longer as early summer emerged.

"How long do you think this expedition will last?" Tiras asked.

"I do not have a good judgment on that. I never did anything like this before. I think a better question is…Where do we start?" Dur replied.

"The reports seem to come mostly from the south. The farmers that are losing crops seem to be from around the Vitirral Mountains."

"That doesn't seem that far from here. I bet it takes less than a day to reach."

"Well, let us get moving quickly. We don't want to be detained and thrown off of our plan."

They each carried a pack, which they filled with various items of food. This consisted of dried meat, fruits and some animal fats. Their naiveté showed as they packed what they could for a day's travel. They did not have the understanding that they may run longer than expected. They did not have the skills for a hunt, but each carried a small knife and their weapons of choice, the bow and a quiver of arrows.

There was no one stirring in the palace when they sneaked through the guest wing and out through one of the back doors to the sparring yard. They felt they would have better luck exiting via that side since it was vacated now, after the celebration.

They each found their favorite horses in the stable, behind the arms depot. Dur chose a black, warmblood gelding which he named Shade. Tiras' pick was also a warmblood gelding, though grey and

62

named Storm. Durable and fast, both horses could be put through a tremendous amount of work.

Moving stealthily, they made their way to the castle wall. The guard on duty spoke as they approached.

"State your business."

"Guard, we are the princes, and we wish to ride in the field to the north along the sea," Dur lied. He was a little nervous as he spoke.

"I know perfectly well that you are the princes. Why are you about at this hour?" He gave them a suspicious look.

"We know that Panalt came this way, and we would like to join him for a ride," Tiras chimed in.

"In point of fact, he did not come this way. Or at least, not this morning."

"Well, he did exit the castle, and I know how he did it," Dur said hoisting up a wine skin. "We'll give this to you, and you can open the gate."

"I see…You have some knowledge of how bribery works. But princes, that action should not be so public. Put that down. At least there is no one here to observe us."

They then dismounted and spoke quietly amongst themselves. Their gamble of calling out the guard paid off. They had gotten lucky and spoke to the same guard as Panalt normally would.

"My name is Strefan. Ask for me when you come here. You have chosen the time wisely. Either myself or one other is on duty during these early hours."

"We want to make the same deal as Panalt," Dur said shrewdly.

"Well, he brings a wineskin and I open the gate. He says he will be gone for three or four days and will return in the morning, the same as when he leaves. I try to time it out so that I have the watch for that third and fourth consecutive day. How long will you be gone for?"

"Today."

"I will not be available to open the gate again later. You must return in the morning."

"As you say then, Strefan. We will see you on the morrow."

They exited the castle and rounded it. Once out of sight of the main entryway, they headed south and around the forest on the west side. They were proud of themselves. They figured out a way to leave at just about any time. This was going to be easy. They were making jokes with one another and having a good time as they rode.

They rode for half of the morning before they came across the first field. Some of the earlier planted crops were already grown to about knee high. Still others were being sown even at this point, in early summer. They spotted a farmer tending to his work.

It took a little longer than they anticipated getting to him. Once they dismounted, they had to travel around the field so as not to disrupt the freshly planted seeds.

"Hey there," Tiras called out.

The farmer stood abruptly and tightly clutched his pitchfork.

"Whoa, kind sir. We do not mean you harm," Tiras continued, holding his hands up.

"There have been gypsies about. Are you part of their group?"

"No sir, we are from the castle," Dur said.

"Well, your attire may be neater than theirs, but it is just as colorful."

"We are only two."

"That is how they work, sometimes. They say they are only two and then bring in many more while you are sleeping."

"You need not take us in, sir. We are not in need of shelter. But can you show us what they did?" Tiras asked.

Warily, the farmer pointed to his field. There was a bald spot right in the middle of it. The crops were plucked clean from the earth. The entire plant was taken.

"Did you see this happen?" Tiras asked.

"With my very eyes. They came at dusk, the night before last. I should have prepared better."

"What would you have done? One against many? You may be lucky they did not burn your field." Dur consoled him.

"Which direction did they go?" asked Tiras.

"They went west, young men. West. Are you going after them? Two against many is not any stronger than one. What do you think will happen when you catch up to them?"

"We have time to plan that out, my good sir. Thank you for the information." Dur said, turning from him.

They left the farmer, who stood staring at them. Then they turned direction and rode to the west; they were only thirty miles south of Albinion. That was a lot closer to home than they had previously thought. The mountain range was still another hundred miles or so off.

They traveled another few hours when they saw a trail of wagon wheels. They followed it for another few miles before seeing that it was joined by many other carts and animal tracks. This was what they were seeking. Having found the sign they were looking for, they stopped for a short lunch.

"What do you think of what the farmer said about our clothing?"

asked Tiras.

"I don't think he understands the style of the city," Dur shot back jokingly.

"What else do we have with us?"

"Nothing, but we can make some changes, even so."

They took off their crimson tunics and flipped them inside out. The underside was darker and looked more brownish. They had to cut off the collar so that it did not scratch their necks. They did the same with their light brown riding pants. Again, the underside of the pants was a darker color, and the outfit seemed to feel instantly more natural and less ornate. Both the tunics and riding pants now showed the seams to the outside, and the princes looked quite humble. They ditched their gloves and scuffed their boots. The look was more complete now. After switching the clothing, they mounted up and resumed their tracking.

"I did not think it would be this long before we overtook them. They must have been farther from that field than we expected. What an enormous head start!" Dur exclaimed.

"We should be devising a plan for what we are going to do when we catch up to them."

"I think I have a plan, Tiras."

They rode and talked about it for some time. The sun was beginning to streak its red rays through the clouds. The glare was reflecting off of the plain ahead of them, but it looked cloudy. The heat waves were rising in front of them, and they had to blink their eyes.

"Look!" Tiras said, pointing.

The cloudy mirage rising was not heat after all, but dust kicked up by a travelling caravan.

"We found them!" Dur remarked, also pointing.

They looked at each other and saw they were each pointing for the other to look in that direction.

"We have to stay low. Let's flank them so that we are not such easy targets to see in the setting sun."

"They may set up camp soon."

It was getting dark, and there were trees looming in the distance. They would have to cover the remaining ground quickly, quietly, and without being caught.

"If we can get around them and into the trees, we will have a better shot at taking them down."

"We can set our plan up there and survey the area to see if changes are needed."

** ** ** ** **

Panalt did not think that he was creating a lot of noise while struggling to free himself of the rope. But he did have a canvas bag over his head, and he could really only hear his own breathing. He realized that he needed to remain steady and give the appearance of being captive for a little longer.

Though the cart had stopped a few minutes earlier, he was surprised to still be left alone. He could not imagine what would be happening except that the captors were setting up camp. It was dark now, and he was having a hard time distinguishing the darkness from the canvas blindfolding him.

He gingerly rolled back over onto his back, with his hands under him. He did not want to take the chance of his freedom from his bindings being detected. It was a long time before he decided that he could finish his escape.

Panalt again wriggled his left hand free of the rope and rolled to his side. He again was reassured that no one was in the space with him, since this was unimpeded. He sat upright and quickly brought his hand up to his chin, yanking the canvas bag off. He was braced for impact in case there was an observer, but he was alone. It did not take long for his eyes to adjust to the failing light. His long time in the blindfold had already adapted his pupils to darkness.

He was in a cart that was about four feet wide by seven feet long and covered by a thin cloth. He could see through the cloth and noted that there were several fires going. There were a few people that walked by the wagon and were silhouetted by the fire. The smart move would be retreating through the front entrance, near where the driver sat. He could not possibly escape undetected by exiting through the back of the cart.

When he tried the cloth, he found that it was very hard to tear. Instinctively, he reached for his hunting knife at his right side, but found it missing. He still did not have any idea of why he was taken, but he knew why he had been relieved of his knife. He needed to get a start in the cart's cover before he could rip a hole in it large enough to get through, so he grabbed it and tried to use his teeth to make a small opening.

Having accomplished the feat of tearing through the covering, he peered outside to take in his surroundings. There was a field to his left and some trees to his right. This could make his escape easier by sneaking into the trees. To his surprise, there was a small sack containing his meager belongings right between the driver's seat and the cargo bay. His knife would come in handy right about now.

Just as he reached into the bag and grasped his knife, he heard voices from outside of the back end of the wagon. He whipped his head around and saw two dark figures approaching.

"Let's see if the prisoner is hungry."

"He has to wake up some time. He has been sleeping for a day and a half."

Panalt slithered through the hole he fashioned in the fabric and got to the driver's seat just as his captors opened a panel in the cover.

"He's gone!"

"Not for long. He can't have gotten far!"

"Look there's a hole in the sheet."

"We'll have him, yet."

** ** ** ** **

The twins managed to flank the caravan and sneak into the trees. They hunkered down in the trees just outside the ring of the caravan. The inside out clothing they wore seemed to camouflage them, and they were pleased. Once under cover, they whispered about their plan and waited a little longer.

"We need fire for our plan, and we cannot risk starting a fire here. We'll be caught, for sure," Dur said.

"They have plenty of fires burning."

"I see that. Look, there is an open cart, without a cover."

"Are you thinking what I am thinking?"

"We may need some extra height to make the shot."

They turned around and looked about them. It was dark out in the open, but even more so in the trees. The visibility was bad, and their shadows mixed with those of the gypsy wagons. They had a hard time finding what they were looking for.

"I see it, Tiras. There's a stump there and a tree on its side. That will give us each a platform to stand on. I don't want to climb up a tree, the downward angle will be wrong."

"And if we climb up a tree, we may not be able to get back down quick enough for a second volley, or defense."

They positioned themselves. Dur took up his placement on the overturned tree, and Tiras stood on the stump. They were about twenty feet apart, and each had a different view inward to the center of the camp. The last step was wrapping up the tips of several arrows with bits of torn cloth and then smearing them with the lard they brought with them. As they were finishing, something caught their eye.

"Tiras, there seems to be some alarm in the camp."

"That may be the sign we are looking for."

Each of them nocked an arrow and took aim. They let the volley fly in an 'X' formation from their point of attack. Dur shot first, then Tiras only a second behind. Each arrow was aimed at the cart without a cover and skipped off of the flat cargo area. The arrows remained true to their original flight path and careened over a blazing fire. The lard instantly ignited, and the arrows buried themselves into the fabric covers of two wagons.

Now the alarm rose tenfold as the gypsies were beginning to cry out and run around. Their caravan had somehow caught fire, two carts at the same time.

"Time for one more volley, then let's move!"

"Quickly now, we don't have much time before they detect us!"

They let fly again and caught another two targets. The clamor was growing, and the animals began stirring outside the circle. They were bucking and braying with fright.

The twins jumped off of their perches and ran toward the other side of the camp when they saw him. A man was fighting a host of the gypsies by himself. There must have been five of them attacking at once, but he was holding his own.

"Who is that man?" Dur asked his brother.

"I don't know, Dur. Maybe it is a prisoner or an outcast. Whoever it is, they need help."

"And we are the ones to provide it."

** ** ** ** **

Panalt could not breathe easy just yet. He may have been loose from his bondage, but he was not to safety. Only seconds passed between him slipping through the hole he made and his captors opening the back of the fabric. He stayed absolutely still sitting on the driver's seat. When he heard the disgust coming from the men behind him, he made a break for it.

The men were much faster than he expected and rounded the side of the wagon in time to see him leap down. He circled around the next wagon and then ducked and rolled under yet another. He was desperate to avoid capture for a second time. It was dark, and his tracks would be harder to see, but he had nowhere to go. There were miles of plains to his left, and the forest was still a few yards off to his right. He would be an easy target if he ran in either direction right now.

He had to remain calm and think. He had a weapon, so his position was of a much greater advantage than just minutes prior. He would fight his way to the forest and then disappear. He had experience on his side. Alden had taught him what he needed to know to survive alone in the rough world nature provided. He was almost ready to crawl out from under his cart when it burst into flames above his head. Bewildered, he scampered out from under the inferno and prepared for an assault. The camp was in chaos. Some of the gypsies were running around wildly. Others were trying to corral the animals, which were beginning to break free of their tethers. And there were more, still, who were waiting for him. His immediate thought was that they were sacrificing a wagon of their own to flush him out into the open, but then there were other carts ablaze as well. He could not think of what may have happened, but he had to defend himself.

The remaining gypsies gathered their weapons and advanced on him. They were of the mind that he had started the fire and would now take their vengeance. He quickly overpowered one of them and stole his sword away from him. In the back of his mind, he was thanking Tobin for his preparation and training with the double sword technique. Armed with his knife and a sword, he could withstand the next few attackers.

With his back to the wagons, he braced himself against his attackers. Their faces were nearly blacked out by the silhouetting of the fires. Before the attackers came for a second round, Panalt was flanked to either side. Two men had come from behind him and sneaked around the wagon at his tail. This caused the gypsies to pause.

"Do you need help?" one asked.

Turning abruptly, Panalt asked, "Are you not one of them?"

"We are not!"

It only took Panalt a second to recognize the voices and put faces to them. His brothers were here.

"What are you doing here?" Panalt asked, in total dismay.

"Talk later, defend now!" Dur shouted and stood next to him.

"Tiras, watch our backs! Dur, take the left side, I have the right!" Panalt directed them.

The twins raised their bows and prepared to fire, but held their arrows under control. Panalt raised both his hands, each gripping a blade. Now with the threesome standing in a tight triangle, the gypsies were less confident than before. The odds were cut down from five against one to four against three. They dropped their weapons in a cowardly fashion and turned tail. The gypsies tried their best to gather their comrades and leave the burning circle.

"Stay out of Gildesh!" Dur yelled at them.

"Let this be a lesson to you!" Tiras added.

Before long, they were the only living souls in the area. The animals had dispersed, and the gypsies gave chase after them. The wagons were still burning, but the brothers now could relax their tense grips on the weapons.

"Well isn't that something now…finding you here. Coming to my rescue," Panalt said.

"Rescue? In a manner of speaking, I suppose. What are you doing here?" Tiras asked him.

"I should be asking you the same thing. I was kidnapped from my cabin…" He shut his mouth quickly.

"Panalt, we know you have a cabin."

"Well then, I was kidnapped and held prisoner."

"For what reason?"

"I do not know. No one even talked to me. I cannot deduce what their reasoning was."

"That must have been dreadful, being taken against your will," Dur remarked.

"Well, we can say it ended just fine though, now can't we?" Tiras asked.

"Indeed, with only scratches as proof it happened. So, then, come to it. What are you doing here? And look at your clothes. You two look like beggars."

"The mighty woodsman is mocking us, Tiras. Look at your own garb, Panalt. Ours is only slightly less dirtied. We needed to fit in with the land during our tracking. You must agree that our palatial clothing is not made for anything but formalities and merriment. Anyway, we were going to try to drive the gypsies out of our country."

"That is a bold plan. I hope that the lesson holds its sway a while. Time will tell, but they will not retaliate soon, I'm betting."

"So, Panalt, do you have anything to eat? We didn't bring enough for more than one day," Tiras asked him.

"Did I not just tell you I was a prisoner? How would I have the means to carry my own food? Relax though, the gypsies have left plenty around for us. We will camp here for the remainder of this night and then head back to the city. Where are we, anyway?"

"I am fairly certain that we are near the Hemage Forest close to the Vitirral Pass. I think we could make out the peaks to the south, before nightfall," replied Dur. "That was about where I expected to find the gypsies."

"Find them you did," remarked Panalt. "And me, too."

"I'm sorry, Panalt, we do not have a horse for you, but we didn't expect to see you."

"I can't blame you for that, but come now brothers…only

enough food for one day. That is the planning of a novice."

"Listen, Tiras, we save him and he tells us we have planned poorly."

"We did plan poorly," Tiras replied, then looked at Panalt. "Maybe a few lessons will be needed."

"They can start after some sleep. The sun is about to rise on another day. Let's cook a breakfast over one of these fires and try to find an intact cart to sleep in."

VI

Kelduun bobbed his head up.

"Have I slept?" he said aloud, before catching himself.

Kelduun was in a darkened room near the front of the castle of Brondin, in the guest quarters. More than once he needed to rely on a spell to conceal him from prying eyes. Sometimes he would distract his would-be captors with a sound of a pebble skittering down the hallway. Other times he would cast a shadow spell to make the very air seem impermeable and thick.

He had successfully kept to himself for the last few weeks and watched as the furry lizards continued adding to their numbers. His chance of escape was minimized with each passing day. The sheer number of them seemed incalculable. How could so many people have been turned in such a short amount of time? Were all of these people from Sehaida?

It was hard to even think of them as people any longer. Their behaviors were transformed as equally as their bodies. They were savages. Each felt the need to lash out at others and try to bite each other, testing their limits. None were as brutal as the former king. There was no regard for killing one of the underlings if they managed to scratch him or assert more than their share of dominance.

They were animals, raw and untamed. Any air of civility had been whisked away. There was blood splattered everywhere. They took to feasting on their own domesticated animals and livestock. Bones were strewn across the once pristine city.

The days never looked different, now. The dark cloud cover was pervasive and blocked out almost every last band of lighting. Kelduun was roused by the sound of thunder and stood to observe the fields.

He felt as if a bolt of lightning flowed through his body as panic rose up in him. When he looked out over the plains south of Brondin, they were empty.

The army must have moved on in pursuit of new recruits, carnage, and massacre. Only questions remained behind. When did they go? Which direction did they head in? How much of a head start did they have?

This was not good. He did not know what should be done first, but he needed to act fast. His panic subsided, and he regained his composure. He needed a way to travel fast. There was no cause for him to defend himself now. He strode out the main entrance to the castle and around it to the stables.

As he expected, there was precious little to be found there. The animals were slaughtered, and their wasted body parts were scattered with absolute disregard. He looked down at the damages and wept inwardly. This behavior could not continue. This wave of disease and destruction would cover the world if he did not step in to stop it. The foe he was against had no feelings or remorse. There was no regret over killing. There was only a need to expand and feed.

He was walking out of the barn when he caught sight of a lame mule, lying on its side. Approaching it, he saw a set of clawed lacerations through its abdomen, and the entrails were beginning to bulge out. It had a broken rear left leg and was bleeding profusely.

He reached down to touch its neck and found it was still breathing shallowly. He could not bring himself to end its life right there, in the stable. Instead, he focused and gave some of his energy to it.

The mule gasped and picked up his head. Kelduun kept his hand firmly on its neck, effectively demobilizing it. His hand began to glow with white light, and more energy was coursing through his arm, into the animal. The lacerations reversed themselves and began to come together. First they ended with a scar as if sewn up; then they disappeared all together and formed a fresh hide. The leg straightened itself, and a subtle crunch was heard before it kicked and flexed strongly.

The mule was wide eyed, but did not struggle. Its damaged body was being renewed, but still, Kelduun held on. He looked the mule in the eyes, and it calmed down even more. Bringing his other hand down and placing it on its back, Kelduun focused what remained of his energy into it. The light was blinding and enveloped both of them.

When the light faded and returned to normal, Kelduun's vision seemed dimmed. His eyes were still recovering from the light burst. The transformation was complete.

"Rise, my friend," Kelduun commanded softly.

In its place a great white stallion rose swiftly and stood. The lowly pack mule was converted to a mighty war horse.

"I shall call you Bolt!"

The stallion stood at sixteen hands and was rippling with musculature across its chest and shoulders. It took several steps to the side and then dipped its head down to Kelduun. Gingerly, he placed his hand on its cheek.

Kelduun was weakened by the exertion required to convert his steed. He leaned against his horse and exhaled a long breath. The horse lowered itself to its front knees to allow an easier mount and Kelduun crawled onto it. Breathing heavily, Kelduun remained keeled over, nearly lying on the horse. He had a grasp on the mane, so as not to fall off as the horse rose to its full height.

The steed brought him out of the stable and around the castle wall to the main entrance. He gently dismounted then and entered the archway. Finding the room he used as a shelter, he quickly stowed what remained of his stash of food. There was no one around for cooking new meals daily, and what he had was depleted and getting stale.

Previously, he would never have risked building a fire in one of the hearths. Besides the fireplace not being designed for roasting meat, he could not afford being caught. Even now, he could not make a fire and lose time. He had to deal with what he had and leave immediately.

He quickly regained the stamina required to mount and ride. Soon he would regain his full energy and be required to put it to the test. When he exited the palace of Brondin, he did not look back. The place had the smell of death in it. It could never be remade the same. The city would be better off if it was razed to the ground and rebuilt.

Bolt was standing by and looked eager to run full out. Having a renewed vigor, Kelduun was now able to mount with ease, without the horse bending downward. The pair raced out of the city's gate and out into the open field. This was where the growing army of beasts was standing, only days prior. There must have been a sign as to which direction they had gone.

When he got to the footprints delineating the front line, he stopped and jumped off of his mount. Examining the ground, he could see the strange imprint of their feet. There were four toe marks with scratches extending from each and the small pad of a sole behind. Additionally, the rear of the foot had another two toe marks with the same scratches. The scratches were presumably claws or talons. These beasts would be merciless killing machines.

The sheer volume of them meant that they covered much ground, even while standing in file, over the plain. The area covered by them was vast, and it took several minutes to find the edges of the formation. When he got to the edge, his heart sank as he realized that this was only one legion and that the next division started only feet away. He continued on and found that there were two more areas of trample. He expected that this was matched on the other side as well and estimated that the army would have had to be in the range of fifty to one hundred thousand.

Scanning further, he saw evidence of tracking and guessed their source as war machines for battery, siege, and catapult. The scope of this army was breathtaking, and he could not begin to speculate the amount of potential destruction this army could deliver.

He knew he would need to alert the other lands of an impending doom, and quickly. There was no way he could deliver the urgent message without the help of his trusty servant. He had not had a need for his falcon in a long time.

Long ago, on a venture along the cliff walled shoreline of the Western Vitirral Mountains, he chanced upon the fallen hatchling. It was lame with a broken wing, but it had fire in its eyes. The falcon hatchling was intently studying the old wizard. Kelduun had to stoop and wait a long time before it allowed him to touch it. After he scooped it up and cradled it, he began scanning the wall above him for a sign of the aerie. Indeed, there was an overhang nearly half way up the vertical face. After debating for a short time, Kelduun decided that he would be sending his new young companion to his death if he returned it to its home. Its avian mother would not allow it to compete with another hatchling for food when this one would surely go on to perish.

He nursed it and trained it since that first afternoon. When the falcon's wing was healed, Kelduun breathed magic into it and gave the falcon the ability to return to his master when needed, as well as an unnaturally long life. Over the course of the next hundred and fifty years, it had grown to be the best message carrier he had ever seen. Carrier pigeons could only fly from one destination to another. Kelduun's falcon was able to lock onto his energy source and find him nearly anywhere he was in the lands. This advantage was paramount at the moment.

His free spirit did not allow him to keep the falcon tied to himself, though. He had always called upon it when needed and released it into the wild after, to have the freedom any wild creature deserves. Given this, he knew it would take at least a day or two for the falcon to home in on his energy and find him. That should give him the time he needed to track down this army and determine where it was headed for attack. Kelduun gave two short chirping whistles, starting low and ending in a high pitch. That was all that was needed, his falcon would find him.

** ** ** ** **

There was a jingle in the window. This was the message that King Vernon Secandor was waiting for.

QUEEN C.R. HEADED HOME WITH PRINCESS A.R.
EXPECTED TIME OF ARRIVAL IS SIX DAYS

He could now determine the state of his alliance with the other countries. Given the delivery time of this message, the queen would be home in another four to five days. He knew that it would take half of a fortnight for Merion to travel the distance from Crute to Creyason, even on horse. The trek to be taken would lead him west around Lake Proseccan and between the mountains. He would have to journey through Gildesh and then again around the Cysterule Mountains near the sea. The time to send him was now.

He sent a servant to bring his son to him.

"Merion, my boy…It is time to see if history still has pull. Go to Caldorn and talk with Queen Crissannah Reesh. Remember to gain as much information as possible. Try not to allow deception to rise in your voice. Have confidence in your conversation."

"I will do as you say. I will not allow her to manipulate the conversation and coerce me into saying anything I needn't say."

"Good luck, my son. May speed be on your side."

"I will return when I am satisfied I have the answers we need."

Merion gave a slight bow and turned on his heel. He strode out of his father's chambers and then down toward the library. He kept his journal there, amongst the other books. It did not take long for him to pack the things he wanted to take with him into a sack. Descending further down towards the main entrance, he exited the inner most ring and circumnavigated the wall toward the stable. He chose a medium sized, sport horse for its speed. It was a spotted horse, and though he was constantly told to get a better looking horse, this one was his favorite. One of its spots seemed to resemble the great Lake Proseccan, and so he called the horse Pro. Then he circled back around and called for a squire to join him on his journey.

There were several young men that he had played with as a youth, but he wanted one he could trust. He chose one from the ranks.

"Gendin, my friend…will you come with me on a journey?"

"My prince, yes, if you command it."

"There is no command. I ask it of you. We shall be equals on this excursion. No titles between us, you may call me plainly by my name."

"Prince, uh Merion, yes. I will try."

** ** ** ** **

"My Lord?"

"Tobin, you only address me like that when there is something on your mind. Come now, what can I do to help you."

"Palantine, have you seen the princes today?"

"Why, come to think of it, I have not. Were they with you?"

76

"That is the thing, sire…They did not show up for their training the day before yesterday or today. I did not think much of it at the time, but I have not seen them for at least a day now, maybe two whole days. That is unusual."

"Indeed. They are oft found around the halls in your wing. Perhaps they have found some new project to invest their minds into."

"Perhaps Panalt. His mind is always searching for a new way to enhance himself. I know he can go missing for a day or two at a time. The twins always seem to have some excuse for him, as to where he is. But he is faithful when it comes to his training. He would not miss it. Dur and Tiras also may have found some mischief to get into. But I doubt that the three of them are all together. Not having any of the three of them around almost makes this castle seem quiet."

"You may be on to something. Let us have a good look around the palace and surrounding area in the city though, before we get too excited."

They did just that. They began a simple search through each of the areas the boys would most likely be in and found nothing. The guards lowered the double draw-bridge system, and Tobin looked around the perimeter of the wall outside. He then asked some of the peasants if they had seen anything. One of them said that there were two riders that left only two days ago at dawn, but he could not have determined who they were. He said they turned to the south.

Tobin had a clue to follow and returned to the castle guards at the gate. There was a new crew coming on duty, and he had twice the amount of men to question about the two riders. After several men denied any knowledge, he came to asking Strefan the same few questions.

"Did you see the princes leave the castle?"

Strefan's face immediately bloomed a darker shade of pink when he heard these words.

"I…" he cleared his throat and stammered, "Which day was this?"

"Do not try to hold it back from me, Strefan," Tobin commanded him.

Tobin was a head taller than the guard and was intimidating him as they talked. He could sense the nervousness in Strefan's body language. Conversely, Strefan could feel the courage draining out of himself.

"I saw them, sir!" he broke down and blurted out.

Tears welled up in his eyes, and he was shaking in fear.

"Easy there, let's keep it straight then, you and I. Let's go over to that rock and sit for a while."

After they moved away from the group, Strefan felt better and began to regain some dignity back. Tobin waited for him to come around and did not say anything when Strefan lifted his head to look into Tobin's face.

"They came to me two days ago, before the sun came up. I did not want to let them leave, but they are the princes, and I did not want to disappoint them. I had also had dealings with the eldest one before, and he always came back precisely when he said he would."

"Wait a minute, Strefan, take it slow here. Start from the beginning. Do you mean Panalt, as well as the twins?"

"Panalt has been coming to me for a few years now. He goes out into the city for a day sometimes. Other times he says that he goes into the forest. That is when he comes back in two or three days. He always tells me how long it will be. He must have a good sense of time or watch the sun and stars because you can rely that he will make good on his word. He is always consistent about when he returns. If he says it is morning or evening for his return, he wouldn't be late."

That was one answer to Panalt. It was interesting, but not entirely surprising. He felt he could sense that the twins were covering for him each time.

"Did Panalt come this way?"

"Yes, he came three days ago. He said that he would not return until tonight after dusk. That gives him several more hours before I would start to worry about anything. The other two though..."

"Yes," Tobin interjected, allowing Strefan to continue with the knowledge that he had an attentive listener.

"As I said, they came to me two days ago. They said they would only be gone for the day. No longer."

"And that is all? Did you alarm anyone?"

"They had never come to me before. I did not know that they would not be good on their word. I assumed that they would be in line with their older brother. I figured they would meet up somewhere and return together."

"That very well may be," Tobin reached up to stroke his chin thoughtfully.

"I regret not coming forward before, sir, but I felt that I would be reprimanded and thrown in a cell."

"We shall call this a lesson, Strefan. No trouble will come to you. It is hard to come forth and tell the truth. But as for your position here at the front gate..." Tobin paused, thinking.

"Please, sir, I will do whatever you need."

"You will remain on guard here until nightfall and then report to me directly. If the princes return on schedule as you say they may, then we continue as usual, but with a new set of rules to follow. If the princes do not return, a different approach will be acted upon."

"Thank you, sir! I will be on the highest alert for their return."

"See that you are, Strefan. I expect to have a report before midnight."

Noon turned into afternoon and continued on into evening. Strefan felt that his nerves would jump out of his body. He scanned the horizon from the top wall of the castle for hours. When the night darkened, small blips of lights could be seen around the city, from the citizens' small hearths warming their homes. There were great fires lit upon the parapets of the castle to cast light over the area.

Several more hours passed and no one came up to the gate of the castle. Strefan reluctantly descended the steps from the top of the fortification to the ground level. He walked glumly up the main path to the stairway leading into the palace.

Tobin was waiting for him in his quarters.

"Sir, they have not returned," Strefan could not look him in the eyes.

"You may leave me," Tobin said solemnly. "Finish your watch for tonight and then return for reassignment in the morning."

"As you wish, sir."

Tobin was thinking. He did not know where the boys had gone or what they felt they needed to accomplish. Worse yet, their absence or late return was foreboding. Could they have fallen to some tragedy?

He took to the southern wing and climbed the steps up to King Palantine's chambers.

"My lord, I have gathered some information."

"Speak up about it, Tobin."

He told him then of what he had found out. The three young men had gone out of the palace walls and most likely departed the city's boundaries. There was a guard that had some knowledge of this.

"I shall hang the guard by his ankles! This shall not go unpunished!"

"I told him no harm would come to him, sire. He was truthful in his admission."

"I am King, Tobin!" he paused, only for a second, cutting himself off. "I am sorry, old friend. I do not mean to raise my voice to you."

"Sire, I am here to serve you. Tell me what you need from me, and it shall be so."

The King was looking away from him. He looked shaken.

"Tobin, I am almost incapable of deciding anything right now. What do you think is best?"

"I can lead a party in search of them."

"Very well. But take my palace guard. They are the finest soldiers in the royal army, and they will serve you well."

"How many shall I take with me?"

"Take them all, Tobin. There are around two hundred of them. That amount of soldiers looking for them should allow for a faster sweep across the surrounding vicinity. As you know, they are all very well trained, and each would recognize my boys from a distance."

"That will cut a portion of fighters out of the royal army, but these have been peaceful times."

"They are the best I have to offer, Tobin. What more important objective is there for them to accomplish?"

"I will take my leave then, Palantine. I will send word when I have found them."

"Use any resource you need, Tobin. May your search be graced with luck."

Tobin turned and left him. He went directly to his wing and prepared for his search. He equipped himself with his traditional leather armor. The chest showed a darker band of leather on each side covering the shoulder and trailing down to his belt. His kingdom's crest, an eagle, was fixed in the middle of the breast. He placed his swords in a crossed sheath over his back. Nearly every part of his gear was designed for swift movement and quick attack. He then went to the armory to choose a bow and a quiver to mount on his steed. Finally, he came around to the stable to garner his horse. It was a stallion like the King's, though kept in a different portion of the grounds. The King's was slightly larger, but still, Tobin's horse was more than capable of galloping for miles at top speed. It was black as night, and he called it Reaper.

Having gathered the necessary weapons, he went to the front gate of the compound.

"Strefan," he called.

"Yes, sir, I am here."

"Your duties will be changing. You are to gather what you need to join me in the search for the princes. Make haste now, lad."

"As you say, sir."

Strefan nearly leapt away. He knew he was getting a second chance to make amends. There would be no hesitation in serving Tobin. In his mind, Tobin had saved him from the dungeon.

Shortly thereafter, Tobin had the palace's royal guard surrounding him as he gave the order of the King.

"We will search for the princes until they are found. Alive or dead, they will be brought home."

The royal guard each held up their right fist at this command and gave a shout of agreement. They exited the palace gate and assembled into a formation just outside the wall. The city extended before them.

They made their way through the city quickly, but without success. It was determined they would have to leave Albinion to conduct a search of the countryside.

** ** ** ** **

Kelduun had his full energy back to him and was scanning the horizon. There was no sign of the dark army. He would have to track them. It would be slow and tedious until he had a direction to turn in.

Mounting Bolt, he quickly rode around the perimeter of the once present formation. The footprints and trample were easy to detect. Coming around to the western edge, he noted that there were a multitude of trails leading in every direction. He deduced that this was the gathering, not the exodus. The trails were worn, but not encompassing of an entire army.

The major path the army took was a swath of grass mowed down by countless footsteps. Travelling due south, it took him a day and a half to come to a change in the trail. Kelduun could not believe he was so far behind them; an army of that size should be seen for miles away. The pace of their traverse was remarkable. Perhaps they were driven by hunger, or blood thirst.

Kelduun jumped off his steed and inspected the ground. There were only two logical directions to proceed. The army would have to try to squeeze its numbers through the Vitirral Pass and the Hemage Forest if their intent was to continue to the south.

After a thorough inspection of the tracking, he determined that south was not the direction of their travel. He took longer than he had anticipated to be doubly sure that he was not mistaken. It could only mean that the direction they took would be to the east.

They were headed for an invasion of Gildesh.

VII

Merion loved his home country of Strayos. The flat plains extended farther than the eye could see. The lake breeze was invigorating. There could be nothing better than to sit on the balcony of the palace's summit and watch the rolling lake beneath him. Each time his father sent him on an errand through his country, it further engrained the sense of pride he had in it. Though Vernon Secandor was King, Merion felt he also had a sense of ownership in the dealings he presided over. He wanted nothing more than to make his father proud of him and prove that he was a worthy heir to the throne.

He had been travelling around his own country for about two years and was confident that he knew the terrain. However, this was the first time his father had sent him out of the country, and alone. There was an untold amount of information to be gathered in the other countries, and he was prepared to record it in his journal. The second day had only just begun, but they had already rounded the southern tip of the great Lake Proseccan and were on their way westward.

The planned arrival in Caldorn's capital of Creyason was to be in ten days. It could even be shaved to nine days if they rode strong and hard. This was not necessary though, and he was busying himself with note taking to ensure he would not miss anything along the way.

The fourth day saw the western tip of the lake and Merion, with Gendin, was able to turn to the north. The two riders were continuously talking to one another.

"I have never been outside of the capital, sir."

"I told you just to call me Merion, but I suppose sir is better than being called Highness. It sounds too much like you are addressing my father, anyway. That will take a long time to get used to when my time comes."

"You said that you had been around our country in the past?"

"Yes, Gendin. I have been through all the land of Strayos. It is a peaceful place. You can see for miles and miles. It is so flat."

"Do you think we have been going uphill since we started today?"

"I think so. I am guessing that is the early rise before we get to the mountains. The peaks you see far off to the west are the Vitirral Mountains. We should begin to see the Cysterule Mountains to the north today and then pass them tomorrow."

"How do you know all this?"

"I have spent many days in my father's library. There is much to study, if you have the time."

They rode then, for a time, enjoying the breezy climate around the water's edge. The Cysterule Mountain range could just be made out on the horizon.

"I have never been out of the country. It will not be long before we cross into Gildesh. My only experience with Gildesh is the journey to its capital of Albinion for Prince Panalt's gathering. Luckily, we do not have to go that far into the country. We can skirt the mountain range all the way into Caldorn. Gendin, do you know how to hunt?"

"No Merion. There is so little game around us and no forested lands near the capital."

"I do not know how to hunt either. You speak the truth; there is no game around for us to practice on, only the livestock we keep. I have been fishing many a time, though. I have been out on the great Lake Proseccan on a skiff before."

"You braved those waters? I heard that there were monsters abound in the deep."

"Perhaps there are, but I have never seen anything. Though I must say, the lake is big enough that it would take days to cross it. That gives a lot of space for sea creatures to be lurking."

"I would think twice before going again."

"Gendin, there is nothing to worry about. Maybe I will take you out with me next time. I think that we should be loading up some fish now, though, before we cross into Gildesh."

They spent the rest of the afternoon relaxing and fishing off of the shoreline of the lake. After camping for the night, they awoke to find the sky dark grey and cloud covered. The temperature was dropping and they hoped the rain would not threaten their progress on this voyage. It had been a relatively dry summer, but both of them knew that the rain was much needed in the plains at home.

** ** ** ** **

Kelduun stretched his arm skyward and held it perpendicularly to the ground. His eyesight was keen. He spied his falcon from a distance and knew it was hunting him down. After a moment, the bird dove and grasped his gloved arm in its talons.

Kelduun gently pulled his arm down to gaze at his helper directly. He spoke softly to it for several minutes.

"It is good to see you, my friend," he said in a low, whispering voice. "Your task is of the greatest importance. You must fly as fast as the wind to the capital of Gildesh. To Albinion. Deliver this message to King Palantine and then return to find me. I will have much work for you to do this time."

He already had the message he wanted to deliver written and rolled into a small tube. He slipped the cylinder into a small clip which encircled its right leg. Then he flipped up a small portion of red meat and threw his arm upward. The falcon leaped into the air, catching the meat as it flew up and away.

** ** ** ** **

The rain continued for the next four days as Merion and Gendin travelled north. Their spirits were diminished but not their resolve. They pushed through the weather, though, it made their travel slower. The terrain, which was nearly flat only days ago, was now littered with rocky outcroppings and stony slabs extending down from the Cysterules.

The rain was punishing the rocky wall to their right, but the mountain's vertical face was enduring, and the rain washed over the stone. The thin layer of water was rushing down the wall of the mountain like a curtain falling down. It seemed connected and moving as one, but it was perpetually bombarded with more watery missiles.

The arid conditions just prior to this storm made for a muddy problem. The windblown dust and dirt which had accumulated on the rocks was beginning to turn into a muddy slurry. The mud joined the rushing water, making everything slick.

The riders were oblivious to this. Their chief concern was the amount of water shooting into their hoods and at their eyes. Their vision was clouded and a chill was taking hold.

It wasn't until rocks started crumbling down the slope that they took note of the brown cascade. The horses were beginning to get agitated, and their footing was unsure. The deluge continued and more rocks and mud balls rolled toward them. It looked like a thousand mice were scurrying to meet them, causing both horses to spook.

Merion was able to retain his mount on the horse as it reared up, but Gendin had no chance. He was thrown from his horse as it bucked and fell backward onto solid rock. He cried out when he hit, and Merion turned to see him crash down onto his back, whipping his head into the rock. Gendin's horse came down only inches from his leg.

Gendin's horse, wild with fright, barreled straight on at Merion's horse and ran into it. Merion was thrown off as well and landed on his side. The rocky slope provided no cushioning, and he yelped out in pain.

Both riders were down, and their mounts had vanished in the

storm. Merion rolled over on his good side and could see Gendin lying on his back. He could not see if he was badly hurt from his position. He slowly inched his way on his stomach toward Gendin. There was a trickle of blood washing down with the rain water, and he knew Gendin was injured.

"Gendin! Can you hear me?"

He was met with silence. There was a flutter through his heart and he began to panic. Merion sat up and winced at the pain in his hip, ribs, and shoulder. He staggered over to Gendin to examine him. Gendin was breathing, so Merion knew he was not immediately killed. He was hopeful when he found the blood came from Gendin's arm and not his head. Gendin had come down hard on a pointed stone, which was lying nearby and was now painted red. Merion positioned himself directly over Gendin's face.

"Gendin…"

Nothing but soft breathing was the response. Merion did not know what to do, and his hands became shaky. He resolved to give Gendin the care he would want for himself. Merion ripped a portion of his tunic off and tied it lightly around Gendin's arm. He did not want it to turn into a tourniquet and become too tight, cutting off circulation.

The rain was still coming down. Merion looked around and spied a small crack in the mountainside. The crevice was not wide, but would give shelter. He slowly dragged Gendin the few feet he needed to get into the overhang. Once positioned, he knew he would not also fit into the tight space. He sat down with his back to Gendin and faced the storm. Drawing his cloak tight to him and over his head, he would have to endure the elements.

Merion awoke to feel his horse, Pro, brushing its nose against his forehead. The warm air coming from its nostrils startled him awake. Merion's quick movement caused him to gasp, as pain shot across his left side. When he looked back into the crevice, he saw Gendin stirring.

"Gendin," he whispered.

"Merion," he said weakly. "I can hear you, but my vision is blurred, and I feel like I'll be sick to my stomach. The world is spinning."

"Stay there, don't move."

Merion slowly stood and walked over to Pro. Gendin's horse was gone. The rain had stopped overnight, but there was no sign of the horse anywhere. Pro remained and was now the savior of the journey. They would only have half of their food stock, but they were not completely on their own. Merion grabbed some stale bread and piece of fish and then returned to Gendin

"Can you see me? Take this."

"Yes, Merion, but it is blurry," he said, blinking his eyes and extending his hand for the bread. "At least you are not spinning, anymore."

"You took quite a blow to the back of the head."

"I feel like someone struck me with a smithing hammer," he said, then took a small break to bite off a piece of bread. "What happened to your arm? It is just hanging there."

"I don't know. It doesn't work the right way. And it is throbbing," Merion said through gritted teeth.

Gendin moved slowly and instinctively brought his hand up to his head. He was still unsteady, and he was visibly uncomfortable. He kept trying to blink the delirium out of his eyes. Finally, he focused his energies and sat upright, head still in hand.

"It doesn't seem that bruised. Poke it."

"What?" replied Merion, confused.

"See if it is broken. Where does it hurt?"

"It only hurts at the joint," said Merion, poking his arm in a few spots and recoiling with each one.

"Then it is dislocated, not broken."

"What do we need to do to fix it?"

"I have to pull on it, but it is going to hurt. I had to do this once for my father."

"Do it."

Gendin pulled and turned Merion's arm simultaneously. Merion howled in pain and was breathing hard through gnashed teeth. The socket did not click together on the first try.

"I thought it would pop back in. We'll have to try it again."

"Wait!"

Merion had to make him stop. He walked back over to Pro and cut a small piece of leather off of his saddle. When he came back, the leather was clenched in his jaw.

The second try also yielded a cry from Merion, though stifled with the leather there for him to bite down onto. The joint popped together, and there was a feeling of immediate relief.

"You can't just move it like you normally would. Grab a bit of your tunic and fashion a sling. I need to rest now. My head is pounding."

"Rest, then. At least now I can do some things to make us a little more comfortable."

The rain broke during the night, but the clouds remained. There could only be a small fire; everything was moist. Only the smallest of twigs would make for kindling. It took Merion the better part of the morning to gather enough twigs to work with. On his return, he found

Gendin sleeping

     Merion woke him by putting his hand lightly on Gendin's shoulder.

"I was only dozing."

"You can have all the rest you need. I have some sticks for a short fire. I did not want you to miss it. There are not any logs around that aren't saturated."

They ate a meager lunch and talked about the remaining trek to Caldorn. They were only one or two days from their destination. The next day would bring them around the northern tip of the Cysterule Mountains, and they would be able to see the sea.

"We have enough food for three more days. It may take us that long, now that we are down a horse. You get up on him, Gendin. I will walk."

"Thank you, Merion. Imagine, a prince walking, while a peasant rides. You have honor in you."

"Gendin, you are the one who needs to rest. I'll hear nothing else about it."

** ** ** ** **

"Sire, you must look at this!"

"Windon, what do you have there?"

King Palantine unrolled the note tucked into the cylinder. It could only have come from Kelduun. The falcon was the calling card. The King thought it was odd that he had not heard from him earlier. On their last conversation, he said he would send word about the goings-on concerning the Fountain. That was weeks ago now. He held the note out at an arm's distance to better focus it in. Kelduun's script could be distinguished at first glance.

Dark Magic has over-run Schaida

Prepare to defend the castle

Army of one hundred thousand approaching from the West

You are days away from attack

"What? What does that mean? Is there more?" Palantine had his hand on his forehead.

"Sire, there is nothing else…"

"Windon, get Tobin in here. Now!"

"But, my lord…You sent him after your sons two days ago."

This statement took some time to sink in. Palantine had been distraught for the last few days thinking of his missing sons. Now, the King would be without counsel on this event, too.

Was war coming to Gildesh? Whose army was coming? Was it the army of King Mata Deland? There had not been a war in the surrounding lands for over two hundred years. Those battles were a distant memory. Once the borders had been set, the Kings had an accord not to overstep their grounds. Of course each country had its own army, but the army was never needed for more than skirmishes and uprisings.

The number of soldiers in the active army had been greatly reduced in recent years. There was not a big need for training and housing a vast regimen so that they may get bored and lazy. Combining that with the fact that he, himself, sent his royal guard after his sons put him in dire straits. The royal guard was mainly composed of the most decorated personnel, the heads of each of the army's brigades.

"Windon, I need help…"

"My lord, I am not good counsel on these matters. Perhaps you can reach out to your allies."

"Which allies can I trust? The message does not tell me who is drawing near. What I cannot figure out is how an army of that size amassed in the first place. How could Sehaida have an army of that size alone? That is almost ten times the size of my combined forces. Is it possible that every nation has banded together, excluding our own, and is now collapsing our borders in to destroy us?"

Palantine continued aloud, "That could be one plausible explanation. It would be annihilation of one country by the others, but for what greater purpose? Have we broken our bond with each country that they would all attack us in an organized movement? But, even if you add up the number of soldiers from each of the lands together, I don't think that you would have one hundred thousand. That would mean that each of the other three countries had thirty thousand troops at its disposal. Even that number would still be almost three times the size of my army. Where did all those soldiers come from?"

"You may try sending a message to Strayos?"

"The message would not arrive in time, and what should it say? 'Are you part of the attack, or not?' Windon, I am afraid we will be on our own in this."

"I am positive that King Secandor is not behind the attack, sire. Send him word of our position. If he responds, you will have your answer."

The King raised his eyebrow at this.

"How could you be positive? How could you know what another country is doing?"

"Just a thought," Windon said, backing away.

"I will think on this, Windon."

"My lord, please do not think long. Time is fleeting."

** ** ** ** **

Kelduun was riding hard. Bolt was a magnificent horse. The two covered ground as quickly as a crow could fly. He travelled to the southernmost tip of Sehaida before turning east into Gildesh. He passed the Hemage Forest on his right side in a mere three hours.

The army's path had stuck close to the shoreline. There could be no question that it was headed for the capital city, Albinion. Kelduun stayed the course and pushed Bolt to his limit in order to catch up to the ever advancing army. He estimated that he was two days behind them when he left Brondin, but they could not have travelled with the same sense of urgency as he did. He would even have ridden by moonlight, but he needed to give his horse the much earned rest he needed.

Dawn struck as Kelduun remounted Bolt. The horse was a pure runner, always ready to give everything in pursuit of speed. Kelduun rode for half of the day when he noticed the army's path changed slightly. Slowing, he noted that the trail turned toward the water's edge. He tracked it for a few miles. When he got to the beach, he dismounted and studied the area.

The army must have come across a small fishing community and razed it to the ground. The only evidence that there was anything existing before they were overrun was a dock for skiffs and the still smoldering foundations of five huts. It was possible that there were more shanties around the area but without a proper foundation. There seemed to be an excessive amount of debris lying around.

There were many tracks leading into the water. Presumably, the army refueled itself on fish after decimating or transforming the community's population. It looked like this took no time at all to accomplish. Undoubtedly, those people were unaware, unarmed, and unprepared. The area was devoid of all life.

He hoped that his message found its way to King Palantine and that he would interpret it as an impending attack. What more could one write on a small bit of parchment?

As he was standing and surveying the wreckage, he heard the screech of his falcon. Dipping to him, the falcon came to rest on his outstretched arm. It had been four days since he released it with his first message. If he had his calculations correct, the siege of Albinion would start the next day. He was going to be too late to help.

He needed a secondary plan to avoid total chaos in the lands. He needed to protect what remained of the free people still left unaffected with the disease being spread by these mutants. And he needed to give them hope that they could fight back.

Kelduun reached his arm across his body, placing the falcon onto his left shoulder to perch. Then he wrote down what he could to convey his mind. Tucking it into the cylinder, he silently hoped to himself that the message would not go unheeded.

** ** ** ** **

It took Merion and Gendin two and a half days to finally arrive in Creyason, the capital of Caldorn. The two men were haggard in appearance and looked like vagabonds. Each was wrapped in cloth of some sort. Merion had his left arm in a sling; Gendin had both his right arm and his head wrapped in what remained of Merion's tunic. Each rider's cloak was muddied but dried since the rain ceased two days ago.

When they saw the city, they each gasped at the natural beauty and geography spread before them. Creyason was unlike any other city in the lands. Nestled in the Cysterule Mountains, the city was spread out along the cliffs. Each area of the city was divided by the natural geography of the peaks. There were great bridges spanning the gaps between the various portions of the city.

The city's defenses lay in the geography, as well. There was virtually no way to make a frontal assault due to the vertical rise to the city heights. The only weakness was from the rear, but one would have to climb the entire range of the Cysterules to gain an access point to it.

The palace of Creyason was equally impressive. There was one main rock formation forming a bridge to the main gate. The palace was carved out of the mountainside. The front facade was stunning, polished black granite, the same as the rest of the mountain range make-up. Each side of the entryway was embellished with a small waterfall flowing down into the depths and causing a misty fog below.

Coming quickly up to them was a royal guard. He had three others behind him, and each had a lance at the ready, poised for a quick jabbing attack. His own lance was held upright and braced against his hip.

"Speak and introduce yourselves!"

"I am Merion Secandor of Strayos. I come in good faith. My

father, King Vernon Secandor sends word to the Queen. This is my servant."

"You do not look like a prince, a pauper perhaps. Two paupers. Do you have proof of your royalty?"

Merion held his hands up and turned slowly to his horse. He was never more thankful than just at this moment that his horse had shown loyalty on the rocky slope and did not disappear as Gendin's horse did. He reached into his pack to retrieve the leather strap he cut from his saddle days earlier. The crest of Strayos was on it, a mighty bull.

He turned to show the guard his crest, when there was a commotion behind the guards. They did not turn from him, though, and kept him in their gaze. Behind them the princess came running.

"Merion!"

"My fair princess, Ashlyn," he replied, with a slight bow.

"Guard, these men may come with me," she commanded.

The guard acquiesced and turned to let the three of them meet.

"I almost didn't recognize you. Look at your appearance!" she exclaimed.

"It has been over a month since the gathering in Gildesh. I am happy that you recognized me at all. We did not spend much time together at the party. You were busied by the prince, Panalt."

Ashlyn blushed at his words.

"Come inside. What happened to you?"

"The story is not as impressive as you may think. We were caught in a raging storm and lost a horse. Each of us had a mishap and acquired injuries. Nothing brave at all."

"We can let you rest easy for the night. I will have a meal prepared and brought to your quarters. We can converse again in the morning. What brings you to Caldorn?"

"I have been sent by my father to speak with the Queen, your mother."

"That meeting can wait until you are well rested."

"I thank you for your hospitality. I would like to send word home that I have arrived. Do you have carrier pigeons?"

"Merion, it shall be done."

"Again, princess, my gratitude to you."

** ** ** ** **

King Vernon Secandor had to sit down. There was a jolt of nervousness in him. He looked at the message a second time.

Dark Magic has over-run Sehaida

Gildesh will fall to invasion imminently

Send no one to Gildesh, Call for a Council with Caldorn

I will come to you in Crute

He was in a stupor and dropped the note absent-mindedly. The King had had dealings with Kelduun in the past. The sorcerer was never wrong about what would come to pass. It was something of his business to know when help was needed. He seemed to be present to help with nearly every tragedy to befall the lands.

But he could not have known that the King just sent his only son directly through Gildesh on a mission to Caldorn.

The King spoke with Merion before he departed, and they decided that dragging a canoe the entire way would be too cumbersome and energy consuming. The rapids of the Gallendar River need not be braved for this voyage. The road would be longer, but Merion decided to ride the entire way, and there was no hurry to get there.

Things were wildly changed now. There could be no mistaking the emphasis in Kelduun's words. A serious event was taking place to the west. And he sent his son into its teeth. He started pacing around and thinking. He walked down to the library and stood in front of the right wall, where a huge mural of a map of the lands stood. He looked at it and pondered. Then he paced more and cast his eyes to the window overlooking the lake. He paced to the window and then back to the painting.

He was deep in thought, scanning and studying the map. The distance was not that great between Albinion and Creyason. A rider could make that trek in three days if he meant to make it fast. Even the distance from Crute to Creyason could be managed in ten days. The fastest of riders may even make it in eight days, depending on conditions and the strength of the horse. It had been twelve days since Merion left him. He stood and studied and pondered. He paced back and forth until the plush carpeting was matted down with footprints.

He was still pacing nearly four hours later when a servant brought a note to him. He snatched it out of the servant's hand, nearly tearing the corner off of it.

Father, arrived in Creyason
Will converse with the Queen

When she invites me to eat at her table
It may take as long as a week

The wave of relief washing over him brought him to his knees. He exhaled loudly and then stood to walk over to a large arm chair to lean on. He was thinking of the last time he saw his son and conversed with him in this room, sitting on these very chairs. He bounced down into the giant, overstuffed, wingback chair and closed his eyes.

King Vernon relaxed for a few minutes to gather himself. When he opened his eyes, he casually looked about him, realizing that he had not yet dismissed the servant. He glanced down and saw that he still had the note in his hand. He crumpled it before throwing it in the dormant fireplace.

"Bring me a wine goblet, then you may go."

This wine tasted better than the last few he could remember. The stress was lifted from him, and he could feel the tension release from his shoulders. He got up and walked the flight of stairs to his bed chambers and saw his Queen standing there waiting for him.

He came up to her and took her in his arms. They kissed and looked into each other's eyes. Vernon broke the close embrace and beckoned her to come over to the bed.

"There is news from throughout the lands," he said to her.

"Has Merion arrived at his destination?"

"Thankfully, my love, he has. As you know, it has been twelve days since I sent him to Caldorn. I know you thought it was a big endeavor, sending him that far…"

"Has something happened? You seem so serious."

"Merion has arrived in Creyason. For that, I am thankful. I have received word from him, in his own hand. It is an honor that the Queen should allow him to write his own message. I am sure she read it before sending it, though. He is a smart young man, not giving away anything of what our planned conversation would be with her."

"He takes after his father," she said to him, smiling.

"And you, as well," he replied, complimenting her. "I received another note just this morning from the wizard, Kelduun."

He reached into his pocket and retrieved the folded piece of parchment, which he handed to her. She read it and looked up at him quickly.

"What is this?"

"It appears that there is magic afoot, and that there is a dark wave covering the western lands. For Sehaida to fall and Gildesh to be invaded…" he broke off.

"You sent Merion through Gildesh! We could have been his murderers!"

"Merkette, he is already to safety in Creyason," he said placing his hand on her knee. "And we did not know about dark magic before this very morning. We cannot blame ourselves for sending him."

"Why did you not come to me when you received this?"

"I did not know what to do! But I am coming here now to have your counsel. We can rest now that we know our son is safe. For now, that is all we need to know. We can talk more about this in the morning."

"Perhaps you saved me from the torture of worrying over a prolonged amount of time. As it is, I should be able to calm down in a few minutes."

"Thank you, Merkette, for understanding."

They lay down together, then he held her tightly to him before they both drifted off to sleep. They awoke to the sound of the bell in the window. This was the third note in the last two days. King Secandor rose and walked to the window to read it.

WIZARD WARNED OF ATTACK ON GILDESH
PLEASE SEND WHAT HELP YOU CAN
KING P.D. DOES NOT KNOW WHO HE CAN TRUST
SHOULD I PERISH, IT WAS AN HONOR TO
SERVE YOU

When he was finished, he walked back over to the bed and sat down. His Queen rolled over to look at him.

"Merkette. King Palantine is requesting help with the attack. But Kelduun said not to send anyone to Gildesh."

"At least we can rest easier, knowing our son is safe."

"That is a matter we can thankfully leave in the past now. I would have gone mad if I knew I sent him to his death."

"So, we should not send anyone to Gildesh now, either?" she raised her eyebrows.

"That is my thought, but why would Kelduun tell us not to aid a friend?"

"You would turn your back on a King in need and embrace a friendship with the sorcerer in its stead? Which plight is greater, that of Gildesh or Kelduun's wishes?"

"I do not know how to answer this quandary…There can be no doubt that Kelduun would have his reasons to deliberately command allies to not help one another. I need more information!"

"His note said he would be coming here, and there is magic to contend with. That does convey a serious tone. He wants there to be a council with Caldorn and ourselves. Surely there will be no representatives from the other lands, neither Sehaida nor Gildesh."

"We will have the information we need at this council. For now, we have been given the gift of forewarning. There is no invasion of Strayos at the moment. We will prepare for war! It shall not take us by surprise. First though, let us keep some good standing with Gildesh. At least we will send them word that we are their friend," Vernon said, leaning back

"You mean to dupe Palantine? Of course, we cannot send him any portion of our army if we are to defend what is ours."

"I do not want to deceive him, but I would like him to know that we have not been a part of this invasion."

"You will do what you must."

** ** ** ** **

Creyason's palace was much darker than Merion expected. The entire rear of the structure was hewn out of the rocky mountain wall. There was not a great amount of natural lighting since the front wall was the only exterior wall. There were many torches along the corridors and the lighting was abundant, but it was not natural as sunlight is.

He had stayed in his chamber for two days and rested with Gendin. Both men were recovering quickly. Gendin only had some residual neck ache, and the gouge out of his arm was healed sufficiently enough to leave the bandage off. Merion had gained almost full rotation back to his arm, though he would only gingerly test this out. The whole area of his left shoulder felt loose and weakened.

Ashlyn had brought his meals to him the first day, but then there was a servant for the next day. He could not guess who would come today. They were pleasantly relaxing and gaining their strength back to them.

Presently, there was a knock at the door. He opened the door and saw that there were two guards standing outside his room.

"Your presence is requested by the Queen."

Merion turned his torso around and said, "Gendin, remain here until I return."

He trailed the guards down the torch lit corridors. Each was braced by pillars running parallel down the length. It gave a sensation of exaggerated length. The columns were polished to a gleaming finish. The hall floor was covered by a thick red carpet embellished with golden embroidered runes along the edges.

When they got to the throne room, he was shocked by the immensity of it. The cavernous room, again, was hewn from the rock and stabilized centrally by four gigantic stanchions. These were white with black streaks through them. The stone work was impressive, and the differing veins of granite were shown off in splendor with a dramatic change to white columns. The room was silent, but their boots echoed as he was escorted up to the Queen. The guards stayed in the room and were at a casual stance. The prince would be no match for well-armed, trained guards.

"Merion Secandor, of Strayos."

"Your Highness," he bowed low.

"You must be bringing me important news. It is not often that I receive a personal request as well as a request delivered by way of carrier pigeon. Your father must have a great need to see me."

"I am here on my father's behalf…" he replied.

Merion was unsure of how to proceed. A message sent by pigeon was not in the original plan. He decided to play coy and gain any information he could from this conversation and deflect suspicion if necessary.

He continued, "I was unaware that he would also send you words through the air. I was under the impression that my presence would be sufficient to gain an audience with you."

"The note requested a council in Crute in the shortest travelling time as is possible to arrive there. I see this as an urgency. It is such a cryptic note, to come to Crute for a council with Kelduun and also not to come by way of Gildesh. It is surprising for your father to ask me to cross over the Gallendar River; he could not know that we have recently completed a grand bridge near the falls at the Tributary Forest. The journey to Crute from Creyason is remarkably shorter with our newly completed bridge; I would not have even thought of going through Gildesh."

"I have come to you by way of Gildesh. The road is quite a bit longer to travel around the whole of the Cysterule Mountains. My father would like to entertain you and strengthen our alliance. We would be honored if you would come to eat at our table."

"Young Merion, an invitation is one thing, but this note has a more insidious tone to it. A council is not called for mere merrymaking."

He seemed caught in his tactic of holding back and changed his direction into what the situation called for.

"Perhaps I was not given the entire reasoning behind this, but if you join me on our way to my homeland of Strayos, my father will make your stay as comfortable as he can."

"My husband has been gone now for years, but the nations had as tight of a bond as any in the lands. I will honor your father's request and travel to Crute. However, I will need some answers when I get there."

"I am sure you will have satisfaction, your highness."

He bowed again and was led out of the spacious, rocky cavern. When he was left to the privacy of his room he leaned back heavily on the door and said aloud, "What just happened?"

"What do you mean?" Gendin asked him back.

Merion looked up quickly, startled. Gathering his thoughts he addressed Gendin.

"I just had the strangest conversation one could expect, with the Queen. As you know, we were to gather information on the upcoming nuptials of either the princess or the Queen. The conversation never even got close to that. As it turns out, the Queen will be travelling to Crute to visit my father. I cannot understand what would cause her to do that. She said that she received a message from my father, but I had no knowledge of that. It sounded like there was a major change and that her help would be needed for something."

"Do you think your father did not trust you to speak for him?"

"No Gendin. I have faith that my father trusts me to do what is best for our nation. This isn't the first time he has sent me on an errand. And he has taught me and tested me enough that he can trust my opinion. But I had the feeling that there was a lot in play that changed since my last conversation with him."

"I suppose we will be in suspense, then, until our return to Strayos."

"We shall see, Gendin. I will try to talk to the princess, Ashlyn, and see if she can give me any information."

** ** ** ** **

King Palantine Dito was overwhelmed. He was without counsel and without help. He had neither Tobin, nor his sons to turn to. There was darkness on the horizon, and it was beginning to rain again. The rain had come almost a week ago and had let up for only a day in between.

He was sitting in his chair trying to decide how to handle his army. With his royal guard assigned to finding his sons, he would need to promote several other ranking soldiers to lead the brigades. He was ready to make his decision and call in his choices for leadership when

Windon knocked at the door.

"My Lord, I have news," he said, as he was shuffling from one foot to the other.

"Yes?"

"Two things actually...we have received a message."

"From whom?"

"From Strayos. King Secandor sends his regards and tells us to hang on."

"What would make him send such a note?"

"Sire, I sent him a message for you."

"You went over me! Who is the leader here?!"

"Sire, I..."

Windon was getting timid. The note to Strayos seemed an easy step to take. Gildesh needed its allies to come forward and offer help.

"I thought it best not to waste time..." Windon offered.

"You..." the King paused. "You are right. Alas, that action could be the saving grace of our country. I have been heavily distracted from anything I once held important since my sons were reported missing. I thank you for standing in for my counsel, even if you acted before I signed off on it. What does the note say? Is he sending help to us?"

"The message said that he is our ally and not a part of this invasion. That should make you feel better, and that you do not stand alone. He also said he would give what help he can. But I do not expect them to arrive with much time left to us."

"I understand that the time it would take to move an army of any size up through the mountain pass and into Albinion would take a few weeks. At least it is something."

"There is worse news, though, to give. A scout has brought word that the invading army is already to the edge of the forest of Albinion. The invasion could begin as early as tomorrow!"

"What! I did not think Kelduun's warning would be so literal. I thought we had more time!"

"Sire, command me. I can help. Tell me what to do."

"We need to build a plan of defense and retaliation."

The King went down to the armory with Windon trailing him. He dressed in his armor and grabbed his sword. Windon chose a set for himself and dressed as quickly as his untrained hands would allow. When he finished he turned around to see the King already riding down to the main barracks on his black stallion. It had also been clad in its gleaming armor. The rider and war horse looked deadly. The crest of the eagle was emblazoned on both of them. Windon looked upon them with awe as they departed the area.

King Palantine drew up to the barracks in the town and selected a new legion of two thousand men for guarding the palace. These men would take up positions around the palace wall and upon the ramparts. Though Albinion's population was mostly comprised of the army, there were several hundred civilians living there. The remaining men disseminated through the rest of the city, recruiting every able bodied man and boy to the cause of defense of the capital. In all, the total number of men ready for battle was just under twelve thousand.

It did not take long for the formations to line up, and soon the regiments took shape on the field to the west of the palace. This was where the first wave of defense would start. Setting camps for the night, they started fires and kept a vigil on the horizon with the highest scrutiny.

The sun was rising in the east over a plain that saw no bloodshed overnight. As Palantine's army stirred in the morning, they could hear a rumble in the distance. The sun was slowly climbing over the horizon, but there was already more than enough light to see the black line to the west. The advancing army was primed for attack.

Spreading over the horizon, from end to end, was the vast host of the unknown army. As they advanced, the number of footsteps made the earth tremble under Palantine's army. War machines and catapults could also be seen.

Archers let a volley fly into hundreds of attackers in the field. This slowed the advancement, but also enraged the fiends into a frenzy. They began howling and grunting. The beasts continued their drive toward the city. The archers continued their aerial assault, and slowly, the bodies began to pile up. Each enemy was taking four and five arrows before finally succumbing and dropping.

Now the attackers had to climb over their own dead to continue the assault. Palantine's army was set up on the defense with three rows of soldiers forming the first barrier. The first wave of attackers ran straight on at them. They carried no weapons, and they did not sway their direction. They closed in on the front line of defense with talons clawing and scratching and fangs gnashing and biting. Palantine's men were confused as they looked upon their attackers. They had never seen such a grotesque form. These monsters could take pain and punishment and hardly slow at all. They had arrows protruding from them, and still they came on at them as if they felt nothing.

They collided into Palantine's army. Most were impaled by the spikes of the first line, but some batted them away and continued into the second row of defenders. The next wave did the same as the first grouping, with still more of them carrying further into the line of men. Another wave was already coming at them and carried all the way through the entire front defense.

There was carnage and bloodshed on both sides. There were bodies strewn over the field, but the onslaught kept coming as if there was no goal other than bloodletting. Palantine's army was set up with multiple rings of lance holders and archers behind them. After the first line of defense was battered and broken, Palatine tried to estimate the damage from the palace wall. He knew there were roughly two thousand of his men gone already. He could guess that the number of enemy fighters among the dead was around five thousand. A two to one ratio was not a good start, especially when he could not even see the rear edge of the attack. The enemy soldiers blanketed the western field for as far as he could see.

The archers kept sending arrows but were given the command to light them on fire. This had the desired effect of killing, with less ammunition spent. More than one fire arrow was still needed to bring down each opponent, but the fire continued burning even after the bodies fell. The field was now dotted with flames.

When the first line of defenders was broken, a terrible giant came to the forefront of the enemy line. He was the juggernaut of Sehaida and wrath was in his eyes. He lifted his arms toward the sky and let out a roar. The beasts behind him returned their cry, which echoed off the palace walls.

What Palantine saw next, he could not believe. Some of his dead soldiers were rising and breaking out of their armor. Their bodies were growing, splitting the armor at its seams. They were transforming into the very beasts accosting them. Some of them started feeding on the carcasses of their fallen comrades. Others began the same behaviors heretofore exhibited by their enemies. They were nipping at each other and testing their reborn bodies. Instantly, the enemy horde had grown by an additional one thousand fresh attackers.

Palantine called for a massive retreat into the palace's fortifications. His army, witnessing the events firsthand, turned tail and fled to the keep. Once they were inside, the outer gate was secured with extra timbers, fortifying against a ramming barrage. The wall was lined with additional archers and fire was brought to them. They rained down arrows across the field. Finding their marks, they eliminated more of the enemy combatants.

This held off the attackers for a short time, until Palantine was given word that ammunition was running low. The arrows would cease to fly very soon. The beasts threw themselves against the walls of the keep and tried to build upward on top of each other.

When this proved to be fruitless, they turned to their catapults. There was no need for large stones to be thrown; and as such, there were none on the battlefield to be had. All that was needed was pure conquer and breaking of the castle. The attrition would prove to be on the side of darkness. Palantine saw that the catapults were being loaded with the monsters themselves. They were going to be flung into the palace walls in a suicide attempt. Several catapults were loaded in this fashion and then released. Nearly fifty of the mutants were flung over the ramparts. Upon landing, they were slain by the awaiting soldiers of Gildesh. More and more catapults were being loaded, and the number of thrown monsters was increasing. Soon there was a small circle of them banding together, creating a perimeter inside the very walls of Palantine's castle.

Palantine knew this was going to be the last day of his life. As his soldiers fought against the enemies, he saw that they would not be killed easily. The final straw was watching the soldiers within the palace being transformed into fiends, as they were on the outside. This was a new form of evil. He could not figure how this could happen, but he was being taken over by his own men. The tide turned quickly as the number shifted from defending the palace to attacking. He disengaged himself from it and went to his tower in the south wing. The swarming attack would overtake the keep within minutes. There would be no escape. Every last soldier that he brought into the castle walls would be trapped there and killed or transformed into the makings of the devil.

He kneeled on the balcony with his head down, his hands resting on his knees. Taking in his final breaths, he thought of his sons. They were not in the capital on this day. They would live on and carry his flag to fight another day.

The chamber door was blown open, splintering off of the hinges. There were footsteps behind him, then blackness.

VIII

Panalt opened his eyes and sat upright quickly. Then he calmed down. He took a moment to relive the last few days. He realized he was no longer a captive in the cart and that he used it last night for a makeshift tent.

He looked down at his wrists and found them to be ringed with red bruises and caked with old blood. He sighed aloud and thanked his lucky stars that he was free. There could be no value put on freedom. He thought again about the events of the previous night. The sheer coincidence that his brothers happened to find him was paramount. He could have been killed or beaten mercilessly if they hadn't come at the right time. There would have been punishment for his attempted escape from his captors.

My silly brothers, he thought. What did they think they were doing out in the world, beyond the castle walls, on their own? They were heeding the call of manhood, perhaps. He answered the call also and ventured into the forest. But this attempt was bordering the irresponsible. They could have really gotten into trouble, hurt, or even killed themselves.

Panalt crawled out of the rear of the covered wagon and cast his eyes about the wrecked gypsy caravan site. There were three wagons that were charred to the wooden base and another burnt entirely to ashes. There were two campfires that were still smoldering; the smoky wisps were lost almost immediately to a light breeze. He poked around until he found some embers and tossed some dried grass onto it, reigniting a small flame.

After stoking the fire back to life, he casually walked over to the two remaining carts. When he looked inside, he found them empty. A shockwave tore through him. Where were his brothers? He turned quickly and scanned the field around the area.

Then he saw them. They were leading a horse to the camp.

"Panalt!"

"I'm here."

"Look what we found!" Dur said excitedly.

"We got you a horse!" Tiras said, right in tune with him.

"Now, I know it isn't as attractive as yours is at home, but you can use him for now," said Dur.

"Brothers, you continually surprise me."

"We didn't want you to have to walk all the way back home.

And we didn't want to keep getting called poor planners," chimed in Tiras.

"Where did you find him?"

"It was one of the gypsy horses. A strong one too; he is as big as any I have seen. Must've been needed for pulling a lot of weight. He was hanging around the camp when we woke up, so we decided not to abandon him. He doesn't have a saddle on him, though."

"I think I can manage him without a saddle. That's an honorable thing to do. Let us have something to eat before we mount up and head back."

They rummaged through the camp to find what food was left. The gypsies were dirty; their food was not well kept. Most of it appeared to be stolen. The vegetables were browning, but the meats were smoked. That would have to be good enough for this afternoon meal. There was a good quantity of meat that they took with them. They would have enough for a more leisurely trip back. There was no need for hurry.

They travelled due east along the Vitirral Mountain range for close to four hours. They decided that they would set up camp and start a fire. In the morning they would turn to the north and make their way home.

At morning's first light, they arose and packed their meager belongings into their packs. Dur and Tiras carried most of the gear. They made a deal with Panalt that if he didn't have a saddle to aid his ride, he would not have to carry a pack with him. It had started to rain during the night, and they were unhappy about it. Their attitude was soured, and they could think of nothing else than the hot baths in the palace. They were quiet for the first portion of their ride.

Not even an hour into the day, they saw a rider bearing down hard on his horse, coming from the northwest. He seemed to be coming in their general direction. They paused and waited for him to draw near. There was not a hint of trepidation among them. They knew that three against one would be an easy match for them to win. The twins sat alert in their saddles and drew arrows out of their quivers.

When the rider came within a hundred feet of them, he cautiously slowed his horse and warily rode to meet them. His horse was trotting at a slight diagonal to their position and was showing its size. The rider appeared unarmed, yet comfortable, his hands loosely holding the reins.

"You need not draw down on me, I am your friend."

"Kelduun!" Panalt exclaimed.

"By the stars, I am happy to see you!" Kelduun remarked in response. There was joy clearly in his face and words. "You have no idea what good luck you have given yourselves. You are all alive and well, I see."

"Does he know of what we have done?" Dur glanced at Tiras.

"I'm not sure," Tiras said to his brother.

"Tell us what brings you to us, Kelduun?" Panalt asked of him.

"My dear princes, I must ask you to sit with me for a while. Come, let us dismount and have something to eat."

They did so at his request.

"Young men, I have grave news to give to you." He had their full attention. "Your country is now a different place than you may have known it. Albinion has been invaded by a dark army."

"Then we must fly homeward to aid in the defense!" Panalt screamed, leaping to his feet.

"You cannot aid them now!" Kelduun said, standing to regain his attention. He placed his hand on Panalt's chest, hindering his movement toward the rogue horse. Panalt snapped his head toward the wizard with wide open eyes.

"Albinion has fallen! There is nothing there for you now!" Kelduun spoke again.

Dur and Tiras both now stood, again making the odds three to one.

"Our father!" they said, in unison.

Kelduun's silence told the rest of the story. He could not have known if King Palatine Dito met his end in a quick death or if he had been transformed into one of the savages. Either way, the result was the same. He was gone, or would no longer exist as the man they called father.

"I have seen it," he said, solemnly. "I have known your father for many years. Since long before you all were born. We had been close and had many a private conversation. This loss will be felt throughout all of the lands."

Panalt motioned for his brothers to sit back down again.

"Kelduun, tell us what happened."

"The last time I saw your father, we were speculating on the condition of the land around the Fountain. It was then that I left for Sehaida to speak with King Mata Deland in Brondin. Unfortunately, I was too late, and I witnessed the destruction of Brondin, firsthand. I was, in essence, a prisoner in Brondin. What I witnessed there was sickening. Driven by a darkly powerful magic, the city and country was completely enveloped in chaos and death. A deadly army was born and ravaged Sehaida. I could not escape with my life before they vacated the city. I tracked them, hoping to overtake them and warn the other lands to build their defenses. It took me days to determine which direction they would steer and by that time, it was clear they were coming through Gildesh en route to Albinion."

"Did you warn our father?" Dur asked, with glassy eyes

"I sent word to him, yes. But he could not have been able to prepare for what was coming for him. The timing was too short and the enemy too great."

"He is dead then…" Tiras whispered.

He was looking down, but Dur thought he saw a tear drop, as well.

"The enemy advancing on your land would take no prisoners. They are harbingers of death, destruction, mutilation, annihilation. There will be no one left alive within the city's walls. I need your help. There is but one way to avenge your father's death. Come with me to Strayos. I have also sent word to King Vernon Secandor. He will have more time to prepare a defense than your father did. We have to get to Strayos before the dark army does."

"We will go with you," Panalt said, clearing his throat.

"I will give you some time to collect yourselves," Kelduun said to them. "We will head for Strayos with urgency the moment you are ready."

Kelduun turned then and strode to his horse.

"I cannot believe it, brothers…" Panalt said to them. "I have only been away from the capital for a week. And you have only been gone for three days. They must have been attacked only a day after you left, maybe that very day. How can a city fall in such a short period of time?"

"The number of attackers must have overwhelmed them," Dur said. "It sounds like the same thing happened to Sehaida. Two of the major nations have fallen. Where did such a force come from?"

"Can we even defend against it?" Tiras asked.

The group of brothers was standing in a tight group. Their heads were all down. Each was full of shock and dismay. Panalt lifted his head and placed his hands on each of their shoulders. Gripping tightly, he said, "There is nothing else to do but try. We will honor our father. We will lead the counterattack. We will triumph!"

** ** ** ** **

It had been almost three days since Tobin left Albinion. The search was not fruitful to this point. His small band of men had been through every building in the city proper and then dispersed into the surrounding countryside. They checked each house, hut, and cabin that they could find along the seashore. There were several fishing communities along the beaches. After another exhaustive day of searching, they turned from the seashore to look inland.

"Bring Strefan," Tobin said to one of the guards.

"Yes, Tobin, you called for me?"

"Did you not say that the princes went to the north?"

"They said that was where they were going."

"Did you watch them? Is it possible they turned?"

"I did not watch them, My Lord. I trusted them."

"They may have duped you. We are going to expand the search. You will remain with us. Do not go back to the capital yet."

They turned to the south and travelled along many fields. They spoke to farmers along the way and finally got their first tip. A farmer said he saw two young men with fancy, expensive looking clothing only a few days ago. He recalled pointing the men to the west, and that they were pursuing a gypsy caravan.

That gave Tobin a starting time and place to begin tracking them. It did not take long to detect the pair of horse tracks leading to the west. They followed the trail for the rest of the day before coming to the Hemage Forest.

Once there, they saw the ruins of a caravan and the evidence of a struggle. There was a skirmish here, and it was only a few days old. Tobin's band of men spread out and surveyed the land. There was no one in sight. There were no bodies on the ground nor were there any burial mounds. Though the princes were not here, there was hope that they had gotten away unscathed.

Tobin searched for more information until the light faded. They set up camp and rested for the night. When they awoke in the morning, Tobin's men again fanned out, searching for anything that would lead to a trail.

They did find some markings of a pair of human feet on each side of a horse's track, as if guiding it back to camp. When they saw that there were more hoof prints going away from the camp, they made a decision to follow them. The markings pointed to the east, so they had hope that they were on the right course. These were three distinct trails though, not only two, as they had followed in the previous day.

After a few hours, the tracking stopped and there was a gathering. More deciphering was needed to find markings. They again found the three sets of tracks and followed them for another short distance. When the trails stopped at another gathering, they found that now there were four trails leading to the east.

Tobin called to a guard that was riding close to him. It was the head of the palace's royal guard and leader of the northern brigade.

"Bayrne, what do you make of this? We followed two trails to the destroyed campsite. That was definitely our quarry. I have no doubt that it was Dur and Tiras. Then we saw three trails leaving it."

"Perhaps they picked up a tag along?"

"Perhaps, but only after the gypsy site. Maybe there was an injury?"

"It is possible that it is not the princes that we are tracking."

"That would be an easy answer. But I have been sure that we had the proper heading, right up to this point." Tobin had his arms spread. "Now there are four trails. Who could have joined them now?"

"There is only one way to find out."

"Follow it to the end."

They had a much easier time following the swath laid down by the four riders and made up ground on them. The path remained parallel to the Vitirral Mountains and continued eastward. Tobin decided they would ride through the night if they could still see the markings.

It was late the next day when they finally saw riders on the horizon. They found yet another burst of energy and rode full on toward them. It took them only two hours to cut the distance between them in half.

Tobin looked around him at his group of men. They were all riding hard. They all had the look of desire and determination in their eyes. They were the best Gildesh had to offer, and they were proving it right now.

The riders ahead seemed to come to a halt. They would overtake them in mere moments. When they came to within a hundred yards of them, they saw a bright flash and then a ball of flame growing upward like an orange plant from the ground.

Tobin held up his arm and the cavalry stopped in their tracks. Only he continued forward, leaving his men behind and drawing attention to himself alone.

Bringing his horse to a trot, he closed the distance. He knew what he would see when he squared himself before the riders. A smile crossed his face and he gave a short laugh. Kelduun was controlling the great fireball, holding it above his head.

Tobin lifted his arm in greeting.

Kelduun had seen the force of men behind them and took the defensive. He told the three princes to keep ready, that he would rain fire upon the advancing force. But when he saw Tobin, he let the magical fireball shrink until it finally went out with a small puff of smoke. He lowered his hand and stood with his arms at his sides.

"I have been looking for you for days!" Tobin addressed the princes. "And now I find you with Kelduun. We thought you were all lost. But in what better care could you be than under the watchful eye of a sorcerer."

"Tobin, my luck seems to grow by the day! And I see you have a small contingency of soldiers with you. For a moment there, I thought we were being hunted. There are strange workings going on in the world," Kelduun said to the others.

"I am so glad I found you. And your father will be happy as well. From here, it will only take us another two days to reach Albinion. But why are you down here? What would bring you so close to the mountain range and Strayos?"

"Tobin, there have been changes in the past few days. Changes you could not know of. The hour is grim. The times are dark," Kelduun answered softly.

He went on to tell Tobin of the occurrences of the last few weeks, starting with the fall of Brondin and then, consequently, of the invasion of Albinion. Tobin was visibly distressed. His reaction was equal to that of the princes. They were all a family, and their bond was sacred.

"I do not know how you came to leave the city when you did, but the soldiers you have with you have been saved from a brutal death. You have the chance to carry the flag of Gildesh still. We can honor Palantine by fighting for him now. And we will be fighting for every free person in the lands," Kelduun tried to reconcile him.

"The coincidence is overwhelming. How could it have been that all of his sons were drawn out of the city, and that I was sent away at nearly the same time. We have all been saved through different routes. This gift shall not be overlooked. I will come to Strayos with you, and we will fight back," Tobin consented.

** ** ** ** **

Merion's return to Strayos from Caldorn only took five days. It was a stark contrast to his journey to the mountainous country. Though he was on the mend, it was decided for him that he would ride in the company of the princess. The caravan was fashioned for comfort, and there were many cushions around his coach's interior to give to the lavish appearance. One could almost forget that it was a large wagon and not a small living area. Even Gendin was given permission to ride along with his master and the princess.

The Queen had her own opulent living quarters in the wagon just ahead of theirs. Hers was not for sharing. Merion did not mind that he did not have to share space with the Queen. He was already feeling foolish for not knowing his end of information upon the earlier questioning in the throne room at Creyason.

What he could not figure out was how the Queen managed to turn the conversation into an interview of him. He had full intentions of making the Queen begin on the defensive and gain information. He was not so inexperienced that he could not talk to another royal and keep his demeanor about him. Yet, when he got his chance to speak with her, he found that the tables were turned and that he was doing the answering, not her. He never got an opportunity to glean the information he wanted.

When he got back to Crute, he would have to tell his father that he failed him on two accounts. The first was that he didn't have any more information that they already knew—that there was a union that could take place between Caldorn and Gildesh. His second shortcoming was than he did not represent power. There was still a chance to turn the voyage into a success, talking to the princess.

The problem with this plan was that Ashlyn had no knowledge of the reasoning behind going to Crute. She said that, at first, she thought it was another invitation for another gathering or celebration. But then she said that it seemed that her mother was reserved and not as talkative about it as she normally would have been.

Merion decided to give it up and hear for himself when they got back to his homeland. Surely he would be able to stand in and listen to the conversation between the Queen and his father. Instead, he decided to allow himself to be taken care of by the princess. She was seeing to it that he was quite comfortable for the journey. They had all the cushioning and food that they could want. It felt as comfortable to him as the journey back home after the festival for the prince in Gildesh.

After the first day of travel, they came to the newly finished bridge over the Gallendar River. Built in memory of the late King Turg Reesh, it was enormous, and its glory stood for the achievement of the people of Caldorn. The bridge was wide enough to fit three wagons through, with plenty of room to allow for riders on each side. Clearly this bridge could handle a large amount of traffic, though it was not built with anything more in mind than honoring a great King with a symbol of grandeur.

The bridge was set over the Gallendar River near the bottom of a great waterfall. This was where the King met his demise. Queen Crissannah Reesh had the procession halted so that she might get out of her car and stand overlooking the area. The waterfall, cast as a backdrop, was mesmerizing to Merion as he gazed upon her. He had not noticed Ashlyn departing, but presently, she was seen approaching her mother to stand beside her. Facing away from him, they were enshrouded by the rising mist from the fall. They lingered for a moment holding hands, and then turned to retreat to the comfort of the coaches.

The rest of the journey to Crute was uneventful and quiet. Merion could feel some restlessness and tenseness in his hosts throughout the entire trip. There was something off-putting about this trip to Crute, but he could not come to a conclusion on it.

When they finally arrived, he was one of the first people to spring from the coach and touch the ground. As he expected, there were many servants around to help with the arriving guests. They were given quarters to stay in and dinner was set for that evening. Merion rushed into to his father's chambers on the top floor of the palace to consult with him. When his father saw him, he quickly embraced him and spoke to him.

"Merion, I have never been happier to see you returning to Crute as I am today. Please, sit, my son. We have much to discuss."

"Father, I have to tell you that the task you had given me went unfulfilled. I failed in gaining the information you desired of the Queen," Merion said, sitting down.

"There is more in play now than the information we sought. There are dark times ahead of us. This is what I know…"

He told Merion of all that had transpired since his departure. He told of the message from Kelduun and the fear over Merion's safety, travelling through Gildesh. He told of the upcoming council with the Queen.

"You will hear more tomorrow, my son. For now, that should get you caught up. Please try to rest for the night. And do not worry over anything you think you may not have accomplished. That information is proving to be a trivial affair in a past world. I hope, though, for our sake, that that world is not totally lost. We must prevail. Kelduun will guide us. We shall see him soon enough."

** ** ** ** **

The council commenced at high noon two days after Merion returned to Crute. Kelduun had arrived the eve before with a cavalry of men and some of the royal family of Gildesh. Present in the room were King and Queen Secandor with Merion; also there were princes Panalt, Dur and Tiras Dito with Tobin; finally there was Queen Reesh with her daughter, Princess Ashlyn.

Kelduun led the assembly and stood before them. They were seated around the banquet table in the throne room of the lowest section of King Secandor's palace.

"My dear royal families," he started, lowly. "It is the greatest of concerns that brings me to call a council and compel you to attend," he turned to look at King Secandor. "Some of you know a little of the news I am going to give you, while to some, this will be the first you have heard of anything," he finished by looking at Queen Reesh.

Kelduun continued, looking at Panalt, Dur and Tiras, "Some of you have already experienced losses, and others may find that even more is required of them," he glanced in Tobin's direction.

The party remained silent, though each was nodding in turn as he addressed them. Each was already deep in thought, yet attentive to that which was being told to them.

"To come directly at it, there is evil afoot. There is a dark magic set loose upon the lands. It was spawned at the Fountain. That magic overtook everything surrounding that once pristine and sacred area and desecrated it. It washed over the land of Sehaida, guided by a warlock who is using the magic to do his bidding. He is the cause of all of the strife, the devastation, the death and destruction. I have seen it with my own eyes.

"I was there when he came to Sehaida. In point of fact, I became somewhat of a prisoner in Brondin. I was a victim of poor timing and wrong circumstances. I had to remain there until I could leave freely, but not before I witnessed a cataclysm of death which has sickened me to my core. I could not fight back at that point. I could only continue watching as more and more citizens fell prey to the attack.

"Had I fought back at that time, I would have faltered and succumbed to death. But my friends, death would have been a much easier route to take than what I witnessed. I have seen the victims rise and transform into fiends! No, I could only watch and be repulsed over and over again. Had I lashed out and come to an early end, there would have been no messengers to warn of the impending doom. As such, I have escaped and come before you to give you the most information I can, so that we may find a way to defend ourselves and defeat our enemy."

"What is this madness that we face?" King Secandor asked, rising for a moment and then returning to his seat.

"Here is what I have deduced from my time in Brondin. The warlock controls his victims with a disease. It renders them into a sickened state. They begin to have chills, sweats, get clammy. We have all had some of those symptoms when the seasons change and so forth.

But this disease also makes the victim docile and open to suggestion. That suggestion is to come forward to meet the warlock, or one of his minions. They are sick in body and in mind. Once they are within striking distance, they make for easy targets to destroy. If they are killed outright by brute force or laceration from the razor talons of the enemy, then the game is over. But if they fall prey to a bite, then they are infected with a dose of dark magic and a transformation takes place. They are resurrected and turned into one of the same minions that accosted them."

"That is beyond imagination!" Queen Reesh spoke up.

"I would have had a hard time believing it, if I did not witness this myself."

"So, what of Gildesh?" Panalt asked him, coaxing on the narrative.

"And what of the King of Gildesh?" Queen Reesh asked unknowingly.

The brothers Dito bowed their heads almost simultaneously. Their emotional pain was still so recent. Kelduun continued slowly and allowed everyone to redirect their attentiveness.

"Panalt, I regret not being able to help your father more. The beasts took nearly four weeks to fully conquer the city of Brondin and the surrounding countryside in Sehaida. As more and more of them amassed, there was less and less chance for me to escape or send word. I had to wait and torture myself daily that I could not be of greater help. When they first attacked Brondin, the group was small. Led by their former King, there were no more than thirty or so of them. Before the end of the first day, that number exponentially increased. I believe there is no one in the country of Sehaida that was not stricken with this disease. I believe that the army of monsters that attacked Gildesh was comprised of nearly the whole of the one hundred thousand people that once inhabited Sehaida.

"When you think that Brondin was taken by a troupe of thirty and that group was further enforced by everyone living in and around the city, you could easily see that Albinion was doomed to fall. Once the army had vacated the area, I had some free space to move in, and I tracked them. When I had a bearing on their direction, I sent word as quickly as I could, but the timing was such that no one would have been able to do anything about it. This was always going to be a battle of attrition. Also, the attackers had no sense of remorse nor regret of death. Killing is their only ambition. They care not for emotions. They have no sense of pain. They are mindless and corrupt. They cannot be considered even remotely human. When you look upon them, they are as far away from humanity as they can get."

"So, am I to think that we are in the path of an army of brutal killing machines which is totaling nearly two hundred thousand now? How long do we have? What are we going to do?" Queen Secandor spoke next, bringing the conversation back on track and towards the end goal.

"Indeed, My Queen. You could estimate that nearly every soul living in Gildesh will be part of that army. Undoubtedly, King Dito managed to kill a certain number of attackers, but their numbers would inflate again the moment resistance was broken. It will take time, however, for the army to gather itself and collect that number of victims. We may have as long as a few weeks."

"What can we offer?" Queen Reesh interjected.

"This will take a concerted effort from all present. We will need every able bodied person, man and woman alike, to fight for the cause. We must fight to avoid annihilation, or worse, a hellish tyranny contrived by dark magic."

"We will make our stand, then," King Secandor spoke for them all. "My army is at your disposal."

"As is mine," Queen Reesh agreed.

"Please, I cannot be the general commander of the armies. I have given you the information, but I am not fit to lead the affair," Kelduun replied. "My plan is this…we will need even more help than what we possess at this point. Combining both armies will still leave us outnumbered nearly six to one. We need more soldiers."

"I have around two hundred with me. I only ask that we be allowed to fly the flag of our King," Tobin said.

"Even more than that, Tobin," Kelduun continued. "We need to take drastic action. I ask you, Tobin, to go into the Valley of Whent and talk to the roving nomads that live there. We need their support."

"I have never heard of an army there. Would they help?" Tobin asked Kelduun.

"You must trust in a hunch that I have. They may not seem like they are a force to be reckoned with, but their numbers are in the thousands. You just do not see them all together at once. That is what you must accomplish. It is no small feat. Gather them together and convince them to fight for us."

"That could take many weeks!" Tobin exclaimed.

"It may not be as lengthy as you may expect. Nevertheless, you must take the time needed to do this. This task is of vital importance. We will be here when you achieve it."

"I will leave my men under your guard then. I will only take a small band with me," Tobin said.

"That is settled, then. I suggest you leave swiftly, once we have finished," Kelduun turned to the others. "The command can be left to one of you two. Chose what you want to do. Each army may follow its own leader, but the general command must be left to one person."

"You may be the head," Queen Reesh bowed to King Secandor. "Your army is much larger, as is your country."

King Secandor bowed to her, silently accepting the lead.

"There is one more thing that must be done," Kelduun remarked. "During my time in Brondin, I had only seen the dark warlock once. That was when he came to the city the first time. After he did his work, the wave was set in motion and had a degree of autonomy. I have not seen him since, and I can only guess he has retreated to his spawning place near the Fountain. He will be too much of a match for any of you. He may be more than I can defeat as well. To put him down, I will need a magic as old as the Fountain. I will need the help of dragons!"

Each of their heads snapped in his direction.

"There are few that can remember them, and no common man alive today. Only the few of us who have the ability to prolong our longevity can remember those times. I ask that Panalt and his brothers accompany me in this."

"We shall!" the reply was in unison from the three of them. Then Panalt spoke alone, "We will do whatever it takes to avenge our father's death!"

IX

The members of the royal council dispersed and each went back to their guest rooms. There was silence throughout the levels of the palace in Crute. Merion went to his father's chamber.

"Father, I want to go with Kelduun and the others."

"Is that so? Are you sure that you are feeling well enough for that undertaking?"

"I feel better than I did before. I am a little sore though."

"Can you heft a shield with it? Show me."

Merion was not armed. He looked around and spotted a decorative sword mounted on a shield above the King's bed. He walked over to it and pointed.

"May I?"

The King nodded. Merion gingerly lifted the sword from its cradle and set it on the bed. He then shifted the shield into his left hand. It felt heavier than it looked, and he noted a ping of pain through his shoulder. He swung the shield a few times and picked up the sword. It did not feel good to be swinging the equipment around, but he kept it from showing on his face.

Vernon looked at him and knew he could not keep Merion from following whatever path he needed to take. It showed honor to continue, to go forward even when he was injured. He would not stand in the way of his son's ambition. Merion would be King some day. These were the very actions a King would need to take.

"Very well, you may go."

** ** ** ** **

Panalt heard a knock at his door. His brothers were staying in the next room. He slowly made his way to the door, but when he got there he swung it open forcefully.

"Oh, did I wake you?"

"Ashlyn!"

"May I come in?"

"Yes. Please," he motioned his arm inward.

She entered and sat down on the bed. He trailed after her but sat on a chair nearby.

"I want to come with you when you go after the dragon."

"Don't you think it will be dangerous?"

"Panalt, I want to be with you, no matter where we are going. I can handle myself. I may not have the strength that you or your bothers have, but I know how to handle a weapon. You may need an extra hand or an extra mind on your voyage."

"I think you may be right. But really, I am just happy to see you!"

"And I, too," she said softly. "Come, sit with me, here," she said, patting the bed's coverlet.

He did as he was told, and the night passed quickly.

** ** ** ** **

Tobin did not sleep that night. There was much to think out, and that planning would lead to his success. He did not want to waste time on searching in the wrong areas of the Valley of Whent. He had to make his mission as swift as possible. There was precious little room for error, and time was working against them all.

The scope of his task was enormous. There were myriad nomadic clans in the Valley. But some clustered together and were comprised of hundreds, if not thousands, of people. They were a native people to the Valley and would set camps in various locations, ever in pursuit of the herds. If their food source moved on, so would they. Most of them were hunters, including the women. This was a population devoted to nothing but survival, in its most primitive form. They cared not for setting roots down in a specific area and developing villages. They followed their own traditions and heeded the words of their own shamans.

Tobin selected his crew of men to help him. Bayrne was his first selection, followed by the leaders of each of the other legions of Gildesh. They were a company of five in all. They prepared their packs and donned their traditional armor.

After riding hard for three days, they made the eastern wing of the Vitirral Mountains. This was the entrance to the Valley of Whent. The climate here was vastly different than much of the rest of the lands. Whereas the major nations each had a border along a body of water, the Valley spanned a great length without any source of humidity. The air here was much warmer and dryer. This was not suitable for growing crops, though various grasses and trees could thrive here. This was a great plain spreading for miles in each direction. There would be many areas suitable for hunting game. But they knew that they were still days away from their prime target, near the rivers.

The plan was to follow their westerly course until they met the

116

Hinton River. They would then trace its path northward to its origin, where it budded out of the Triffin River. This was the only water source in the Valley, and sure enough, there would be animals around it. If the herds were there, then they would find the nomads.

It took another day to get to the Hinton River before travelling upstream. After another day of searching, they finally saw a herd of Einads in the distance. The Einads were a form of antelope, native to the Valley. They had two spiraled horns protruding from their heads with a bony connective tissue webbing them together. There were hundreds of them milling about and leaning down to drink from the riverside of the Hinton.

Tobin's group stayed south of the Einads, watching them for a day. There was an alarm sent through the herd, and they began separating. Tobin's first thought was that they may have been disturbed by hunting nomads, but they saw the true cause just a moment later. The Einads were spooked from a pack of wild dogs.

Scattering as if on the wind, the Einads shot in every direction, before coming back together again. Their swarming behavior kept most of them safe and seemed to confuse the dogs briefly. But the dogs had their prize; a small section of the younger Einads had been separated and would not live to rejoin their group. The rest of the herd moved on and accepted their losses.

It took Tobin's group another day to find them, further upstream. They flanked the herd, this time to the east, so that they could come over a bluff and have the advantage of looking down over them. Taking position on their stomachs there, the group of men was only another mound on the bluff. They could see for miles in each direction and would not disturb the herd.

The sun came to its zenith and started its westerly descent when Bayrne touched Tobin's shoulder. He spotted the nomads before the hunt began. They were painted with stripes to match their surroundings. There were fifteen of them crouched low, approaching from downwind. They took up a formation to ambush a wayward group of Einads. A grazing Einad perked its head up and twitched an ear. Others joined it, and they again had cause for flight.

The nomads, hunters to the last, were upon them instantly. Their strategy was one honed through generations, and they were exceedingly good at bringing down their prey. They had some excellent marksmen in their band, and they quickly brought down two of the Einads. They were so skilled with the bow that each man got off two shots for each target, ensuring a kill.

When they were finished, there were four more Einads downed

in the grassy plain. The prey was not far spread from one another, a sign of the efficiency of the hunt. While the nomads were cleaning the carcasses, Tobin made his move from the bluff down to the plain.

Approaching them, Tobin had both of his hands raised high in the air.

"Friends!" he said, thinking he may not have time to say more before they drew down on him.

The nomads turned and took their aim at the intruders. No one let their arrows fly before more was said. The intruding men were still yards away from them and posed no danger to their newly killed dinner. They saw that each of the five men had their hands extended skyward in an obvious sign of submission.

"We mean you no harm," Tobin continued.

He instructed his men to halt where they were, and he continued alone several more yards. Keeping his hands raised, he moved forward several more paces before lowering them.

The leader of the nomads rushed to him with a dagger in his hand. Tobin did not waver or move. When the nomad got within striking distance he feigned an attack before stopping himself. Tobin remained motionless; the dagger was still far enough away from him that he could have dodged it.

"Who are you, and where do you hail from?"

"My name is Tobin. I am from Gildesh, to the north," he said, rising.

Tobin found that he had to look up to the eyes of the nomad. He was a good four inches taller than Tobin.

"I see, Tobin from Gildesh. What is your nature?"

"I came to ask you for help. Will you do me the courtesy of giving your name?"

"My name is not important. What do you need?"

"I ask that you and your people help in defense. Our nation has come under attack," Tobin said, stretching the truth.

"I do not see Gildesh coming to the help of our tribes. I see no reason to help the people of Gildesh."

"You must know that, if we fall, your people may be attacked next."

"The great Mountains divide us. Our Valley is safe. We need no help from the outside. Gildesh does not concern itself with us. We do not concern ourselves with it. We have no allies. We need no allies. Nature will guide us."

Tobin raised a breath and then exhaled. There was not going to be anything else worth saying. "I will take my leave from you. We will not interfere with your hunting grounds. Let us leave in peace, and we shall not return here."

The nomad said nothing but continued to bore his eyes into Tobin's.

Tobin backed a step away and then turned to return to his men. They retreated up to the bluff and mounted their horses. When Tobin looked back over the plain, the nomad was still standing apart from his kinsmen, watching them. This was one tough man. He would have been a deadly adversary if given cause for attack.

Tobin looked at Bayrne.

"One man does not speak for them all," Bayrne reassured him.

"Aye."

They continued north another day and a half, until they came to where the Hinton River split off from the Triffin River. At the fork, they decided to cross the Triffin and continue west instead of crossing the Hinton and searching south, between the rivers. That night, they saw a cluster of fires dotting the landscape. There were no carts here, so they did not suspect gypsies. They knew they had come across another band of nomads. The tips of their characteristic folding huts could just be made out in the failing light. Here today and gone tomorrow, they could strike camp and fold away their belongings in a few short hours.

The group from Gildesh watched them from afar. They did not light a fire of their own in order not to call attention upon themselves. They did not want to invite an attack during the night. They set a watch and took turns resting until morning.

It was late in the night, but the moon was brightly lit in the summer sky. The second man was on watch, Sheft, commander of the former western brigade of Gildesh. He was just about to wake his replacement when a shadow caught his eye. Darker even than the night, he saw movement. No sooner than the moment he stood, the shadow sprung and caught him squarely in the chest. It was a Bengoss, a lion with the great horns of a ram. There were spikes lining its spine all the way to the tail.

Sheft's scream was cut short. His cry awoke his comrades, but it was too late for him. The Bengoss had done its job; going after the jugular, it made short work of the unarmored skin. Sheft's body was dragged off, into the darkness, before anyone had a bearing on his position. They all remained awake then, for the rest of the uneasy night.

When daylight broke, they noted more than one set of tracks around their small campsite. There was more than one Bengoss stalking them. It was common for them to hunt in pairs; there was the instant realization of how lucky they were to have had only a single loss. They found the spot on the ground that was painted red and then dragging marks left around it. Sheft's body would be a long way off. They had to leave his memory behind and pursue the nomads. Five messengers turned to four overnight.

The nomads were preparing to move their camp. They could be seen in the distance lowering the folding huts and placing them on their pack horses. This was a good chance for Tobin and his men to make contact without looking like they were thieves, beggars or rogues.

They rode around the main portion of the temporary settlement and came up to one of the men at the perimeter. They dismounted and introduced themselves as travelling through the country. Presently, they were taken to the leader of this grouping.

"My name is Argenit; these are my people. There are two thousand of us here."

"My name is Tobin. I come from Gildesh. I must speak with you about dark times that are ahead."

"Go on…"

"We need your help. There is a wave of black magic spreading from the Fountain."

"The Fountain!" Argenit cut him off. "We have had some of our tribe not return from a recent visit to the Fountain. What more do you know?"

"A dark army was born and has sacked Sehaida. Gildesh lies in ruins. That army is moving toward the last free grounds of civilization. We are in desperate need of your help!"

"There are strange things happening in our Valley as well. There are changes in the winds, changes in the ground. There are changes that we cannot see but can feel. The earth is changing. I will stand with you."

Tobin nearly embraced him, he was so joyous. There would be help to be gained here.

"You cannot know the gratitude and appreciation I have for your gesture. There is no hope for my country now. My King has fallen. But we have a chance to make the difference in the battle. We can fight back. We are fighting for our lives and the lives of everyone here, around you. Thank you for your support."

"Two thousand hunters will not put fear into the eye of our enemy."

"It is a start. I have already been travelling in the Valley for some days now. But, I came across another clan, only to be turned down."

"There is a better way of going about things. A gathering must be held!" Argenit coached him.

"A gathering?"

"The people of the Valley may look to be broken into separate clans, but our culture is universal. We have the same customs and worship the same gods. We have shamans to help enlighten and direct us, but they do not speak for us. Even if my shaman would say that I will die in battle, that does not mean it does not merit my presence. The leaders must come to a gathering when one is called."

"You have a progressive mind, Argenit. I am at your mercy. Please, help us and call the gathering."

"It will take only a few days to send word to the others. The gathering place is not far from here. It's at the river's divergence. We will spread word that the Valley is coming under attack. That will perk the people's interest."

As the next two days passed, nomads started to set up camps across the plain. It was another five days before the gathering was held. By now, there were thousands of groupings of people. There may have been nearly twenty thousand people there. Tobin thought the turn-out was more than adequate. There may not have been as many people as the four great nations, but then again, there was not a great city in the valley for the population to flock to. These people lived in a different way than any that he had known. They would make a strong addition to the cause.

Before Argenit spoke, a bonfire was lit as a signal for the commencement of the gathering. It quickly picked up in ferocity, raging against the wind. Argenit was first to speak when the leaders gathered, and he found that he needed to raise his voice to overcome the surging fire. The gathering was his doing, so he was the temporary leader of the meeting and would stand as mediator if the situation called for it.

After he welcomed everyone, he turned to Tobin to give his piece. Tobin delivered the message he intended to and the clamor began. He had not even sat down before the arguing started. Some opinions were conveyed louder than others, and soon there were two main factions in the group.

One portion said they should join Tobin to fight for their freedom. The other was arguing that they already had freedom, and they would not fight voluntarily, unless they were forced into it. This second group firmly believed that there would be no invasion of the Valley, and that they had not seen, nor heard of anything to prove it would happen.

"Who is that man?" Tobin said to Argenit, pointing.

"That is Husto. His clan is the largest in the Valley. He may have five thousand in his group. They all follow him in whatever he does.

He fancies himself a king but is god-like to his people."

"That is the man we ran into before coming to you. He abruptly declined to help us."

"He feels he is a conqueror and that may be. He is the strongest hunter I have ever seen. It is said that he has slain a Bengoss by himself, with no help save for the spear he carries. No doubt, he feels that no harm will come to him. He will not easily be swayed to help."

"I did not think there would so much unrest between the groups. I thought more people would see things the way you did. Is there no way to join everyone?"

"Let me try to talk to Husto and see if I can change his mind. If he does, maybe he can tip the balance in our favor. We may gain the whole of the nomadic people if he joins us."

Argenit left Tobin and strode to Husto. Tobin could see that they were arguing just like many other circles of men. Finally, Argenit returned sulking. Tobin turned to him.

"That did not seem to go well."

"Husto asked the one thing I was hoping would not be brought up. He is asking for the survival trial."

"What is that?"

"When a clan is requesting assistance, it is common to send a warrior to pass a test given by the clan offering aid. It may be perilous, or benign. If the clan needs assistance badly enough, they must send a warrior to achieve whatever trial is set before him. If he passes, the offering clan is obligated to help them. If he does not, there is no accord. If he perishes, the original clan may be in even worse condition, having lost a warrior."

"I must do it then. I need help from as many as I can find."

Argenit bowed his head. He paused a moment before returning to the clan leaders. The clansmen drew lots to determine the order of them to call upon Tobin. Husto went first, then Argenit, and then the other seven major leaders.

"Send him to Cletra! We will see who is brave or who is dead!" exclaimed Husto.

"I will not have him perform a trial. I will stand with him," Argenit said, casting his vote.

"I am with Argenit, no trial. I will go with him to fight," said the next.

"I would have offered another task, but I think Husto is right. Send him to Cletra," the next spoke up.

"Cletra!"

"Cletra!"

"We will go with him to battle."

"As will we."

"I agree. No trial."

The vote was cast. Five clans would back Tobin and go to war with him. Four clans were demanding a trial. There was enough in a vote to win, but the decree was such that he must still pass the test in order that the others would come with him.

They dispersed after the vote, each happy with his own decision. Argenit came back to Tobin with a saddened look in his eyes.

"You look thoroughly dejected, Argenit. The way I see it, I could have had to perform four different tasks. And look, there are some clans that agreed with you not to have me do anything more than lead them into battle."

"It may sound good to an outsider, only having one task to accomplish. But it is the task itself that is troubling me."

"We can work through it. Where is Cletra? I have never heard of it."

"Tobin, Cletra is not a place. It is a person..."

X

Kelduun was seeing to the final details of the voyage north. His band was assembled, including a few last minute additions. The group would have six members now. He would take the lead; Panalt, Dur, Tiras, Ashlyn, and Merion would follow him. They each had their trusted steeds packed and fed. A gallant looking party, Kelduun was seated on the majestic, white stallion, Bolt. As always, the twins looked alike on their horses, Shade and Storm. Panalt decided to keep the draft horse they recovered from the gypsies. Nearly as big as Bolt, he was a medium brown color. Panalt grew to trust him in the last few weeks and would not abandon him now. He called him Chance, in honor of the twins discovering him. Merion stuck with his trusty spotted horse, Pro. Ashlyn would not settle on a pony and picked a mare out of the stable of Crute, though she did not give it a name.

They were just about to exit the main gate to the palace leading into the city when they heard a cry. Running hard around the corner of the inner wall, Gendin raced up to them.

"Is it too late to join you?"

Merion looked at Kelduun, who nodded back. They would wait for him to pick his new horse from the stable. It did not take long, for Gendin had already packed a satchel for himself, which was stowed secretly away near the stable doors.

The group grew to seven then, and they left without further issues arising. Their path took them to the east and around Lake Proseccan. They would not venture into Gildesh for any reason.

After a day of riding, Dur came along the side of Kelduun. Panalt was already riding beside him on the other side.

"I don't want to sound silly, but just how is this dragon mission going to be successful?"

"I can understand your concern, Dur," Kelduun answered him. "I was just talking to Panalt about this very thing. Let us speak more after we set up our camp."

"Agreed," Dur said and fell back to join the rest of the group.

They had gone into the evening before stopping. They were still just south of the turn of the lake's shoreline. Tiras and Dur walked up and down the beach in search of driftwood to make a fire. Panalt and Ashlyn tended to the horses. Merion and Gendin placed the group's belongings around where the fire's circle would be.

Once the fire blazed to life, they each made a meager meal. They could fish as long as they were around the lake. After that, the fishing would be sparse, as the Gallendar River had many areas of rapids. The sky was nearly black before they finished. Kelduun cleared his throat and spoke "Dur asked me a question this afternoon, and now you will all hear the answer." He looked at Dur.

"What I want to know is…well, what are we doing?"

"That sounds about right," Kelduun smiled. "To begin with, you, that are surrounding me at this moment, cannot have the first idea of the terror that is coming toward the remaining free kingdoms. I do not say this to make you feel inadequate. I say this because no one has ever seen this type of force in their lives or in any of history. When you think of the population of Albinion to a man, there may have been fifteen thousand people living there. But you would rarely see even this number all together at once. To multiply that by ten or twentyfold, and then to see that mass of enemy soldiers in formation at once is almost incomprehensible. Even with the most successful military tactics, the army of Strayos and Caldorn will need reinforcements. I hope that Tobin accomplishes his task, but even so, we are going to provide the help that is desperately needed.

"That is where a dragon can be of great use. It would be able to fly over the battlefield and spray its flamed breath over a vast number of enemies. Burning them down to the ground, this would purge the onslaught. A dragon may be able to take out a thousand of the monsters before even becoming wounded."

"That sounds pretty far-fetched, but could it actually work?" Tiras asked.

"Dragons are magical creatures. If dark magic created the scourge coming our way, we can combat that with our own. The dilemma is that there are so few dragons left."

"I have never seen one," Ashlyn remarked.

"I suspect you have not, Ashlyn. They have not been in the known world for some time. Even in the olden days there were not many around. They dwelt in the mountains and each range had its own small group. When the nations were forming, their territory was discovered. After that, they were hunted to near extinction. They migrated north and left man to conquer each other."

"Do you know how to find them?" Merion asked.

"There are parts of the world that even I am not well versed on. I will go with my gut instinct that they have gone as far north as they can. There is not another mountain range anywhere around the nations until you cross the Semolend River and into the Horgangee Mountains. That is where I hope to find them."

"Semolend River. Horgangee Mountains. I have never even heard of them. I cannot believe how vast the world is beyond the land encompassed by the four great nations," Dur remarked.

"So, assuming we find the dragons, what will we do with them once we have one in sight?" Ashlyn asked.

"That is a much deeper question, which requires a somewhat flexible answer. As I was saying to Panalt before we stopped, this is the hardest portion of this mission. In short, I do not know what we will ultimately do…"

"What?" Gendin perked up, though he had stayed quiet for so long.

"Let him finish, Gendin," Panalt gently coached him.

"A young dragon may be able to be captured and trained. Though, this is an outcome that is fraught with potential disaster. Even a newly birthed dragon is large — as big as a standard cart. They are trusting only for a short period of time before they begin to develop their own independence. If we come across a dragon that is already actively hunting, then our chances of luring it and training it are drastically lowered. Even the chances of finding a hatchling are minimal. The danger, as you may be guessing, is that the parent will not be far off. There is double the peril in this approach. The hatchling is certainly capable of defending itself, but it also has the security of a guardian close at hand. And, no doubt, we shall be caught trying to move an egg or the hatchling itself. They are too big not to go unnoticed. I do not feel it likely that we will be able to succeed in this fashion."

"Is that the only way?" Merion asked.

"It may be an option we have to entertain, but it is not the only way. There are spells in the annals that could be adapted to this objective. There have been tomes written on transformations. I have studied these at great length and I have had success in my dealings in this. Would any of you suspect that my mighty war horse started as a lowly pack mule that was nearly eviscerated by our foes? Even the enemy we face is a gross interpretation of what can be done with transformation, though that course is born out of disease and shaped by black magic. I propose that we find a remnant of a dragon. Anything we can find: a scale, a tooth, a claw. We can use it to make ourselves a dragon!"

"That would be much safer. We can scavenge to find what we can and then retreat to a more sheltered area to put the magic to use," Panalt chimed in.

"Our dragon would be loyal to us, but it is going to be small. We will create a baby, only the size of a hatchling. But, my friends, you would be surprised at how quickly it can grow. It may be twice or even thrice its starting size by the time we return to Strayos. In the few weeks it will take us to return home, it may be the size of an adolescent and deadly powerful already. You have not witnessed this in your lifetimes, but the power of a dragon cannot be underestimated. Our enemies will not know how to deal with this new terror on our side."

They finished their conversation and rested for the night. In the morning, they rose just after dawn to pack what little they had. They rode for another two days. Coming around the Lake and pointing north, they came to the great bridge of Caldorn that crossed the Gallendar River. Further north, the Gallendar proved to be hard to follow along its banks. Many boulders were strewn about its beaches, and they soon broke away entirely to take an easier northerly route.

As they did so, the rocky shoreline gave way to a grassy plain, and travel was light for another day. As they continued north, the grade started to increase, somewhat slowing their pace with the uphill trek. Soon they could make out a dark line on the horizon that was the Tripean Forest. It extended for as far as they could see in either direction.

The sloped plain proved to be a greater distance than expected, and it took them another two days to reach the Tripean Forest. By now, most of their reserve food store had been depleted. They would have to hunt. Only Panalt seemed unfazed by this, and there was a small amount of grumbling to be had from the others.

"Brothers, you wanted to learn how to live in nature. Here is your chance. I can teach you, but you must be patient. It is much more delicate than you may guess," Panalt instructed them. "You are each very good shots with the bow, and Merion can join you in the hunt. Stay low, move slowly and quietly. Follow my lead. Stay downwind. Watch and listen. I will set some traps as we go."

The men advanced into the trees leaving Ashlyn, Gendin, and Kelduun to set up camp. Kelduun did not join them, but told them not to go far into the Forest.

"This territory is wild. More so than the forest outside of Albinion. Do not venture too far into the forest until we are all together as a party."

They managed to shoot two game hens and set many traps to check on their way through the next day. The sun was beginning its descent and turning the sky fire red mixed with lavender. Panalt and his group made the decision that two birds would have to be enough for the lot of them and turned towards the campsite just outside the forest. Merion was leading the way back, followed by Dur and Tiras; Panalt was trailing.

Panalt was walking and listening and looking upward when his foot sunk into the earth, changing his balance. He looked down to find he had stepped into an imprint in the earth. He stopped cold as he realized there were larger and more dangerous predators in this forest than the hunters he was with.

"Stop," he whispered. "Stay quiet for a moment. Get low."

They did at his request.

He bent down to inspect the ground. The print was almost twice the size of his foot. It was shaped as a paw and showed massive claw marks. It was driven into the earth; he guessed its owner had a sizable weight. The track was dried on the edges, so it was not recent, but also not older than a day. Scanning the area, he found another track of the same dimensions and guessed it to stand on two feet, rather than four. He estimated that it may stand about six feet high, based on the stride distance. This would be a dangerous predator to come across.

They marked the direction it appeared to be going in and took the opposite route. When they got back to the camp, they held up their prizes. Gendin started working on a fire for roasting. Panalt came up to Kelduun and told him of what they found.

"An Anget. They are apelike. They stand on their hind legs much of the time. They have four arms coming from their torso, but their muscular strength keeps them from coming unbalanced. They commonly drop down to four when running and eating. We should be mindful when we enter the forest. Let us set a watch for the night."

The night passed without incident, though the sounds emanating from the forest were foreign to everyone. Everyone was relieved when the sun rose.

Kelduun addressed them. "Today will be the last day of easy travel. From here, things will be much more difficult. I am afraid that our horses will not serve us any longer. Pack what you need to travel lightly."

"We cannot leave the horses behind," Tiras complained.

"I know that, Tiras," Kelduun reassured him. "Gendin, I am asking you to guide our horses back to Strayos with you."

"I…will," he replied . There was disappointment in his face and words.

They entered the forest warily: Kelduun in the lead, Panalt in the rear. The twins and Merion each had their bows at the ready. They trekked for a long time; no one dared to raise his voice to suggest stopping. There would be no comfort as long as they were surrounded by the trees.

After a time, they noted that the ambient lighting was changing.

The foliage had blotted out much of the light over the course of the morning's haul, but now, there seemed to be some rays punching through to the forest floor. The trees thinned in density, and then they came out into a vast clearing.

There was a collective gasp and Merion pointed.

"Look!"

The clearing was accentuated with a grand lake. Behind that, to the northeast, there was a giant structure built. They could not make out the details of it, the distance being so great. There was a collective decision to investigate it, as well as the other side of the lake. A plan was agreed on to travel around it from the south, then to the east before turning north again.

It took half of the day to circumnavigate the lake. When they reached the other side, they were again impressed with the structure they saw. It was a massive pyramidal building overlooking the lake. At its peak was an area, or room, walled in with pillars on all sides. No doubt, this was held as sacred ground. Further to the northeast, there was a string of stone buildings in a semicircle, all facing the pyramid. A second row of buildings was behind the first, though straight in orientation and running parallel to it. Each of the buildings was set upon four stanchions, keeping them propped in the air. There was no way of getting to the entrances without climbing a ladder.

The silence was profound. There was nothing stirring. The air was calm. They stood motionless, looking from right to left and back again. The buildings cast their shadows over the party. The open air windows and doors held blackness within.

Ashlyn called out, "Hello."

After the pervasive silence, the sound of her voice seemed intensified, though she just spoke normally. Their ears pricked with the slightest sound. The area was like a vacuum.

"Something terrible happened here," Panalt said.

"Perhaps, but that may be an early assumption. Let us do a cursory search of the area. I have no knowledge of this place or its people," Kelduun said.

"Why are the houses elevated?" Ashlyn asked.

"My guess is that they provided some amount of defense from most every predator in the forest. Even an Anget would have little success with this. You saw the prints, Panalt. They do not have the hand-like extremities of regular apes. The talons they possess are for hunting only, not dexterous manipulations of tools. We may need to use one of those dwellings for the night."

They walked around the area for a short time before turning

their attention to the pyramid. Climbing to the top, they found that there were one hundred eighty steps ascending. The peak was crowned with the room surrounded by pillars. An altar was in the center of it, stained black with sacrificial blood.

"It is hard to say how long this place has been abandoned," Kelduun said, as he studied the rocky flooring of the pillared room. "I think we should prepare for the night before the light fails. We do not want to be taken off guard should there be predators around. These people may have done us a favor by showing us how vulnerable we are in this forest."

The group descended the pyramid and selected one of the closer raised huts for their stay. They quickly fashioned a ladder using smaller trunked saplings and vines to lash the rungs into place. There was little light left by the time the task was finished. Panalt climbed the ladder first to check if the area was secure. He also tested the flooring and was reassured that it was sound. After he gave the word, they quickly climbed into one of the elevated buildings. They retrieved the ladder and settled in for the night. The building was surprisingly drafty; a chill hung in the air.

Just after darkness enshrouded the clearing, the sounds of the forest began. This night was much harder for the party to endure. They were ill-at-ease nearly the entire time. There was no need to sleep in shifts, for no one slept at all. It seemed a long time for the moon to rise over the tree line to give what little illumination it could to the weary travelers. When it did, they were able to see the edges of the clearing and the ground around them.

Kelduun nudged Panalt without speaking and then pointed to the eastern edge of the clearing. Panalt was already scanning the area, but he turned at Kelduun's bidding. He stifled a gasp as he saw several white lights and knew they were many pairs of eyes. There were at least twenty animals at the perimeter watching; their eyes were lit up white with the moon's luminance. The light was not great enough to make out what kind of animal they were. After some time, they disappeared back into the darkness from which they came, another reminder that they were not alone.

Panalt was starting to dose off when he felt a chill run up his spine. His instincts served him well. When he looked to the ground, he could see shadows of things racing around the building's supports. They were big things, but they were as quiet as wraiths in the night. How such a big predator could move so quickly and remain quiet was frightening in its own right. This forest was not like the one around Albinion. There, he was the hunter. Here, he could easily be a meal for a better killer.

He looked at Kelduun who was still awake. When he touched his shoulder, Kelduun looked back at him with questioning eyes. He did not know what was below either.

Finally, the sun peaked over the horizon, and things quieted down. The party was exhausted after the ordeal. When the rays of light began coming through the open windows of their shelter, they could see it was minimalistic in décor. A bench and a table against the wall were the only pieces of furniture. There were no pleasantries for sleeping, only a rumpled old blanket. The layer of dust on the table and the holes in the blanket signified that this place was uninhabited for quite some time.

They moved the ladder to the next dwelling and found it to be nearly identical in furnishing. This shelter had a crude drawing on the wall, a roughly drawn stick image with a word under it.

CENTREPEN

There was nothing of use in the next two buildings and no more information to be gained. Moving the ladder around was getting tedious, and they were ready to move on. There was a feeling that they could not be entirely safe at the village, but they also knew it was dangerous to be in the forest as well. In the end, the settlement was no closer to their goal, and they were forced to leave it.

They moved away from it as quickly as they could. After covering some distance, they felt a little better about their situation.

"What did you make of those black hunters last night?" Panalt asked Kelduun.

"They were not Angets. Even an Anget down on four, or even six of its limbs, does not look quite like that. The body was different, more stick like and less muscular. They might be the likeness of the drawing we saw."

"And don't forget about the tracks we saw at the base of the buildings. They were not the paw prints from the forest. It was almost as if the earth was stabbed into. The print was as if a sword was plunged into the earth. They were not like a paw at all," Panalt finished for him.

"We may have a name for them, Centrepen, if you want to trust the drawing. But we should be cautious. We may need to set ourselves in the trees to sleep so that..."

"What was that?" They snapped their heads in the direction of the sound.

"I don't see anything. Let's move, quickly."

They began moving hastily and put even more ground between them and the lake. After another hour, they took a short time to rest. Ashlyn sat on a log, but it was decayed through and broke under her weight. She stood and aimed to kick it in disgust. When she placed her foot firmly on the ground, she was surprised as it gave way. She broke through a thin layer of branches and debris and tumbled into a deep hole. One minute she was angry at the decayed log, the next minute she vanished before their eyes.

"Ashlyn!" Panalt screamed.

There was no answer.

"Did you see that?" he asked his brothers rhetorically. "She just disappeared."

They nodded.

"Let's take a look," Merion said to him.

They went cautiously to the spot where Ashlyn slipped into the hole. It looked deep and dark.

"Let's throw a stone in and see how deep it is," Dur offered.

"We can't do that. What if we hit her?" Panalt said.

"I didn't think of that!" Dur snapped his fingers.

Kelduun stepped over to the lip and peered down. "Well, we cannot leave her. Do you want to climb down to her Panalt? I will give you some light from up here."

Panalt nodded. Kelduun held his hand outward and let a flame spark to life on his palm. It took longer than he expected to climb to the bottom. The hole was not large at the top, but only inches under the surface the bottleneck expanded. This made the climbing more dangerous, as he was hanging more than anything. He had to tightly clutch onto the few handholds that the rock provided, which caused some balancing issues. Finally, the wall straightened out, and the climbing was more vertically downward.

When he got down to the bottom, he found Ashlyn wrapped in a greenish, ropy, plantlike substance.

"Ashlyn? Are you hurt?"

She turned to him. "I was lucky this time. I fell through all of these vines. They slowed my fall but did not stop it entirely. I still landed pretty hard on my leg. My ankle hurts, but I can move it."

"I do not think it is broken, but nevertheless, you cannot climb like that," Panalt said, then looked around him.

The cavern was large and supported by a sturdy column through the middle. There was a stream flowing on the other side of the rocky brace. The ceiling of the cavern was littered with pock marks. Ashlyn may have fallen through one of them, but any one of them could have at any time. The earth above them was likely to give way entirely at some point in the future. The walls curved upward, also supporting the dome, but the surface was perilously thin. Around the stream and perimeter of the cave, he saw holes in the walls leading in several directions. He called out to the group topside.

"She cannot climb. Use the rope and come down here."

Panalt's voice echoed back to him in the rock, but on the surface it was barely audible. Kelduun heard him and instructed the rest of them to descend. It took only a short time for them all to descend, and they left the rope dangling there.

"What should we do now?" Dur asked him.

"We can try to hoist her," Tiras offered.

"That is true, but look at that ceiling," Panalt pointed upward. "It looks like it could give way at any time. It might not hold the weight of us pulling her. And what if she drops? She could be hurt even worse. Remember, the vines broke her fall before, but they are all ripped down now," Panalt countered.

"Perhaps we can do it even easier than that," Kelduun said. "The ground is fairly level down here, at least around this place. The forest is not. We can follow the stream. It should come out of the cave somewhere, and it looks to be flowing in a northerly direction. This must be an underground river flowing from the lake. Grab some of those branches, and we will use them as torches."

Kelduun used his flame spell once again to light the torches, and they gathered Ashlyn's belongings. She could stand on her own but was slightly hobbled when walking. She placed her arm across Panalt's shoulders for support.

They walked for an hour, staying close to the underground stream. It twisted this way and that, and even Kelduun was having a hard time determining their bearing. There were no clues to go off of, only the stream. If it turned too many times, they may head in the wrong direction.

Another hour of walking led them down a tunnel that seemed to have light at the end of it. Their excitement grew, and they began to hurry toward the end. Even Ashlyn was walking on her own, her excitement overcoming the winces of pain.

When they got to the end of the tube, they saw that the light was not coming from the open sky, but only another large opening in the ceiling of a vast cavernous area. It was similar to the cavern Ashlyn tumbled into earlier, but this one dwarfed the other. If she would have fallen here she would likely have broken a leg, or worse. The tunnel they were walking in deposited them onto a precipice that was acting as a balcony to the rest of the cave. They could look over the edge to their right and down into the depths. The walkway disappeared into the darkness in a rather straight line, far above the bottom. There was a little light in this area because of the roof's collapse, but it could not serve as a substitute for their torches. The stream they were following flowed out of the tunnel and cascaded down into the cave, creating a vast underground lake.

The drop from their walkway to the lake was nearly vertical. Rather than wasting another length of rope, they decided to continue using the walkway and keep the lake in sight below them. They needed a good way of descending before trying to follow another outflow from this underground lake.

After several yards, they came to the site of a rockslide. It effectively cut off their path, while also giving a declining slope for them to get to the floor. They were cautious in their decent and even Ashlyn had no trouble getting down. Her ankle was feeling better, but not pain free.

Once they reached the floor, they continued along the lake's side. The atmosphere was different down here. It seemed warmer, and wetter. The air was humid, and there were muffled sounds carrying through the air. With the stream's waterfall far behind them, the cause of this was unknown. There were even more holes in the walls going back into the rock.

"Look at this," Panalt pointed to the ground.

They gathered around him. He was crouched down, inspecting the rocky floor. There were scratched marks leading down to the lake's edge. Closer to the shoreline, the rocky floor gave way to a more muddied appearance, and there were stab marks in the softer earth. This was similar to the tracks they found in the village near the pyramid.

"This is not good," Panalt said to Kelduun.

"Those things may be down here," he answered.

"Is that the sounds we are hearing?" Tiras asked.

"It could be. Though they were eerily quiet when we saw them in the village, they were likely on a hunt then. If this is their territory, we could be near the nest. We must be quiet and make haste. We have to find a way out of here," Kelduun replied.

They found the outflow they were looking for in the form of yet another stream. It disappeared into the rock, but there was not another tunnel paralleling it. They had to get wet. They waded into the stream and ducked under the rocky arch in the wall. This arched tunnel was only several feet long and emerged on the other side onto a plateau. There was yet another drop-off, this time to their left. The grandeur of this cave system was immense. The stream continued flowing on the plateau. As they walked, the sounds grew in intensity: screeching and scratching.

Kelduun walked over to the edge of the drop-off and peered over the side. What he saw almost took his breath away. There were hundreds of the Centrepen monsters below. They were crawling over one another, slashing at one another, and communicating with each other in whatever way they did.

The others gathered around him before he could warn them. Ashlyn screamed, but cut herself off. It was too late. The alarm was sent through the hive. The hunters had a target; the game was started. The Centrepens immediately sprung into action and reared up.

Kelduun could see exactly what they were up against. The bodies were black. It was hard to see them in the light, but he could see what they looked like. They were sleek and almost tubular. There were eight legs along the carapace. The first two appendages were curled in a mantis-like clawed appearance. The bodies were slender and were complimented with a barbed poisonous tail of a scorpion. The whole body length stretched out to a full seven feet.

They clawed at each other to gain access to the ledge that Kelduun's party occupied. Kelduun rushed backward and directed his group to cluster around him.

"We cannot fight them. They are too many. We have to run! Go ahead of me."

"Take the rear then. We will need your magic to give us some time. I will lead us!" Panalt said to Kelduun.

The Centrepens were already coming close to reaching the plateau's top. They were stacking on top of each other and mercilessly throwing themselves at the wall in waves. The ones on the top of the pile would breach the ledge in minutes. Already they were shooting a spray of poisonous fluid from their tails. It was wretched smelling, and no doubt, toxic if it landed on their skin or clothing.

Panalt led the small group across the stream and into the next tunnel. They had to turn twice in only a few feet; this tunnel was more winding than any they had come across in the cave. Before he knew it, the stream was gone. They had to keep running, no matter if the stream was at their side or not. Another twist led them to a dead end. They had to backtrack through their last turn. Inspecting the wall, Panalt found that there was a hole at the floor that they may have to squeeze through. He threw his torch through the hole. It bounced off of the walls and almost extinguished itself. The fit would be tight. He could not gauge how far the tunnel went into the wall or where it would lead them.

Kelduun rushed up to them as they were inspecting the wall.

"They are coming. I will blaze them with fire, but I cannot hold them for long."

"There is no time! We have to squeeze through this hole. I will go first, then Ashlyn. You all follow after," Panalt instructed.

He ducked down and thrust his shoulders into the hole. It was a very tight fit. He could only inch his way forward. Now that he was at ground level, he could see that the fissure widened in two feet. After that, it narrowed even further. He could only fit now by sliding on his side. It was hard to breath. The closeness was overwhelming. He could feel his feet scraping the sides of the wall. His shoulders were getting stuck at every movement. Each breath was filled with dust. He could not see what was happening behind him; he could only move forward.

When he thrust his head through the last tight portion of the crevice, he took a deep breath. He was free of the confining, stone coffin. He scrambled to his feet and waited. And waited. And waited. Where were they? He got back down to his knees and saw Ashlyn was almost to the end. He reached for her and pulled her free.

"There is going to be trouble. Merion doesn't think he will fit into the tight space!"

"He has to!"

"Your brothers are coming next."

"I was not even worried about him. I was more concerned for the old man, Kelduun."

It seemed to take a painstakingly long time for them to emerge from the crack. Time was slowed down. Panalt could not imagine what was going on at the other side of the hole.

"You have to go," Kelduun told Merion.

"I will give it a shot," Merion returned.

He had to. There was no time to waste. He stooped and got down to his stomach before crawling through. His shoulders were just a little broader than the other three men. His shirt was snagging and soon the rocks were slashing at his bare skin. When he emerged from the hole, he was bloodied and ghastly in appearance.

"What happened back there?" Ashlyn asked. "Did they break through?"

"No, this happened in the tunnel."

Kelduun wriggled through as he was speaking.

"We have given ourselves a window of time. But these creatures know these caves better than we do," Kelduun said to them. "I see we have found the stream again."

They looked and saw that he was correct, but the small chamber that they were in was only big enough for the stream and the small band of earth they were standing on. Getting out of this small pocket of a room would require swimming under the rock.

"I will go first this time," Merion said. "I am a good swimmer. Let me try to see where this ends up."

"Wait," Kelduun reached down to pick up an oblong stone. "Take this."

"A stone?"

"Transformed."

Kelduun lifted his hand, and the stone began emitting light from within. There would have been no light to help him determine the course of the stream without it. The torches would not survive in the water, but this stone was magically encapsulating the light inside it. It would be impermeable to the water.

He waded in to his hips before the stream deepened to where he was clearly treading water. He disappeared under the water and glided below the rock. The light slowly faded away. It took a long time before anything happened. The time had gone for one full minute; then two minutes elapsed and passed into three. Could he still be down there?

When the time grew to nearly four minutes, Ashlyn felt like jumping up and down. She could take it no longer. She was about ready to crack when there was a hint of light approaching from under the ledge where they last saw Merion.

He thrust his head out of the water and took a great gulp of air. Merion swam to the side of the stream, crawled out and collapsed. He turned over on his back. His chest was heaving up and down and he took enormous breaths. When he composed himself he spoke to the others.

"It is close to sixty feet to the other side. It is so dark, even with the stone lit up. It was hard to tell any features. There is a point a little over half way there that you could try to get a breath, but there is precious little room. I will go first again. When I get to the end, I can stay in the water and hold the stone, so you can see your goal."

He left again without saying another word. They did not have time for argument. Kelduun once again stayed until the end, but gave each of them a stone to hold. Each was lit like the one he gave to Merion. Panalt dove in and disappeared. Dur and Tiras also went, eager to be done with this.

"My ankle still hurts, I do not know if I can make it," Ashlyn complained to Kelduun.

"I will be right behind you, Ashlyn. There is no other way," he coached her.

She got into the water. The pain in her ankle was much less in the cold water. It felt soothing, and the weight lifted off of her foot from swimming instead of standing made for a much better outlook. She took her breath and slipped under the water.

The water was black. Even with her stone, she could not see more than a few feet before her eyes. She kicked and paddled a long time. Her lungs were starting to hurt, and she stopped to look behind her. There was no other light in the passage, neither at the end, where her goal was, nor at the start. Kelduun had said he would be right behind her, but she could not see anything. She started to panic and fear began to grip her. What if I cannot make it? Where is the middle point to get some air? Did I pass it yet? How much farther until the end?

She kicked onward but was feeling weak. She was feeling sleepy. Her lungs were burning. She was swallowing the air left in her mouth; her reflex to open her mouth was rising and she fought to continue. Do not give up! Is that a light? Maybe there is more than one light…She felt herself sinking; she was so tired.

Then she felt a rush as she was grabbed and yanked out of the water. Panalt was there standing over her. She gasped and coughed, arms flailing; her eyes were bleary. But she made it. Panalt saw her start to sink and dove in to grab her. She may not have made it if he did not see her light stop. It remained motionless for a moment then moved, but not toward them. He needed to use his instinct to rescue her.

A moment later, Kelduun emerged making the party whole again. Ashlyn still needed to take some time to regroup.

"Ashlyn," Panalt said to her softly. "Can you walk?"

"I think so."

"That is good, we have to move. We are not safe here."

She coughed and opened her eyes fully. There were bones strewn across the floor and round looking stones. They were eggs with the Centrepen pupas inside. They were in the center of the hive. She stood up quickly and had a moment of dizziness. She was frightened and clung to Panalt.

"We know why the village was deserted. But we have to run," he said to her.

The scratching sounds preceded the rancid smell. The Centrepens were coming to protect their larvae. They would be in this chamber within seconds. The group turned and ran to the stream's next outlet tunnel before wading through it.

Behind them the Centrepens burst through a different opening into the room. It was as if a black geyser opened up, spraying the poisonous creatures inward. They were upon them as the group entered the tube.

Kelduun let another ball of fire grow in his hand and threw it at the egg structures. This slowed down the assailants, as many of the Centrepen drones were sacrificed. Their reinforcements kept up the pursuit.

"I think I see a light ahead!" Panalt called back.

"Run!" Kelduun screamed. "I cannot hold them for long!"

Panalt turned another corner and was rewarded with the long sought after prize of daylight. There could be no mistake that this was not another sun ray lit cavern but purely natural light. The stream thinned somewhat, and there was a rushing sound. It ended in a waterfall. When the group emerged from the hole, the stream dropped in its fall some fifty feet down.

"Should we jump?" Panalt asked Kelduun.

Kelduun looked at Ashlyn.

"I think I can climb it. At least a short distance, so that the fall will not be so great."

It was agreed. They could not take the chance that the river would not be deep enough at that point. It did not appear that there were rocks at the base of the fall, but they could easily be hidden under the water's surface. None of them could afford to be further hurt. They would climb as far down as they could before making a decision to jump.

The group took to the vertical mountain face and slowly eased their way down. The Centrepens rushed to the opening. Most of them stopped, but the masses behind collided into them, sending several over the wall, down into the river below. They flew over the heads of the party clinging to the precipice.

They had some sense of relief. The Centrepen hunters would not continue to follow them down the crag, but they were not out of danger. After descending halfway to the riverbed, they came to a platform. There would be no further climb to make. The shelf stuck out only a short way, but the river below had eroded enough of the bank to make the bottom portion of the climb too inverted. There could be no way for them to hang upside down for so long and all make it without dropping.

"At least we do not have to jump now," Tiras said. "I'd trade this for a broken leg."

He held up their last length of rope.

"It may get us to within a few feet of the water," Dur agreed.

"I will help you set it," Merion chimed in.

They found a rocky outcropping and wrapped the rope around it. Testing it, they found they could put weight on it without it giving way. One by one, they lowered themselves down and off of the rope. The water rushed by, swiftly whisking them downstream.

XI

Albinion was in ruins. The dark army of Sehaida conquered Albinion and started its demolition of the surrounding countryside. Soon the whole of Gildesh would be captured.

The once pristine garden outside of the Dito palace was burning. The castle itself was being ripped down, stone by stone. The tower that was once the domain of the king was stripped of its exterior layer, and the stairwell could be seen. The double moat ran red with blood during the assault and was now a dark, cloudy mire. Everywhere the signs of decay were present. The city looked hundreds of years older than it did only weeks previous.

The fall of the city was cataclysmic. The soldiers inside the castle walls only had a small chance of success against a force so large. But when the monsters flung themselves into the walls of the fortress, the disease had new life and spread. The mode of attack was as genius as it was simple. Attrition would prevail. The fiends were their own ammunition. Fling enough of it at the target and the mark would be sure to be hit. The more of the attackers that got inside of the walls, the faster they would be brought down.

There was no remorse in sending themselves on suicide missions. There were no thoughts of their own deaths. Killing was the only goal. It came with transformation in many cases. So many victims were put through brutal pain. It would have been a lethal amount, but they were destined to rise again and suffer longer, through the transformation. The bodies grew and changed. The hide stretched and ripped and scales formed.

The enemy force outgrew the defenders and overwhelmed them in strength and in numbers. Now there were no citizens or soldiers left in the city of Albinion. Everyone was dispatched.

The dark wave spread from the city, seeping up to the shoreline first and then into the forest. The numbers of marauders grew exponentially, as more and more people fell. The farmland was next, and the country was soon laid to waste.

Two of the major nations had been captured. The signature left behind was death, decay, and pestilence. There was no area left in its previous condition. The very earth itself looked as if covered in grimy soot. The fields, once used for farming, were burned and stripped of all nutrients. All that was left of a great civilization was being erased and replaced with nothingness. The brutal nature of the conversion would have been stunning to any onlooker.

Having rebuilt the numbers of attackers lost in the battle at Albinion and augmenting the invading army with the souls of Gildesh, the enemy was now twice its original size. In the span of a few weeks, the attackers would count their numbers as two hundred thousand strong. This was a force that no one in the history of the lands had ever witnessed.

After extinguishing the resources in Gildesh, they would need to move on. As water flows around boulders, they took to making their way across the land to the Cysterule Mountains. The mountains diverted the army and split it in half. Some of it went to the north to attack Caldorn. The other portion of it was channeled south between the Vitirral Mountains and the Cysterule Mountains toward Strayos.

** ** ** ** **

"I expect that we only have two to three weeks," King Secandor said.

"Can we get everything we need to do finished in that short amount of time?" Queen Merkette Secandor asked him.

"We will be pushing everyone to their very limits. But it is what must be done. The invading army will give us no quarter. We are fighting for everything that is dear to us. We may have slightly longer than a few weeks, but we have been given a gift of warning. We cannot waste it."

"Very well. We will consider any time after the two weeks as a bonus to us."

"Indeed. Let us call our guest, Queen Reesh, to us so that we may discuss a plan."

Queen Crissannah Reesh had stayed in Crute at the palace while preparations were made. She had her coach readied though, so that she may get back to Creyason as quickly as she could if the need arose. She had a hard time with the part of the plan that her daughter Ashlyn took, leaving with the sorcerer on a quest for dragons. Though Ashlyn did confer with her about it, it was not any easier knowing she would be in harm's way.

The King sent a servant to Queen Reesh's guest chambers. It was not long before she came at their calling.

"I have an idea, and I want your input on it," Vernon said to Crissannah.

"You have my attention."

"There is little doubt that we may be attacked in each of our

142

countries, but the timeline is what is in question. The attack may occur nearly simultaneously. Though it could not be perfectly timed out, given the distance between the two countries, breaking the advancing army in half would allow an attack on both fronts. They certainly have the numbers to do it."

"Go on."

"We must not make the mistake of waiting until they arrive at our door step. We must ride out to meet them in the field."

"I agree. Though, Creyason has many natural defenses. The city itself is spread along the mountain tips. It would be hard to breach, and we have massive stores. We could wait out an army for quite some time," Crissannah said defensively.

"That may come to pass, but I think a more proactive approach may prevent that alternative entirely. For our part, Crute is also protected by the lake, but that only leaves one course to flee if we are hemmed in. We would have to take to ships and cross the lake if that was our only choice."

Vernon walked over to the wall and hoisted down a large map of the area. He brought it over to where the queens were seated, lightly setting it on the table.

"My plan is this. Our armies will have better success if they are joined into one, but we have to defend two borders at once. Let us place a small regiment of men at the pass where the Cysterule Mountains come to the sea. There is only a thin strip of land there that we can use to our advantage. If we lure the oncoming marauders there, we can set off an avalanche and eliminate many of them. At the same time, the more successful this avalanche is, the greater the possibility that it will cut off the strip of land and thus protect Caldorn. It will be cut off from the attack," Vernon finished, pointing at the map and directing their eyes.

"That will cut us off entirely from Gildesh."

"I know that, but it is the price to pay for the survival of your country. We can then use more of your soldiers to fight for us on the other front. We will defend Strayos at its bottleneck entrance, between the Vitirral Mountains and the Cysterule Mountains. We may have to fall back and use the lake as another form of cutoff. This is where we must make our stand. We cannot allow that army to reach Crute. If Crute falls, the gateway will be open for Caldorn to be invaded from the south."

"I see your point. It is most valid and worthy of further discussion," Crissannah agreed.

"You know the landscape better than I. What size regimen will be necessary to give the illusion that there is a full army ready to defend the shoreline?"

"Two or three hundred men should be enough. Another hundred men poised on the cliffs above may be needed to set the avalanche in motion."

"Very well. I will leave this matter in your hands."

"I will place the duty of overseeing the preparations and the command in the hands of my most trusted general, Mido Sinne. He is here with me, but I will send him back to Caldorn promptly. I will continue to stay here and help with the rest of my force under your lead. What else can be done for Strayos?" Crissannah offered.

"Let us say five hundred men for the avalanche diversion. We are left with thousands in service of Caldorn. That is many thousands more than Strayos could lean on, by itself. I thank you for lending such a great number of soldiers to the cause.

"This enemy is far different than any we have faced. We cannot chance them getting within hand to hand combat distance. We must take them out from a distance. We will make arrows, hundreds of thousands of them. That will be our main weapon against this threat. We will keep them at bay, from a distance. We will rain down on them and continually fire more and more. I do not expect that this army will let up. We may have to be prepared to fight both night and day.

"I will task every man to begin gathering wood and fashioning the weapons we need. My proposal is to make each arrow twice the girth of a standard arrow. We need more stopping power. We need more of the arrows to deliver a kill, not only to mortally wound. Because of this, we will also need a new method of firing these arrows. I want to deliver as many arrows as we can, in a near continuous loop.

"That is the first part of the plan. The next part will occur after the raw materials are gathered and the arrows are being made. We will dig trenches. We will cut chasms into the earth so deep that climbing the walls will be hopelessly difficult. There will be row upon row of them. We will dig until we meet the distance that our arrows fly. Understand that the depth of these trenches will make it all but impossible even for our army to retreat, so we will position ourselves fully on solid ground and launch our aerial attack. The distance may be over four or five fissures. That will slow any invasion down.

"This army may even overcome those obstacles. They may fill the trenches with their dead as we fire round after round of arrows. But even this will be a success. We may reduce their numbers by thousands. If they advance past the first trenches, we will ignite the very earth they tread upon. We will spoil the earth both in the trenches and the strips of land between them with tar. A fire burning arrow will be all that is required to set the blaze off. After the inferno is born, we will convert all of our remaining ammunition into fire arrows," Vernon finished, letting his plan wash over the two women he was in company with.

"That seems well thought out," Merkette complimented him.

"This may only be a stopgap. They will come at us no matter what measures we take. I am positive there will be enemy fighters that come to within a spear's throw, or even to our swords. My Queens, we will be in grave trouble then. The moment they get that close to us is the time that our tide may turn for the worse. We may go from defending against an enemy to finding that we are fighting the very men who stood at our sides. We must not let that happen."

"I hope it does not come to that. Let us get our preparations underway," Crissannah said.

She left the King and Queen of Strayos and went to her chamber. Then she summoned Mido Sinne and told him of the plan. There was no hesitation in his answer, and he took his leave immediately.

Mido Sinne was fifteen years older than Queen Reesh. He was there when her King fell, and regrettably, had to make that report to her. He had a strong mind and was crafty when it came to military tactics. Once he had the command to return to Caldorn, he wasted no time. He was the only personnel from the army of Creyason to join the Queen and princess on this visit to Crute. He was the only rider to depart the city of Crute to return to Creyason. There was no fanfare or send off. He left once he gathered his supplies.

He rode hard. It only took him three days to return to his home city. It may have gone down as a land speed record if anyone was interested in clocking it. But that was not on the peak of his mind. His mind was in constant motion, clicking through ideas of how he would bring down the most damage.

When he arrived in Creyason, his first order of duty was gathering the army to him and relaying the information he had received from the Queen. There would be five hundred men staying in Caldorn, while the rest of them would be mobilized to Strayos. He selected a battalion to remain and sent the rest to gather the supplies needed to make the journey to the neighboring country. They would need more time arriving there than the trip he had just completed, but he had faith they would make every effort to speed the voyage to its maximum.

He then went to the geologists and civil engineers of the city. Creyason was supremely unique for its architecture. Nearly every building was hewn from the rock. The structure's integrity was secure. This city would be hard to destroy. The flip side of this is that these were the men that created it, and they would be the best men to help in its defense. These men could tell him how to create a devastating rockslide.

It was only a day's trek to the site where they would make their defense. Here the strip of land was the narrowest. The mountain was sheer on their left side, and the sea was accented by many rocky peaks jutting up from it. It appeared as though a major landslide occurred eons ago and was slowly eroded away by the waves. The rocks in the sea created a sense of a corridor. This would be the perfect bottleneck.

When Mido Sinne arrived at this corridor, he noted how the wind strengthened in it. This would help neither side, but he may be able to gain an edge because of his knowledge of it. He looked upward. The mountainside would easily fill the wind tunnel between the sheer mountain face and the pillars in the sea. It was not a large landmark, but this would have to be the final stand.

Mido Sinne sent a scout to post himself at the very border of Caldorn and Gildesh. His only job was to relay when he first saw the invading force. They had to have their plans readied before then.

He climbed the mountain with his team of engineers. They took surveys of the landscape at the summit. Each of them seemed pleased with what they saw. The wind had worked its magic on the rough stone here as well. There were several areas that were windblown and sandblasted, leaving large boulders on pedestals. If not for their intervention, this area would see another collapse in the future, how ever long that may have been.

The stone workers got busy tapping here and there. Creating stress marks was all they wanted to accomplish at this point. They did not want to cause the rocks to fall prematurely. Mido was at the top with them. He peered down and checked to see how the boulders would fall. Aiming was not part of the game; they would have to rely on luck to guide the boulders into place below. He called out to the soldiers at the bottom, but no one responded. He yelled a second time, but his words were carried away on the wind. This experiment proved vital, for now he knew there could be no communication between the men on the mountain and the men in the passage. This would not stop him; he would make it work.

He instructed the engineers to continue their work and create a continuous line of boulders ready to fall. They would take no chances on them not falling properly into position; the more rocks thrown down, the greater the chances of their success.

At the bottom, the men set up a great number of makeshift camps. Each man tended to his own tent and camp fire. This gave the illusion that there were hundreds of groups of men, or a whole regiment. He needed this ruse to lure his prey into the area. The attacking army needed to think they could overcome a great defense.

Once the fires were started, they were continuously doused with tar. They would flare and settle, but the tar was much more combustible than wood. The idea was to ensure the fires would burn even after the soldiers abandoned them.

Most everything was prepared. They waited three days. Then they waited two days more. During their time, they made hundreds of cracks in the mountainside. They built hundreds of mini camps. There were clusters of fires.

When the scout ran to Mido Sinne to report of the approaching force, they knew the preparation time had drawn to an end. This next day would determine the course of everything afterward. If they were successful in this battle, the war may have a chance to be won.

Mido Sinne climbed to the summit to oversee the siege. He had devised a communication route for his men. The commands would come from on high in the form of an arrow. There were colored cloths attached to the tail end of each arrow that gave directions for each battle scenario. Each man on the ground also carried with him a full quiver of arrows and a bow. They had swords, but everyone knew this was a last resort. If the enemy drew that close to them, the tide would surely turn against them.

The soldiers were in position and lined up in firing squad formation. They would only need the word to let fly. The men all had full packs on their backs, in addition to their quivers. These men were well trained, and the extra weight did not bother them. There was no need to leave anything in the tents they had just occupied.

The monsters approached with their characteristic reckless abandon. They carried no weapons. They ran straight forward. The soldiers held their ground and enticed them in, taking care not to fire upon them until the trap could be sprung.

Mido gave the sign. His first arrow plunged into the earth with a green cloth on it. That was the word to fire. The soldiers drew back and released. The arrows found their marks, dropping hundreds of attackers in the front line. Their replacements were quick to take their place, and the wave continued to advance.

The onslaught was faster than anyone had planned. They did not expect such disregard for life. The monsters were unfazed at losing hundreds from their line. The soldiers of Caldorn did not have much time to reload arrows before shooting again, and they gave up precious ground between them for this costly overestimation.

Mido allowed his men to stand in the path of the passage. He did not yet release the retreat signal. He wanted to let another volley loose before that. The archers sent another round into the foes. Mido was quick this time to shoot his arrow downward with the yellow flag. The message was to fall back but not to retreat completely. The attackers were only just into the corridor. He could see the fiends gaining ground on his men.

When his men were beginning to fall back to the foremost tents, a new signal was sent. The red flagged arrow plummeted down. The men dropped their packs and left them open. They were filled with hay, and soon they fell over on their sides. The enemy still engaged and came to within several yards of the soldiers. The wind tunnel acted as if on command, blowing a gust throughout. The hay was ripped out of the packs and blown through the air. It immediately ignited, taking another few hundred monsters out of the line.

Mido's last arrow was nocked, it bore a black flag. He looked over his shoulder.

"Now!"

He released his final arrow; the call to clear the area. His soldiers on the ground turned and fled down the corridor toward the shoreline of Caldorn. Seeing this, the monsters started their pursuit with renewed vigor.

The soldiers on the peak were grouped together and carried great battering rams. The rams were fashioned from the oldest pine trees in the Tributary Forest. The soldiers heaved the wooden cylinders at the cracked mountainside.

Nothing happened. The boulders did not break free of their moorings.

"Again!"

They heaved again. Nothing moved. Spider cracks were seen spreading at the base.

The monsters were upon the men below. They could strike them at any second. If they got through and into Caldorn, all would be lost. This was their only chance to preserve their country.

"We have to hurry! Again!"

The rams collided into the stone. There was a screech heard as the last of the cracks snapped their grip. The boulders were free. They careened down the slope and over the sheer cliffside. Below, the intruders were flattened. They had no defense from the tonnage of rock hurled down on them. More and more of the gargantuan stones broke free. The weight of the boulders caused damage of its own and other large sections of the mountain face ripped off. The trigger was set and there could be no turning it off.

Mido's men escaped, barely. The corridor was cut off, but some of the fiends made it through the gap before it was hemmed in. They were wild with fury but stood little chance of survival against the men of Caldorn. The soldiers took aim and slaughtered the fiends before they could further advance. The onslaught was stemmed; the devastation was complete.

The men on the ground could not see what was happening on the other side of the wall they had just created. They could barely even hear anything from the other side. That was the goal. There was no remaining way to traverse into Caldorn without taking to the sea.

** ** ** ** **

The legions were assembled in formation on the plains just west of the great Lake Proseccan. King Vernon Secandor looked down on his army with pride. They would all be needed. Reinforcements from Caldorn had arrived and were integrated into the divisions. Everything was set in place; they would wait until the dark army came. There was no doubt it would.

A scout found the King on the field and handed him a note, which he read to himself. He smiled in spite of the dire situation he was up against.

Mission Complete And Successful
Caldorn Secured
No Further Invasion Without
Sea Navigation
Will Join You As Soon As Possible

The King called attention to himself by having a squire blast a note into a horn.

"We have our first taste of success! Caldorn is saved! Let us pick up where they left off! We will win this battle!"

The legions spread before him let out a cry and raised their arms in salute. They were as one.

XII

"A witch!"

"Sorceress. Conjurer," Argenit replied to Tobin. "She goes by many titles."

"I would not have expected this turn of events. I figured that I may have to perform a task for each of the clans. I did not expect a unanimous vote to do one thing. It must be a terrible affair. What is the truth behind this?"

"To be forthcoming as much as I can, you do not have to do anything Tobin. You already have five of the nine leaders behind you. That would make a sizable militia."

"I hear what you say, Argenit," Tobin answered. "But the leaders not standing with me hold some of the largest numbers of hunters. Taking on this trial, with success, will nearly double the force of men on my side."

"As you wish," Argenit conceded.

"Now, what am I up against?"

"I will tell you what I know. The Fountain has its allure, but the Cloggon Bog has a virtue of its own. That is the end of the Triffin River, and the area around its delta is lush with vegetation. The animals there are more exotic than any in the Valley, or anywhere else, from what I have heard. The area is plentiful, and even animals from miles around come to drink the water. There is a small, rocky, rapid system at the very end that seems to filter the water before depositing it into the small lake. There are mangrove trees there at the edges with mighty roots exposed. Crocodiles patrol those waters. It is not the safest place to begin with, for there is still the game of predator versus prey folding out at all times.

"If you follow me, this is where the best meat can be found. The water is so pure. The animals there seem to be healthier than any in the Valley. For this reason, we try to send a hunting party there a few times a year. Earlier, I told you that there were some of my kin that did not return from the Fountain. That is something new to us. But there is nothing strange about hunters not returning from the Cloggon area. There is always a chance they will meet their fate at the hands of Cletra.

"Only one in five parties will make it back to us. Those will have been the lucky hunters to get into the area and back out before she turns her attention to them. We know there is great risk in sending men into her territory, but once you have tasted the meat, there is none that compare. It has almost grown into a compulsion; to gamble and turn a profit, or to send hunters to their doom."

"She has tricked you, my friend," Tobin said. "There must be magic permeating through the Cloggon. It sounds like it has seeped into everything in the area. It is not that the meat is so sweet; it is a spell that draws you in."

"Surely you don't mean to say..." Argenit cut himself off. "Only an outsider could put meaning to that. I am in your debt for revealing that insight to me."

"That debt will be absolved if you help me get to her."

"Aye."

They selected three other men to join them. The group was eight: four left from Gildesh and four nomads. One of the men was Argenit's son, Negano. There was such a striking resemblance. The two of them looked as if the same person stepped out of his own skin and aged twenty years.

Their voyage south took only a day and a half before the Cloggon Bog was in their sight. The mounds around the area were but foothills between the arms of the Akkerand Mountain chain.

When they got closer to the mounds, they found that they would need to use the Triffin for further access into the area. The hunters quickly and skillfully fashioned rafts to continue downstream.

They slipped downstream quickly and found a clearing to beach themselves on. This would be their base to start from. They were close to the water and could escape if needed. There were fish in the area that were hungry for the bait the men dropped for them. Their dinner that night was a feast. All of them were pleased and rejoiced at their good fortune to this point. While they were eating, Argenit took his son to speak with Tobin.

"This jungle spreads for miles to the south of us. It seems such a large area and that we are only a minimal party, but still she comes for us. We need to keep a good watch for anything suspicious."

"Perhaps she is lying in wait for you...maybe she is the hunter here and is setting a trap for all who enter," Tobin offered.

"That could be. I have never thought of it that way. I have always thought that we were unlucky, in the wrong place at the wrong time. But it happens so frequently that hunters do not return. All of the clans agree with this. You may be correct in saying that," Argenit agreed.

"Some people say that she is hundreds of years old," Negano spoke. "That she is crafty. She must be; no one ever sees her. She has powers that are foreign to us. They say she can change the area around her. She has guardians with her that do her bidding. They are camouflaged into the jungle and then take you by surprise. No one ever

151

returns that she has come across."

"How do you know if they sneak up on you, if no one survives to tell of it?" Bayrne tested the young man.

Negano flushed momentarily.

"It may seem far-fetched to an outsider…" Negano started.

"He was jesting with you, Negano. We will take your advice. We must be wary," Tobin apologized.

"We must be serious about this," Argenit admonished them. "You do not know of what you speak."

Tobin and his men were quiet now. He needed their help. He could not afford to anger them. If the clans all believed that this sorceress was evil, then he had no choice but to accept it. There was not one report to the contrary.

The next morning saw little light. The jungle's foliage was thick; few of the sun's rays penetrated to the floor. They travelled a fair distance before coming to the clearing at the mangrove lake. The water was pristine. One could see directly to the bottom of it as clearly as if it were only inches deep.

Tobin reached down and cupped his hands to gather water into them. When he turned around, he found he was alone. Startled, he whipped his head around and found that the small band had continued forward and was behind another grouping of trees.

They reconvened and followed the shoreline of the pond. Nearly half way around, they came across what appeared to be a path. Though it was thin, it seemed to be well worn.

"This is it, Tobin. I am sure this path will lead you to what you seek," Argenit coached him. "We will go no further. I will take my men back to the rafts. We will wait there for five days, or as long as we can."

Tobin placed his hand on Argenit's shoulder.

"I thank you for helping to put me in a position that I can aid my people," Tobin told him.

He made eye contact with Bayrne and then Gren, and finally, Theagon of the former eastern and southern brigades. The men from Gildesh returned his look. They would be coming with him through whatever may await them. The nomads left them and turned toward the river, taking the path from which they came.

"Arm yourselves, men. Take every precaution," Tobin instructed them.

Tobin crossed his swords across his chest and gave a nod. The others drew theirs and readied shields. Tobin led them down the muddied path and found the end at a solid vertical wall of rock. The path turned sharply to the left and continued only another few feet before a gaping hole opened up. Other paths lead right, left, and center of the opening into the lair. The hole ran deep into the mountain but was lit with torches. They burned with a blue tint; another sign that all was not normal here.

The maw of the lair looked ordinary and could be passed by any hunter trying to avoid a bear or worse. Inside, though, was crafted with fine detail. The corridor was a perfectly square shaft. The torches were held in silver sconces. There were tapestries lining the walls. Along the main corridor, statues of wolves were lined in succession on each side of the walkway. There were piles of weaponry laid at the foot of each of the statue's pedestals.

"Gren. Theagon," Tobin called to them. "I want you two to stay at the cave's opening and watch for these 'Guardians' that had the nomads spooked. Bayrne, you are with me."

Once the commands were given, they were heeded unerringly. There were no questions asked; the men did as they were told. Gren and Theagon moved to the outside of the cave's entrance as Tobin and Bayrne moved further in.

After a few minutes, Gren peered inside the opening. Tobin and Bayrne were long gone, having vanished into the recesses of the mountain. He looked from side to side and noted the statues were also missing. The pedestals were bare, but the weaponry remained.

"Have I missed something here? The statues?" Gren said to Theagon.

"Magic! It must be an illusion. Keep your guard up," was the reply.

They stood for another half of an hour before anything happened. Presently, they heard singing. It was angelic and coming from everywhere at once. There was no directionality to it. Theagon could not understand the words. He turned to ask Gren if he heard it and was confronted by an ogre with snakes wrapped around it. He fumbled for his sword, calling out for help. Gren heard his cry and turned to Theagon. What he saw was a burning pyre, writhing and gripping a sword. It was shouting at him and advancing. He drew his sword as well.

The burning figure and the ogre clashed and fought, each a formidable match for the other. The ogre plunged his sword into the flames, eliciting a roar. The fiery form slashed down and cleaved off the left arm of his opponent.

As quickly as it started, the singing stopped. Each man dropped to his knees. Theagon had a sword buried to its hilt in his abdomen. Gren was already keeled over on his side; the amount of blood lost from his severed arm was tremendous. His face grew grey, but he caught sight of Theagon's eyes. There was fear in those eyes momentarily, then blankness. The cave was once again cloaked in silence.

Further into the hallway, Bayrne trailed Tobin by a few steps. The cave entrance could not be seen behind them. After the entrance hall with the statues, they had climbed a few steps. The next shaft was a replica of the first, complete with running statues of wolves on either side of the hall. The two men continued a short distance until they came upon a three way intersection. They could turn left or right, or retreat.

"Shall we split up to cover more ground?" Bayrne asked Tobin.

"My instinct says we must stick together.

"We cannot be separated. Stay…"

"What was that?" Bayrne asked Tobin.

"Behind you!"

Bayrne turned to see a dozen wolves rush up the staircase they just climbed. As if on call, the statues in the corridor they were standing in also mobilized and turned to them. They were out matched twenty four to two.

"The statues are the guardians! Run!"

"We've been duped!"

They ran down the left corridor. It was another duplicate of the first, but ended in a four way intersection. Possessing blue torches and tapestries, there were another dozen wolf statues here as well. Once they passed them, these statues again uprooted their limbs and gave chase. They were losing the battle of numbers from the very start, but each hallway they entered was the very same as the hallway before. It was a maze of identical rooms. Each time they turned a corner they were confronted with more statues and then chased by more foes.

"How many turns have we made? Do you have your bearings?" Bayrne shouted to Tobin.

"I don't know. I think we have nearly doubled back."

The next turn brought them to a hallway, but this one was different. The pedestals were empty. These wolves must have already left their posts to give chase. They could not rest; they could not retreat. They were only moments ahead of the surging wolf pack. Tobin thought turning right was the same turn they took before in this room. He paused slightly, then decided left. He was just about to direct Bayrne when the wolves rounded the corner and discovered them in the room. Other wolves were just ahead. Their choices on where to turn were reduced. Tobin ran left, but Bayrne ran right. The wolf pack successfully separated them.

Tobin could see out of his peripheral vision what direction Bayrne took. They were on their own. He cursed himself for not yelling out before turning in this direction. Now they would be easier targets. Tobin decided he would no longer turn. He would continue straight until he came to the outer wall of this maze. If he could find the outer edge, he may be able to get an idea of how the area was set up and then search for Bayrne.

Tobin rushed forward but found that the wolves had stopped chasing him. Their sounds were diminishing behind him. He came to a stop and breathed easier. He turned his head and saw the torches flickering as though there was a draft in the room. When he fixated his view to the hall before him, he saw a light at the end of the tunnel. He slowly stepped forward to follow it.

He cautiously stepped though another two rooms without catching sight of its source. It stayed far enough ahead of him that he could only see that there was something lit up. As he hastened his pace, the light got slightly brighter.

When he thought it stopped moving, he hurried to catch it. Tobin rounded the corner and stopped short in utter surprise.

He found the witch.

Tobin stood and studied her. Cletra made no advance toward him. He took little notice of the large room he had entered. The room was round and lined again with the characteristic wolf statues. These did not move, but he did not look in their direction; only at her.

She was tall. She was not as tall as he was, but tall enough for a woman. She was clothed in a silver robe that rolled down to the floor. Adorned with platinum blond hair and fair skin, she was strikingly beautiful. Her blue eyes captured his. He could feel power in her gaze. He could almost hear voices in the room, though they were alone. She stood as motionless as the statues around the room.

There was an aura about her. She was creating light from her being, and it was reflected outward by her robe. The very air in the room felt electric, and he felt a tingle down his spine. The air felt like it was moving. He felt like he could see it swirling around her. She was wrapped in what appeared as a heat-wave induced mirage.

"Why have you come to me?"

Tobin blinked his eyes. She did not move her lips, but he heard her clearly.

He could not speak. He was taken with her.

"How may I serve you?" she spoke plainly this time.

"I..." Tobin relaxed. "You are not as I expected."

"Have the natives been talking about me again? They never stay long enough to get to know me."

"They fear you."

"Perhaps they should. It is an age old myth, to fear what you do not know. Do you fear me?"

"I thought I would. They spoke so many terrible things about you."

She was weaving her spell. It was taking root in Tobin. He was off guard and relaxed. He should not have been, but he could not stop looking at her. She was mesmerizing. He had all but forgotten about the wolf pack, the chase, and his comrades.

"What is your name, My Lord?"

"My name is Tobin. I hail from the nation of Gildesh."

"Are you King there?"

"No, m'lady."

"Would you do something for me, Tobin?"

He nodded.

"Come with me. Sit on this chair. Do you like what you see?"

He was sitting on the only chair in the room. It was directly in the center of it. Cletra was facing him, only a few steps away.

"This could be your new nation...I could be at your side."

Tobin was comfortable. He liked this. He began to feel thirsty, and he realized he had not eaten in a long time, as well.

"Could you bring me some wine?" he casually asked Cletra.

"I would do it for you, My Lord."

She brought him a cup. There was no food around. He took it and sipped from it. When he was finished, he noticed how tired he was.

"Perhaps I should show you to your chambers, my Lord. Come with me."

Tobin obeyed her and followed. The chamber was just down another hallway off of the throne room. He peered into it and was greeted with opulence. He entered it without question. Cletra was behind him as he did so.

"Enjoy your stay with me, Tobin," she said mischievously, then closed the door and walked away.

Tobin was alone again. He missed her already and was looking forward to having dinner with her. He was imagining how things would go.

When he turned around, the room appeared different. The cushions that were there only moments before were gone. The bedding was missing as well. There was no rug covering the floor. It was dark and cold. It was a cell. This was no opulent chamber for a king. Cletra led him here and fooled him. He had fallen for her ruse.

He was her prisoner, but he would think of a way out. He was in solitude for another day before there was a knock at his door. He perked up quickly. Tobin could see the telltale light streaming into the door as it cracked open. To his surprise, he felt excited again. He had been a prisoner for a day and a half, but he felt elated that he could see Cletra again.

When she rounded the corner, his eyes deceived him. The light vanished instantly, no longer needed, it had done its job. The vision left to his eyes was of a goblin's dark, leathery skin, a long bulbous nose and blue eyes ringed in red. The voice was soft, uncharacteristic of the shape before him. He recognized it as the voice of Cletra.

"Are you hungry?"

Tobin said nothing. He was in shock. The voice changed partway through the question. It went from soft to sharp and gruff.

With no response, Cletra left him. There were no pleasantries on this visit. He could not figure out what had just happened. He was excited and then crushed in the same moment. What happened to the shining woman he saw yesterday?

The next day was the same. There was a knock at the door and the light shined in. His excitement grew and was then dashed as he saw a ghoul, diminutive and pink skinned.

"Are you hungry?" it was the same croaking voice as she used the day prior.

"Yes! Yes," he pleaded.

He had nothing to eat or drink in the last two days.

"Good…" she spat.

She left him again. There was no food or drink provided.

Tobin took a turn downward then. He was stuck here. He was hungry and thirsty. He was a prisoner and going through torture.

He noted that his vision was changing. Everything had a red hue to it. At first he could barely perceive it. But as the red dots connected themselves, it was as if he was looking through a red filter. His bones were aching as well. The armor he was wearing seemed to chafe him around the neck area.

His vision continued its decline. He decided to remove his armor and found that his chest felt better, less confined without it. He could breathe more easily after that. His arms started to itch, as well as his back. He felt like his hair was growing longer. There seemed to be more hair along his forearms, as well.

After awaking from the night's sleep, he stood slowly. His back was creaking, and he was wholly uncomfortable. He found he was much more at ease when he dropped to all fours. He could still stand, but it was almost painful to do so. Being on his hands and knees was more natural feeling, if not natural in his mind.

The door of his cell announced another knock. He was just as happy to hear it as the previous days. There was no light, but he knew who would be coming to see him. She entered looking as the goblin he saw on the second day of his entrapment.

"You are evolving quite nicely," she croaked out. "I have brought you something."

Cletra threw a freshly cleaved leg of a lamb in his direction. The raw meat was as enticing as anything he had seen. With total disregard to its origin or make-up, he came to her and snatched it. He gnawed on it, satisfying his hunger and insatiable thirst.

"Very good. You are almost ready."

Cletra left him again. This was the only thing he had gotten to eat in the last four days. The raw meat was heavenly to the animal he was becoming. He found that he could almost cut the meat with his fingernails. They were longer than he remembered, and deadly sharp.

After his meal, he curled up near the door and waited for more. Nothing happened until the next day when she visited him again. He was now her servant; there was no need for lighting theatrics, or niceties. He was ready.

"Are you hungry?" she said.

The voice sounded so soft. He turned his head acknowledging he understood, but he did not speak.

"I have something for you. Come with me."

He trailed behind her, half walking but also sometimes dropping down to his hands. He could cover more ground, and much more quickly, this way. He felt so much stronger now than before.

She led him to another room where a prisoner was shackled. The prisoner was in the center of another circular room and was hanging with his hands tied above his head. His feet were barely scraping the floor. He was tall, but bludgeoned and bloodied beyond recognition.

"He is all yours."

The werewolf that was Tobin rushed at the prisoner, slashing at him with his razor sharp claws. The chest was brutally ripped apart, and the face and neck were gashed and lacerated until there was blood covering everything around. A red geyser was opened up and sprayed for several seconds. When it was over, Cletra left Tobin in the room. He was free to do what he pleased with his new plaything. She need not worry about her newest pet. It was under her control.

The werewolf stalked the room around his victim. Still dangling by ligaments, the legs were the next thing to be ripped open. Continually circling, it noticed there were items lying on the floor in the corner of the chamber. He sniffed the air in that direction and sauntered over to it.

When he shuffled through the pile, he found there to be nothing edible and lost interest. Turning around, something shiny caught his eye. He looked at it. It was a pendant. It looked like a shield with an eagle on it.

He thought a moment. In his twisted mind, this meant something. He took a few steps toward the body and then returned to the shining crest. The eagle was stunning. It was important. He could think of nothing else.

The werewolf was not surprised that he was left alone. There was meat here for him, but the eagle pendant in the corner kept drawing him to it. He thought he knew what it was and left the room with the body. When he returned to his cell, he sniffed the pile of garments in the corner. He rummaged through it and found the same crest, with an eagle on it.

The connection clicked in his mind, the crest of Gildesh! He needed to find his armor before it was too late. His clouded mind was full of twisted thoughts. He was free here, but he was not the master. He needed to get out of this cell and find his weapons.

He slinked out of the cell and pretended he was returning to the chamber with the body. He then scurried to the last hallway before he entered the throne room. There, leaning against the wall were two swords and a small pouch. He sniffed the things and began fumbling with the pouch. His fingers were harder to manipulate than he remembered. Finally, he opened it and found what he was searching for. The vial was small but filled with the last remnants of the glorious clear liquid from the Fountain. He managed to open it and drink its contents down.

The liquid flowed through him, and he let out a wolf's howl in pain. The poisonous damage done to his body was reversing. The witch's venomous spell was being drawn out of him. The hair on his arms and back withdrew; his hands regained their gripping strength and his nails reduced their size. His vision cleared. He stood erect for the first time in nearly a week with no pain. He was Tobin, reborn. The commotion drew the attention of the sentry wolves.

He was aided by the narrowness of this final hall. The wolves could only attack him one or two at a time, rather than grouping around him. He felt new strength coursing through his body and met his attackers head-on. He wore no body armor or boots. They were still within the cell of his torture, but his weapons were right here in this room where he set them down. His chest was bare; he wore only his pantaloons that he had not taken off.

Tobin cut down the wolves one by one and two by two. Sometimes it was easier to make a kill, and sometimes he felt threatened.

He inched his way down the thin hall, gaining ground on his adversaries. The room before him was still teeming with wolves ready to pounce.

One very agile, and lucky, wolf leapt and flung itself toward him. Taken slightly off guard, he was knocked into the wall and dropped one of his swords. He still possessed one in his left hand but quickly made his way to the nearest pedestal. There was a bow at this one, and he made good use of it. He emptied the quiver into another dozen wolves before spending his ammunition supply. The next pedestal had several spears at its foot, which he used to pummel and kill still more of them.

Each skill he mastered with the varying weaponry was being called upon for his survival. By the time he got to the last pedestal in the room, he found there was a sword and shield. His opponents were dwindling in number, and he chopped at them from behind the relative safety of his shield.

The amount of energy he spent defending himself was otherworldly, but he still had strength to spare. When the last of the wolves was put down, he turned his attention toward the throne room. He knew he would find Cletra there.

He walked cautiously into the round room and saw her in the center. She was magnificently adorned and shining with her lighted aura.

"You have killed your brothers and shown your allegiance to me. Now you are truly ready to stand here as King," she said gracefully.

"Your poisonous words mean nothing. Your conjuring will not work a second time," Tobin said.

The water of the Fountain was surging through him still. He was fully restored.

"It is a pity. One as great as you would have been a strong leader," she still was hoping to convince him.

"Your time has come. It is time to end this."

He raised his shield and readied the sword. While not his weapon of choice, it was as good as any. She shifted her shape again, this time before him. She could make herself look like anything she desired. That was what the nomads meant when they said she could change things.

She morphed into a Bengoss, though twice the size of any on the open range. Her talons were inches long, and the spikes along her back and tail were enormous. Cletra made to ram him with her horns and collided into the shield. He gave ground but then slashed with the sword and sheared off the tips of the spikes along her back. She lashed out with her paw, the claws tearing off the bottom of the shield.

Then she transformed herself into an Anget. Standing now on two legs instead of four, the four arms swung in unison clapping around the shield and wrenching it from his hand. He was forced to let it go, but again brought down his sword removing two of the arms.

Cletra shrieked and drew the stubs in to her body, protecting them. Next she morphed into a cobra. The snake shape showed no appendages that were able to be hewn off and she appeared healed. The cobra reared back, showing its size. The head was nearly to the ceiling, and the girth of the body was as large as a cart.

She snapped and struck downward at him several times, but he was nimble enough to avoid disaster. He rolled to his left and then agilely jumped to his right. He was in continuous motion, but his target was set. After jumping again backward, he lunged and caught her in the abdomen. The entrails began to push through the severed opening he created. The snake coiled, but the wound was still gaping. Cletra made a final attack and sprayed venom from her teeth. Her size was miscalculated and too large. The twin streams of poison split around Tobin. He was still unscathed.

She aimed to strike, and the head came down at him. He stood his ground and raised the sword to plunge into the chin and drive upward. Nearly severing the head in half, the sword emerged from the top.

The damage was done; Cletra fell limp. Her power was spent. There was no more evil to battle.

Tobin withdrew the sword. There was blood spilling down his arm as he did. The blood of Cletra started to crystallize around the blade of the sword, transforming it. The blood grew and changed the metal into a fearsome blade. The weapon began to lightly pulse in his hand.

Tobin looked down at the newly forged weapon he carried. There was power in it. He knew instinctively that the magic within the blade would bring terrible wrath to its opponent.

He brought himself to reenter the cell where his armor was. The shining eagle was his savior, and he proudly donned the chest piece. He gathered himself and then went to the room with the body. He guessed what he would find. It was impossible to identify the body, but the garments and armor belonged to Bayrne. He had killed him in cold blood, as the werewolf slave to Cletra.

Tobin picked up Bayrne's pendant and brought the necklace over his head to wear. Then he grasped the savage blade that Cletra created. It was no longer pulsing; there was not enough magic in the area that was strong enough for it to detect. He fixed it to his back and picked up his other two swords.

He found his way to the entrance of the cave. The sun's light hurt his eyes at first. He had not seen it for days. Once he exited, he found the bloody remains of the last two of his countrymen. He hung his head and picked up the amulet each had, showing the crest of Gildesh. Placing them in his pouch, he made his way down the path and past the pond, to the river.

Argenit and his crew were packing their things onto the raft.

"Argenit!" Tobin called.

"Tobin! You understand my surprise to see you! We were ready to give up on you. Look at you, you are painted red. What of your comrades?"

"It is over, Argenit," Tobin said softly, avoiding the answer to his question.

XIII

"I believe we have reached the Semolend River. This will take us to the sea," Kelduun panted.

After their frantic escape from the Centrepens and subsequent drop into the river, they were carried downstream for a hundred yards. There was a bend in the river taking the brunt of the erosive forces, and they were deposited there. When they gathered themselves, they found there was no imminent danger present. They were able to stop here for a while and catch their breath.

They were in a deep gorge cut into the rock by the river. The canyon raised its heights a half of a mile into the air on either side. To their left, the canyon walls were accented by many outlets like the one they just exited. There were many waterfalls, indicating a large underground water system issuing from the Tripean Lake.

"Is anyone hurt?" Ashlyn asked, noting that her ankle felt better.

No one spoke, but each shook their heads, denying any pain. There could have been worse outcomes, and they agreed that they were just happy to be back out in the sun and out of the cave.

They walked along the edge of the river. This was much harder travelling than the earlier part of their journey along the Gallendar River. The Semolend River's edge was soft, and chunks of earth broke away at the slightest touch. The riverbank was sloped, and their footing was unsure. They could go nowhere but downstream. The walls of the canyon hugged them on both sides. They were at the mercy of nature. There were no trees to build a raft, and they could not hope to climb to the peak of the gorge.

It took a day of travel before the wall on the left side to the south dropped and leveled off. The mountain range was ever present on the northern side of the riverbank, but they could travel and camp much easier on the left bank. They trekked for three days before they could see the distant sea glistening in the sun.

When they came to the sea, they saw that there was a port at the river's end. Knowing they needed rest and recovery, they decided to try to make accommodations at an inn on the outskirts of the city.

The weary group approached the city and set their sights on the Catfish Inn. It was dingy and not as well kept as its competition just a block away, the Drake Inn. There was a whimsical sign of a flopping fish out of water above the entry. The building was only two stories tall. There was a saloon on the first floor and rooms above.

"May we speak with the proprietor of this establishment?" Kelduun inquired.

The man acting as host was a big man. The behemoth was nearly as round as he was tall and must have weighed four hundred pounds. He had the look of a bruiser back in his time; his arms still had the girth that hinted of muscular tone. He stood partially leaning on the door jamb with his arms crossed; an enormous plug of tobacco was in his cheek.

"He's out. Not be back for another two days. I'm in charge in his stead. The name's Torung."

"May we use a room for an evening?"

"What have you got for pay?"

"We have no currency. We can work in the saloon as barter."

"You can work, indeed. But you'll sooner sleep outside than here, if you don't have money," Torung shot back at Kelduun.

"Wait! What is the harm of having a few guests?" a voice shouted from behind the bar counter.

They turned their heads and saw a youth rounding the counter and approaching them.

"My name is Swint. My father is the owner here." He turned to Torung. "I will vouch for them. We have not had guests in a long time. I don't want to turn them away. They can stay in my room."

"Will you be sleeping on the floor, then? Very well. But if your father says anything about this, the blame will fall squarely on you," Torung warned him.

"Many thanks to you both" Kelduun said sincerely.

"Come with me," Swint called. "Welcome to Azloth."

He was already heading toward the staircase at the side of the room. It creaked in protest as the troupe headed up. The top floor only had six rooms. The staircase was at the head of a hallway that passed two doors on the left and one on the right. There was one washroom to the right to serve for all of the guests. They passed these rooms and found the same pairing of rooms on the far end of the hall.

"This is my room," said Swint, pointing. "Torung stays on the other end of the hall, near the stairs. I know I said you could stay in my room, but the rooms opposite my door are vacant. You can stay there, if you are quiet."

"What can we do to repay you?" Panalt asked him.

"Just come sit with me downstairs and keep me company. I'm sure outlanders like yourselves have all sorts of stories to tell. All the sailors do when they come into port. Our business has been very slow since they built that new inn down the way."

"I would be happy to oblige you," Panalt said to him.

Panalt and Kelduun stood up as a pair and walked downstairs. They were followed by Merion and the twins. Ashlyn remained behind, resting.

Swint hurried around the counter to retake his post behind the bar. He was a few years younger than Dur and Tiras, maybe thirteen or fourteen years of age. But he was already showing signs of a much more mature person. He handled himself well and worked deftly, mixing drinks, pouring draughts of ale and settling squabbles. Though Torung was the elder, the patrons seemed to defer to Swint, knowing that his old man was the true master of the house.

There were not many people in the saloon that day, but it was a different story during the evening. Many fishermen had come off of the sea and were now back in town. The saloon was alive and crowded with dirty men. They all came to have their fill of ale, wasting their meager salary doing so.

Though Swint was busy, he still took time to talk with his guests. He went up and down the bar asking what each man did and how successful he was at it. He could really work the room.

"What brings you up to Azloth?" he asked Panalt.

"There are some bad things going on in my homeland, Swint. We are headed to the Horgangee Mountains."

"There isn't anything up there. No men live north of the Semolend River. The land is too dangerous."

"I believe you. But we are not looking for men, or refuge. We are looking for a dragon. We need it to help us."

Swint was quiet for a moment, and then said, "I don't know if that is a good idea."

"It may be the only option we have."

Swint busied himself again.

The second night was a replica of the first. It was not quite as busy, but many of the same men were back for another round. One of the favorites of this party was a drink Swint mixed up. It was a dark liquor smelling of fruits, but having a foreboding taste of nuts and roots. There was ale served, as well, and even Torung seemed to be partaking.

When the sailors started getting drunk, Panalt asked Swint if he needed any help in dealing with potential rough-housing. Swint said the he had seen all of this before, and that it was common. There was not much to break, and if something did, he would fix it, like usual. Some of the men had brought women in with them; they were beginning to inquire about rooms.

"Swint...I told you we would need rooms!" Torung clapped

his hand down on Swint's shoulder. "Now where will your charity case friends stay?"

Panalt made to move toward him, but looked at Kelduun, who shook his head. Panalt stayed a short distance away, continuing to observe the scene before him. Torung led some people up the stairs. On his way down, his boot slid, and he tripped down the last step. Trying to compose himself, he shouted at the nearest drunkard.

"What are you looking at?"

Swint quickly went over the end of the counter and offered another drink, diffusing the situation. When he returned, he talked with the travelers.

"Don't mind anything he says. He's not even drunk, just clumsy. He's a bit moronic. Hardly anything that comes out of his mouth is correct or even meaningful. My father lets him stay here because he needs someone he can trust. They have been friends since they were boys."

"What does your father do? Why is he out?" Merion asked.

"My father is a fisherman. He goes out with his crew to catch marlin. One or two of them makes for a successful outing."

"Sounds like honest work. I wonder how Torung got to be able to have these duties instead of joining the crew," Dur said, nonchalantly.

"He was part of the crew a long time ago. There was an accident, and he was flung overboard. While he was thrashing around, he was bitten in the leg by an orca. They didn't even know if he would survive. His recovery was very long and drawn out. That's how he gained the weight. He would sit around and eat all day long. He got so big that my father would not take him out anymore. He was always afraid that Torung would fall overboard again, not being as nimble and all."

"I see," Tiras replied.

"Now, he pretty much sits around here. But he is quick to remind me of how this is repayment for my father not letting him come out any longer. That he needs a job…He never thinks about how my father saved him…"

"I'm sure things will right themselves, Swint," Kelduun encouraged him.

The hour was late when the Swint ushered the last man out of the saloon. Torung was already upstairs in his room. Panalt and Merion both said that they would stay down in the saloon to help Swint with the cleaning. The twins and Kelduun retired to their quarters.

They wiped everything down, and Swint dragged himself toward the door to lock up for the night. Before he got there, it clattered open, and a sailor fell inward. He was panting and sputtering. His clothing was soaking wet, and he was shivering.

"Pirates! Swint!" he called, rising up to his knees.

"What Veston? Start again," Swint said, then looked at Panalt.

"Veston is part of my father's crew."

"Pirates! They came for us! They came at night. We didn't have a chance, Swint. They came across the water, silent as a ghost ship. We were almost home. We didn't see them until they were right on top of us. They threw their hooks over our gunwale and reeled us in."

"What happened? What happened to everyone?" Swint asked, fear rising in his voice.

"They took them. I was able to jump overboard. Your father told me to do it. I had to swim for my life. It must have been two miles!"

"We have to do something!" Swint pulled at Panalt's sleeve.

"We will, Swint. We owe it to you for your kindness these past two days. "

Panalt rushed up the staircase and roused Kelduun. After quickly relaying the story to him, they made a decision. They would help Swint since he had shown them such generosity from the start.

The group made its way down to the saloon. Though it was very late, everyone was wide eyed. Veston was wrapped in a blanket and had a mug of ale. Swint was pacing to and fro. Kelduun asked if everyone would sit around a table to begin the conversation.

"What more can you tell us, Veston?" Kelduun asked him.

"We hear of the pirates, out on the seas. But no one sees much of anyone else out there. The water is so vast. We did what we always do. Head out to catch what we can. If we do well, then we stay out. If not, we come home. This was an average run, nothing out of the ordinary. We decided to return a day earlier than planned. Night fell upon us, just like normal. That's when they came."

"My father says they collect people," Swint started. "I don't know for what. There's a place he talks about. He never saw it, but he says that's where they go. It sounds like a fairy tale. I have heard about it since I was a young boy. They call it Entopiny."

"Entopiny! The home of the Wizard's Ring!" Kelduun spoke up.

"You know of this?" Veston asked him.

"I know a little. The Wizard's Ring is a group of sorcerers that live together. They fancy themselves as the saviors of the earth. They are always working on spells and conjuring plans for enlightenment. They are mostly harmless, for they do not leave their stronghold. It is a place considered to be of high regard, but to some it appears as if it is a cult. A young wizard may be recruited by them to join their ranks, but that would be the last you hear of them. No one returns once they have been 'enlightened'."

"My father is no conjurer. He is a hard worker. He knows nothing of magic," Swint defended him.

"I understand that. But these wizards, they consider themselves the upper echelon. They live in an utopian world. They can only live in the manner they are accustomed to by keeping slaves! The pirates must be doing their dirty work. The sorcerers, they do not even see it as slavery. They view it as people that are willing to help them. The slaves are kept in the dungeons and furnace rooms far below the keep. They never have contact with each other. They needed your father because he is a hard worker. I suspect this happens often in these parts."

"Indeed," Veston replied. "Boats go missing all of the time. But the sea is fickle and not easily predicted."

"Aye, some boats may go down to the depths. But, no doubt, others are captured," Kelduun corrected him. "We need a plan so that we do not suffer the same fate. We do not want to join the ranks of slaves while we are trying to save them."

"What do you propose?" Panalt asked him.

"Entopiny is at the end of an archipelago. My bet is that there is a high probability that the pirates also call this chain of islands their home. If we can navigate a skiff to the islands, we may be able to sneak onto one of their ships and hijack it."

"Why not just let the pirates take us on the sea as they did before?" Veston asked.

"They would have the upper hand in that scenario. We need stealth and secrecy on our side," Kelduun countered.

They made their plans and slept the rest of the shortened night. In the morning, Torung was banging on the door to Swint's room.

"You better not be sleeping! There's work that needs done."

Swint opened the door. Torung peered inside and saw each of the travelers already awake and packing their things.

"Time to go?" Torung asked. "I don't know if Swint could afford to have you stay another night, what with you not paying and all. Swint, it is time to mop the floors and then go to the market."

Swint turned his head downward. Panalt and Kelduun both walked to the entrance of the room. Swint was standing in the doorway with Torung.

"The chores will fall onto your list of duties on this day, sir," Panalt said to Torung.

"But…He has to, that is what he's here for!"

"I believe you have gotten your roles mixed up. He is a boy, albeit, eager to please and energetic. But he does not run the Inn. He will do what it takes to put a good reputation to his father's name," Kelduun said. "There is a matter requiring his services. He will not be under your direction for some time."

"But I can't do all of this myself. Wait until his father hears of this mutiny…"

"I believe his father will hear of it soon enough," Panalt replied.

They left Torung in the hallway, surprised and angry. He did not move for a long time, but then caught up to them at the bottom of the staircase.

"What if the Inn fails?" he called to them in a last ditch effort to guilt them into leaving Swint with him.

"See that it does not. Or else, that blame will be in your name," Merion shot back at him.

They departed and headed to the marina. Torung watched them leave, standing in the doorway. His bulky figure was slouching; he was neither happy nor excited about the endeavor ahead of him.

Veston did the negotiating, and they acquired a sloop big enough for the eight of them. He had some money saved up, but this was as noble of a cause as he could think of to spend it on. He wanted to do his part in saving Swint's father.

When they boarded their small vessel, Veston took the lead. He had assumed a leadership role, since he was knowledgeable about these waters. Merion stood with him, lending his experience from sailing on Lake Proseccan.

"Alekan and me, we go way back. Torung may have known him first, but you could argue that we had a closer friendship," Veston spoke of Swint's father. "When things get hairy out on the sea, we are always there for each other."

They raised the small sail and let the wind fill the jib, taking them out into the open water. The tide was helping them and seemed favorable to guide them toward the ocean. The wind, as well, sped their voyage, and they made it to the archipelago in three days. They saw nothing of other ships on the water along the way.

The water around the islands was crystal clear. Even though they were still a mile away from the shore, one could see to the bottom. The floor of the sea surrounding the islands was very shallow. It ranged from five to twenty feet deep. Many corals could be seen, and the fish were brightly colored

They beached their craft and scouted the area. They could see the other islands from theirs. Each was only a short swim away, and the sea was very shallow in between. They could scout an entire island in a day and move on to the next. The party disguised their dinghy in the trees by laying fronds of leafy branches over it. They may have a need to use it again, but not until they scoured the islands for signs of the pirates.

On the second day, they found what they were seeking. As they stood on the beach looking across a narrow waterway, they saw the very next island was bustling with people. It was a contrast to the island landscaping they had observed the past two days. The island they were on, as well as the previous one, was untouched by human hands. Everything was natural and quiet. The scene before them was opposite. There was a small city built on the shore. Many of the trees had been felled to accommodate the need for ship building and population expansion. But there was still dense foliage just beyond the town's limits, toward the island's interior. This was the biggest island they had come across yet and practical for a base of operations for the pirates.

"We shall swim across after the light fades," Kelduun instructed the team.

"It will be tough to approach the island and be completely unseen," Veston replied.

"The darkness will give us some cover, but you are correct. The boarding will be the most perilous part of this expedition, yet." Panalt agreed.

"The risk is so high," Ashlyn said.

"But we have to do it!" Swint called to them. "For my father. And I have a plan."

They turned to him.

"I've seen it done before. Some of my friends would stow away to see their fathers in action on the sea," Swint continued. "We have to see how they load their ship."

The sun shifted its balance to the west, and the hours ticked by. Before it was totally dark, the group took to the water, slowly swimming to the other side. They chose to swim right up to the dock and gathered beneath it before emerging. Their thought was to get as close as they could to their goal and not to infiltrate through the entire port.

The ship moored to the docking was ominously quiet; the captain's quarters were darkened. Beyond the dock, there was merrymaking to be had in the saloons. The sounds of shouting and laughter were heard along the wind.

Swint volunteered to rise out of the water first and determine if his plan would work. Kelduun took precautions. He weaved his hands and asked a cloud to drop, enveloping everything in fog. Swint then climbed to the shore and slowly scouted the area around the dock. He was just about ready to make a report when light shined out of an open door.

The saloon closest to the ship spit out one of the pirates into the night. The scallywag was plastered drunk and wobbling on his feet. He made his way to the dock and looked toward the ship. Swint spotted him first, but had nowhere to go. The booze hound was singing a song while meandering right and left, completely oblivious to his surroundings. Swint spied a barrel next to the pallets he was looking for and scurried to it.

The buccaneer turned to the tavern to yell something that no one could understand. He tripped and fell to a knee. Gathering himself, he sauntered over to a row of barrels. Once there, he unabashedly dropped his pantaloons to relieve himself over the side of the dock.

Swint remained motionless. He was only inches away from detection. He was breathing rapidly, and he could hear his heart beating in his eardrums. If the pirate turned his gaze downward, he would be caught; however, the pirate kept singing and draining himself, oblivious to his surroundings.

The drunkard finished his business and reached down to pull up his draws, but fell backward in the process. Swint breathed a small sigh of relief; he was no longer in the brigand's line of sight. The man started laughing and laid back, feeling the cooling moisture on the wooden beams of the dock. After only a moment, there was silence.

Swint waited for a little longer before venturing to peek around his barricade. When he did, he almost laughed out loud. The scoundrel had passed out cold, with his trousers still around his ankles. Still garnering caution, Swint returned to the others just under the dock to tell of what he saw. The others had seen the pirate encounter and could not believe the good fortune.

"There are two pallets ready to be moved onto the ship. We must hurry if we want to get settled," Swint coached. "There is a pulley system rigged with counterweights to lift and swing it."

One by one they cautiously moved to the pallets and situated themselves in the center of barrels and crates. The lone pirate on the dock rolled over, but remained asleep. Swint found a blanket to cover the first group. He then covered the second group with a fishing net that was lying on the side of the dock, before scrambling under it. This second group would be more exposed, but there was no help for it.

The sun had not reached the eastern horizon when they felt movement. The pirates were loading up the ship. There was no concern over the pallets. Using the cantilevered pulley system, they moved each of the pallets. More weight was needed to counterbalance them, but no one made to adjust the loads.

The goods were set down into the main hull and covered with the decking. Once the deck was secured overhead, they quickly moved out from the barrels. The ship had the fetid odor of dung. It was creaky and possibly not watertight. There was a fine layer of water rushing back and forth. There were rat droppings rolling in the rushing water.

The plan from here was simple. The twins would grab any man entering this area, and the team would demobilize them. There were two doors, one toward the port side, the other, starboard. They set themselves up to defend each. Sooner or later, the missing men would be looked for, and another few would be dispatched. After a time, their adversaries would be diminished enough to take the ship.

This came to pass, but took much longer than expected. The crew manning this mission was rather small, and they were easily taken care of. When Panalt's group emerged onto the main deck, there was much surprise, but little fight. The men were unorganized and acted as if they had never previously defended their boat. They were accustomed to quick undertakings and kidnapping a skiff's crew at night. These were not battle hardened men; they succeeded more on scare tactics than anything.

Having successfully bound and gagged each man, they turned their attention to the captain.

"You saw how easily we took your ship, captain," Panalt said to him. "Will you cooperate with us? Or should we send you to the bottom?"

He nodded his consent.

"We will release as many men as you need to sail. But you will take us to Entopiny. Once there, you will ask for quarter for your men."

"I have never done that before. We simply drop off our shipment and take our leave as richer men."

"This time will be different. Regardless of how unorthodox that request must sound, you must insist on it. Of course, we will stand in place of those men and enter the keep at Entopiny."

"They will catch you. They will know things are amiss."

"They do not know at the moment. Do they? Perhaps it is your survival that hinges on your performance at the gate of the keep. We are just men pretending to be under your guidance. You are the one who leads and thus will fall, if things go wrongly. Many men may serve you, but the wizards know you as their captain. How much trust do they have in you?"

He did not answer.

"Remember. When the time comes…"

He nodded again.

Kelduun noted how Panalt had grown as a leader in the last few weeks. Each time there was adversity to overcome, he stepped up. He overcame anything in his path. He was quick witted, yet easy going. He had the faith of each of the party members that he would lead in the proper direction. Though Kelduun's power exceeded those present, he could step back and let Panalt lead them. He was making hard decisions and doing it with a trained eye.

The tower rose out of the sea. As if on command, the moment they set their eyes upon it, the water became choppy. Waves began crashing against the sides of the ship. Swells were thrashing all about them. They were in the area where the inlet of the sea met the vast ocean beyond.

The tower was black and ringed by an enormously tall breakwater. The wall surrounding the tower was built concentrically around the base; it was split only at the entrance. The 'C' formation of it protected the tower's base from nearly all sides. The ship was able to slip between the opening of the protective barrier into a very calm lagoon.

The tower soared overhead. The shore was lined with boulders that would dash any trespassing ship to splinters. The captain used his time honed skills to maneuver around the tower to the dock on the opposite side of the barrier's gap.

The captain walked down the gangplank and stood on the pier.

"I have wine, ale, and spirits for the wizards. I would like to speak with Shentille of the Ring."

The request was heeded, and the leader of the Wizard's Ring was summoned.

"Bultan, my friend. To what do I owe the pleasure of your company?" Shentille's voice was smooth and seductive compared to the sharp barking tone of the ship's captain.

"Our voyage was much tougher than expected. The waters took a toll on my ship, and some of my crew was injured, while others were sickened by the great waves. I am asking shelter for a few days to recover and refit my ship."

"It is not my concern what may happen to your crew, only that you survive to carry out the orders we give you."

"I assure you that I am fine. I was born on the sea. But I cannot set sail without a working crew. Give me one day, if anything."

"You drive a tough bargain, Bultan. But we have grown comfortable with your services. A day you shall have."

The captain walked back to his men lining the rails of the brig. He mentioned something to one of them as he walked by.

"You are on your own. You have one day."

Panalt nodded to him and then led his band ashore. They each had the look of being beaten by the travel. Two of them were limping, one was a woman. One had a bloodied patch over his eye, while the last one looked to be over a hundred years old.

The pier was long, ending in a grassy area just beneath the gate. They were led into the tower but then down a hallway to what appeared to be a stable.

"You can sleep with the pigs. No one may ascend the staircase, save for the sorcerers," the servant said to them, before departing.

"We haven't much time," Swint said.

"At least we are not locked in a cell," Ashlyn offered.

"And we are closer to the dungeons here, rather than being taken up the stairs," Merion said.

"Dur and Tiras. The same as the pirate ship. Watch our backs. If deadly force is required, take down anyone aiming to deter us," Panalt guided them. "We need to do this as quickly as possible and then sail with Bultan. He will not leave. He knows he has to continue this charade in order to keep his contract with the sorcerers. They would know there was treachery if he abandons us."

They silently came back to the main shaft of the tower and looked at the grand spiraling staircase. There were no window openings at this level of the tower, and the staircase rose up into the darkness. They could not guess what was up there, but it did not concern them.

The staircase was guarded by the same servant who ushered them into the pig pen and another with him. Kelduun used an age old trick. He made it sound like a door was creaking open from far above them. The guards turned to look up the steps. They began climbing to answer whatever request was being made of them, leaving the tower's entryway deserted.

"Where are we to go? How can we find them?" Swint asked.

"When looking for prisoners, it is best to follow your nose," Kelduun answered. "They will not be well kept and are short lived because of it."

They chose to descend and were met with a slightly pungent smell of burning coal. It confirmed they were heading in the correct direction. The room below opened up into a vast cavern. The tower was built over a gigantic mine. The mine extended far into the rock, seemingly farther than it could have. Kelduun wondered how close they were to digging too far and releasing the ocean's water into the mine.

The slaves were working in shifts. Some would break rocks and gather coal. Others would shovel it into the red hot furnaces. There were more locked in their cells, effectively controlling them until their shift started.

There was a foreman on duty at each station. Kelduun walked up to one of them. He appeared clad in a green robe, trimmed in gold. "I am delivering a new batch of slaves for you to process. Where should I leave them?"

The foreman was not looking at him and casually answered. "The cells are to your left. You can leave them there until they are processed and assigned," he looked at Kelduun. "Who are you?"

"I am a new wizard here, making my rounds. I am learning what there is to know about the tower."

"Wizards do not do that. They do not come to this level," was the suspicious reply.

The foreman turned quickly, meaning to confirm the identity of these strangers but stopped immediately. He dropped to his knees and exhaled as a huge gash opened across the breadth of his back. Panalt was on the delivering end, and he eased him the rest of the way down to the floor.

"We cannot afford an alarm to be sent."

The others nodded their agreement. What was done needed to be. They had gained the information they needed. Their time was already running thin. Merion rummaged around in the pockets of the dead man and found a key ring. They stashed the foreman's body behind a pile of rubble and quickly made their way to the cells. Kelduun once again changed the appearance of his garb to mimic the same as the others.

When they got to the cells, they found that only a few of them were occupied. Swint and Veston began calling softy for Alekan. After a few minutes, they heard a response. The cell was medium sized, but there was no bedding; only straw covered the floor. Merion tried the keys until he found the correct matching one. He turned the lock, and Swint rushed in to greet his father. The others stayed outside, watching for trouble. Alekan stood and strode to the exterior hall and thanked them. He extended his hand in greeting and shook Kelduun's first, then the others.

"I am Alekan Broce. I see you have met my son, Swint. My sincerest gratitude to you. I cannot believe that I got to see my son again."

There were tears in his eyes.

"We must hurry. We do not want to be caught and placed in the same position we rescued you from," Dur said to him.

"We came in the pirate ship, father. It will take us home again.

My new friends are going to the Horgangee Mountains. They are looking for a dragon!"

"Slow down. I don't understand any of this."

"The story will be told to you in full, but after we get safely away from here," Tiras replied.

There was a shuffle behind them, and they turned. There was no one else in the corridor, but they heard a croaking laugh.

"I know something of dragons."

It came from the cell directly opposite from Alekan's.

"Did you say something?" Merion asked.

"He is always talking about something. He never shuts up. He is always going on about how he almost got away with it. Or that he would be part of the Ring," Alekan relayed to them.

"What do you know about dragons?" Panalt asked the prisoner.

"If you let me out, I will tell you all I know. My name is Vonne Rekt, and I know things about this place."

Merion looked at Panalt and Kelduun. This was not the purpose of this journey, and there was something odd about this man.

"We will let you out if you tell us more. How do we know you won't give us away to the slavers?" Merion goaded him.

Vonne Rekt threw his hands up and walked about in his cell muttering. Then he came back to the gate quickly.

"Why would I give you away? Can't trust anyone in a cell, can you? You trusted him," Rekt pointed across the hallway toward Alekan.

Merion dangled the key ring from his finger.

"I know how to control them! The dragons! I know things. I was the wizards' servant. I could be a wizard too someday. They didn't trust me. I couldn't show them what I knew. They would have sent me away, but they knew I would come back. I can control the dragons!"

"He may be of value to us," Panalt said to his mates. "Let's take him with us and have some straight talk. I want to know what he knows."

Merion let him loose. Vonne Rekt almost stumbled in his haste to flee the cell.

"Freedom! Precious freedom."

"We are not free yet. We have to get out of this place," Ashlyn reminded him.

"I know secrets. I know ways. There are hidden passages through the keep. The wizards do not use them, but we servants do. We need to get up and down and bring them things. They do not want to see us, so we have to use the back ways."

He led them to the entrance of the corridor to the cells. There was a hidden door, intricately disguised as a rocky face. He pushed on it, and it gave and opened, sliding into the wall.

"We use the newest slaves to help with delivering their goods. New slaves are not as dirty. Once they are processed, we take them up."

They sneaked into the hole in the wall, and it closed behind them. There was a narrow set of steps hewn out of the stone that went upward. It branched after several flights, and Rekt made a choice to go to the left. When they emerged, they were back in the pig pen, where they were supposed to be resting.

"I don't know how you managed to get down to the mine without using one of these back ways. You must have been lucky not to run into a loyal servant. Wizards do not come below the second floor, but servants do all of the time. It is where we separate the goods before ducking back into the hidden passages."

"Why do you help them? The wizards?" Ashlyn asked him.

"They let you do things. They said I could be a wizard some day."

Kelduun thought this may be the answer, but this line of thinking would only work on a weak mind. If you bought into this, you would make a good servant. If you did not, your time would be spent dreaming of escape, or cut short.

They went to the rear end of the stable area and simply unlatched the door. It opened to the side of the grassy area around the pier. The pirate schooner was still there, as Panalt predicted it would be.

"And now for my trick…" Vonne started to say.

"Do not do anything!" Kelduun scolded him. "We will leave you here if you give us away."

"But, I haven't gotten to use it yet," Vonne complained.

"Whatever it is, it can wait," Panalt said to him.

The grassy area was busy with slaves packing crates, rolling barrels, and stacking sacks. They would try to blend in the best they could. Each walked over to the delivery point and milled around. Then, one by one, they casually walked up the gangplank and back onto the ship.

"Captain, set us free. Let us make haste while we go," Panalt said to Bultan.

"I do not know how you manage the things you do. You must have luck with you," he replied.

"It does not hurt to have a sorcerer on your side," Ashlyn said.

They quickly cast off the mooring lines and were underway. Even the captain was eager to get out of the lagoon. It was not customary to stay, and he did not like to be in the company of the Wizards of the Ring. Too many stories were told about the powers they had. He did not care to see any of it, only make his runs and get paid.

By the time they were nearing the mouth of the lagoon, there seemed to be a commotion around the docking area they just left. Fortunately, they slipped out of the entrance to the tower's breakwater before they could be stopped. There was only a minimal sigh of relief. Outside of the confines of the breakwater, the ocean picked up in ferocity until the archipelago was in sight. They made land, and the captain spoke to the group.

"Be gone with you. You managed to make a mockery of me and may have sabotaged my contract with the Ring. I wish never to set eyes upon you again. If I do, I will be prepared to kill."

They left without fanfare and paddled their way back to the safety of the next island. As they lounged on the beach, Panalt reflected on the whirlwind of events spanning the past two days. The pirate captain would surely have to provide answers on his next visit to the tower in the sea. His lot in life had surely changed, and he may have even been listed for an early death at the hands of Shentille. It was only a matter of time before the sorcerers in that tower were made aware of the escape of the prisoners. Panalt had a pang of remorse over the way that they used Bultan, but their plight was much greater than the scallywag's at the moment.

Panalt then turned his mind to the events in the dungeon, and more emotions flooded his consciousness. He had never taken a man's life before. It had to be done, but it did not feel good. He did not feel like a hero. Panalt was silent for a long time thinking on this. Presently, he cleared his head and stood. He strode to where their new guest was sitting, and then he spoke to Vonne Rekt.

"Now, tell us what you know."

"They trained me to do things. I was a good helper until they turned on me. I was the one who made the potions."

"Wait, you have to start at the beginning," Panalt coached him.

"They always look for new spells," Rekt said, confirming what Kelduun had told them earlier. "They want to be able to have control of things. They use the land to the north as their play ground. They change things and reform the landscape. They use the dragons to do it."

"How?" Merion asked.

"There is a sequence of things to do. There is a flower that grows in the Horgangee Mountains. It can be dried and crushed into a powder. You then mix it with bee's honey and sweet coconut water."

"It doesn't sound like much," Dur said.

"That is all it takes though. The hard part is getting the dragons to eat it. The flower is potent. The petals have a chemical in them to

178

hypnotize the dragons. Each one will come when called, and it lasts for many days. I got into trouble because I heard one of the calls used by the wizards. They did not want me to have that power, so they locked me away."

"What is the call?"

"Listen…" Rekt whistled loudly. "The first tone the dragons hear is the call that they will respond to. If you do not do it exactly the same each time, they will not come, or you will not be in control."

They turned in for the night. Making simple lean-tos, they had a meager shelter for the night. When they awoke in the morning they were confronted by a new terror.

A dragon was sitting on the beach. It was enormous and adorned with red armored scaling from its eyes to the tip of its tail. The belly showed a broad silver stripe. The watchful eyes were green, surrounded by gold. The wings were folded and tucked behind it as it sat upright.

"It worked!" Rekt exclaimed

"Vonne, what do we do with it?" Ashlyn asked.

"I don't know. I never called a dragon before," he replied.

Rekt approached it, but the dragon reared up and brought a clawed attack down only inches from him. Rekt quickly whistled his tone, and the dragon settled. Having been imprinted by his master, the dragon was now docile.

Rekt stepped close to it and touched it. The scales were slippery but sharp at the points. He leaned into it, but it did not budge. It acted like a house dog, trained yet ready to play.

"Unbelievable!" Kelduun said in awe. "This is unlike anything in the tomes. This is a power that no one else knows of. The Wizard's Ring is responsible for this, but we can use it to our benefit."

Rekt leapt onto the dragons back and gently whispered to it. It reared and flapped its great wings.

"I'll take my leave now," he called down.

"You cannot leave now, we need your help," Ashlyn begged him.

"I have repaid my debt. You set me free. I told you what you needed. What you do with the information is your own business."

The dragon rose up and jumped before sweeping its wings down, gusting the small group and lifting away.

"Can you stop him, Kelduun?" Merion asked.

"I could, but would the dragon charge us? He is correct. He owes us nothing more than what he gave. Let us concentrate on obtaining the ingredients we need. If we can find enough, we will have a dragon of our own, rather than just one that needs time to grow. Think of the power a fully grown dragon would possess!"

"We need to get to work then," Panalt finished for him.

XIV

The battle took its toll on the attacking army for the first three days. King Vernon Secandor had planned well and had even foreseen where the shortcomings in the plan would come. The combined armies of Caldorn and Strayos had not had a loss yet, but they could not hold this enemy at bay forever.

The archers lined the battlement just behind the nearest deeply dug trench. Over and over, they let rounds of arrows fly. The arrows were delivered in such a torrent because of the system devised by the king's engineers. The set up consisted of a long plank that could be swung up and down to change its angle. On the plank many bows were affixed, and each had a catch point to hold the taught wire. Arrows were nocked at each catch point and fired in rapid succession. Rather than having a single shot ballista, this multiple shot approach ballista system took a little time to load the contraption, but the results were deadly. One man was capable of firing many arrows. With the ballistae set up every few feet, the barrage of ammunition spent nearly stopped the onslaught.

The first day saw a great victory for Strayos, as they saw that the arrows had the desired effect. The thicker arrows stopped the fiends dead in their tracks. There was hope along the ranks of men that their planning may let them live. They watched as line after line of enemies fell.

There was little retaliation, and the forces for freedom were unharmed. The monsters did not carry weapons and had no bows to fire the arrows back. They relied on their grotesquely created bodies as the killing machines. They took massive losses because of it, but the numbers were still heavily in their favor.

As King Secandor predicted, the dead began to pile up before the first trench. Soon after, they began to fall into it. The horde was not made of intellectuals, and it took them almost the entire day to figure out that the dead bodies could fill the trench before they could advance. The moment they made to use their own dead as a bridge, King Secandor instructed his archers to load fired arrows and proceed. The arrows struck down the monsters and ignited an inferno. The tar had caught fire and blazed high into the sky. There were black tendrils whisking from the tips of the flames. For several minutes, the men of Strayos could not see the enemies at all, the flames were so great.

The enemy horde was scorched and had to withdraw. The inferno persisted for many hours and effectively ended the fighting for the day. Knowing that there were six trenches all prepared in the same fashion, King Secandor estimated he could last at least a week, before a new plan would need to be devised.

The next day was nearly identical with the exception that the monsters started this day by filling the trench with bodies. The inferno had died down, but the earth was still hot. This ultimately was not an issue, as the bodies thrown down acted as a buffer to those marching over them.

Again, the arrows were launched. Then the fire arrows after, and finally the bonfire was ignited in the second trench, ending another day of fighting. This tactic was scoring kill after kill, and even the King was thinking he could pull off the defense of his country. The problem with his planning was that there was no great recourse after the trenches had all been filled in. There was no secondary area to retreat to and set up another effective defense.

The next day began with the continuation of that thought. They would need more kills before they could be satisfied with a retreat. This was a disease he was fighting. It could not be left free to transmit itself to the other peoples in the lands. There could be no enemy left standing before he would rest. He was pondering this as the third trench flared in the background behind him. There were only three remaining.

He strode to the very rear of his camp and found what he was seeking. There was a squire waiting whose only job was to keep the falcon of Kelduun. The sorcerer left it with the King, reminding him to keep him informed. Kelduun told him that he could leave the falcon with the King and that if he needed it, he would call it. Any message that needed sent by Strayos would be received when the falcon found Kelduun's energy again.

Vernon Secandor wrote a note and tucked it into the cylinder. Then he released the bird and watched it until it was only a black speck in the sky.

** ** ** ** **

The coconuts were easy to find. Each of the islands was plentiful with them. The bees proved to be annoying adversaries. They looked for what seemed hours to find the hive. When they did, they heard it before they could set their eyes upon it. The great orb hung in an ancient tree that stood above the others in the jungle. It was buzzing with life. Hunters surrounded it, and gatherers came and went.

The twins shot through it with arrows and severed its ties to the limb. The hive fell and crashed into the jungle's floor, exploding with thousands of angry stingers. The ferocity of the hive was set loose upon any living creature in the area, and the group had to retreat. When they returned, Kelduun struck up a fireball in his hand that he quickly extinguished into a ball of smoke. The magical smoke stayed spherical, though one could see it rolling and reaching to be freed of the invisible bond.

Kelduun thrust his smoke ball out and over the hive, effectively diminishing the rage of the bees. They slowly dropped down and were immobilized. This enabled the twins and Swint to gather what remained of the nectar and honey after the crash. It seemed to be enough to make a good quantity of the elixir they needed.

The next step was to use the dinghy to bring them to the northern shore and the base of the Horgangee Mountain range. Once arriving at their destination, Alekan, Swint and Veston departed and headed back to their coastal port of Azloth.

"Many thanks, my friends," Alekan said to the group. "It is because of you that I can be free. My time from this day to my death will be given in thanks for a strange band of heroes that came to my aid."

"You are most welcome," Panalt started. "If it were not for Swint's kindness, we would not have been able to recover and pursue our goal."

"You are welcome in my house in any time of need. I am eternally in your debt," Alekan finished, with Swint beaming behind him.

The group nodded back.

Panalt's crew was left alone then, being much farther up the coast than they would have gotten on foot alone. The treacherous voyage over the mountains was avoided by their detour over the water.

"Vonne Rekt said that the flower was located on the mountain. We had better get started," Merion reminded them.

"Keep your eyes open, now. We may see a dragon at any time," Kelduun coached them. "If we do not have the elixir made before we see one, it may be tragic."

They started up the slope and found it still dense with forestry. Further up, as the trees dwindled, they found more grasses and flowering. None of the flowers seemed to match the description of what they were looking for, so they continued their climb.

The day grew old, and they decided to stop for the night. There was no cover, as the trees were lower in altitude now, and the wind was constant. Night fell upon them, but it was less dark than any of their trip to this point. The moon was lit brilliantly white; the stars in the sky hinted of the greater vastness of the universe behind them.

Just as Ashlyn's tired eyes were closing, she thought she saw a flash of light. She opened her eyes and sat upright. Maybe it was her imagination. She waited for a moment before deciding to lay back down. This time she left her eyes open and watched. It took several more minutes, but there was a shadow flying through the air just to the east of their position. There was another flash, and she knew that the source could only be fire from the mouth of a dragon.

It was guarding its territory from an intruder and swooped into the valley over the crest of the hill they stayed on. She quickly woke the others, and they scrambled to the summit to peer over it.

The two dragons were squaring off. The instigating dragon was smaller, but no coward. It was pawing the air and letting small spurts of fire escape with each exhale. The defender that Ashlyn saw flying in the sky earlier was much larger and had a powerful looking stance. It walked around the intruder on all four legs. Possessing two pairs of wings, this formidable giant was easily twice the size of the dragon that Vonne Rekt rode away on.

The larger dragon scorched the ground before pouncing and clipped the wing of the challenger. They tussled for just a moment before the smaller dragon tried to escape. It was already wounded, and it lumbered to fly away. The resident dragon did not pursue it after winning the rite to remain in this valley.

It was very quiet now; they could see the brooding dragon circling a few times before laying down. Their target was in sight. They only had to find the flower and mix the elixir.

The next sun rose a few hours later, and they cautiously crept to the summit again to see if the dragon had moved. Their hearts sunk when they saw open ground beneath them. The dragon had moved stealthily on during the night.

They continued along the ridge of the peak they climbed. The descent on the opposite side of the rise had a bright purple clump of flowers half way down. That was what they were looking for. The purple petals were accented by a white variegated center; the stems were a muted grey. As they got closer to the flowers, they began to pick up the mildly burnt odor emanating from the ground around the dragon's conflict the night prior.

Once Ashlyn gathered the flowers, Kelduun drew out his fire. They quickly withered and became drier. Just as they were about to grind them down on a stone and make the powder, they heard a shriek to the east. When they turned, they saw the same dragon from the previous night racing toward them. The group dropped to take cover and hoped that their grey cloaks would camouflage them on the peak.

The dragon flew overhead, not giving attention to the cluster of lightly colored boulders. It headed straight into the valley as if it was its home. Satisfied that there was not another dragon in the area, it circled again and lay down. It stayed there for a long time then. The afternoon was waning and evening crept on. The dragon got up and flew off without looking in their direction.

The group was stunned, until Kelduun spoke up.

"They must be attracted to the fire. Clearly, this one keeps returning. Maybe it has its lair around here. At least, it thinks this area is worth protecting against other dragons. Last night it was a dragon indeed. Today, when I fired the flowers, I must have invited it. It probably thought there was another dragon coming to call this valley its own. Dragons have keen eyesight. We are fortunate it did not spy us out. Our cloaks provided just enough cover to deceive the dragon. I suspect we got lucky in that a dragon was the only thing this one was after."

"If that is the case, then I have a plan," Panalt said to them.

Ashlyn stayed on the ridge with Kelduun and ground the flower petals down into the pasty elixir while the men descended into the valley. After a short time of searching, they found the spot that was the center of the commotion. Tucked lightly into a bowl shaped eroded rock were four eggs that were cracked open.

They had the answer of why this dragon was so protective. It was protecting its future offspring. The eggs had hatched already, but the dragon still maintained the area as its home. How long it would stay in this area could not be predicted, but they would need to act fast. They couldn't miss their window of opportunity.

After joining Ashlyn and Kelduun, Panalt told them of what he planned to do. They layered some of the elixir on the eggs and lit a fire. The dragon came as predicted, the same silver beast with the double set of wings. It was a magnificent creature. They held their breath as it stalked the area, sniffing and exhaling small bursts of fire. It inspected the site around the eggs, getting very close to them.

"Stay here," Panalt instructed them. "I am going to try calling it. Do not come down the ridge. If it goes wrong, save yourselves. I do not know if he has taken the bait, but I have to try it now."

Panalt crawled away from the group, so as not to sacrifice them as well as he, should he fail. After he cautiously slithered half way down the hill, he gave a whistle.

The dragon turned sharply to address the sound and jumped into the air. It landed only feet from Panalt and studied him. The group on the ridge was unable to do anything to save him now.

Panalt whistled again and stood. The dragon reared but stayed on the ground. Panalt stood motionless. The dragon inched toward him, sniffing. The exhaled hot air smelled of burning and was all about Panalt. The gusting breaths actually ruffled his clothing. Panalt whistled very softly a third time, and the dragon laid down at his feet. He was its master now. He turned to call to the group behind him, and they joined him.

"It can be done. We know how to do it. Why stop at one dragon, when we can each master one and put the evil army down for good?" Panalt said to them.

It was what Kelduun was thinking, and he smiled that Panalt again took the lead here.

"We will not have to work so hard for the next ones. I have a different plan," Panalt said.

They slept the night and prepared in the morning. Panalt mounted his new steed and took to the air. From an aerial vantage point, he could see for miles and could direct his team below to where they needed to go.

Once they found suitable targets, the plan was to hunt down elk, kill them, and coat them in the elixir. This would be the offering to the next dragons. They separated and each got their elk. They then set fires and called their dragons. One by one, they were successful in obtaining their battle companion.

Kelduun would ride with Panalt. His dragon was by far the largest; and therefore, Kelduun did not need to call upon the dragons.

The final night in the Horgangee Mountains was a picture that no one would ever forget. The team slept in a tight circle surrounded by five fully grown dragons.

Kelduun awoke first. The sun's first rays were just easing into the black blanket of night. The graying band was being displaced by the faint orange light. It was before the sun peaked over the mountains that he heard the familiar screech. He turned and raised his hand to let his falcon perch on it. This would be an update on the war to the south. He read the scrawled note from King Secandor.

WE HAVE HELD OUR GROUND
ENEMY NUMBERS ARE OVERWHELMING
WE MAY HAVE KILLED HALF OF THEM
STILL OUTNUMBERED FIVE TO ONE
ONLY HAVE THREE DAYS UNTIL WE RETREAT

The news was grim. The enemy force seemed insurmountable. The battles could not be fought like any in the past history of men. Not one of the fiends could get through the lines. If it did, the disease would spread and all would be lost. Kelduun knew that time was running out for everyone.

His falcon could cover ground faster than any carrier pigeon ever known. Still, this message was already a day and a half old. He wrote his note back to the King and held onto hope. It would be close to arriving late, if not for the great speed of the falcon.

** ** ** ** **

"Tobin! And not a moment to spare!" King Secandor nearly jumped on him as he dismounted from his horse.

"How do we fare?" Tobin asked him.

"Things have gone according to the plan we devised. We have kept them at bay. We have not had a single loss. There are still two trenches left, but the monsters have been trying to launch themselves in their catapults. So far we have been able to intercept these aerial attacks and have shot them down. You can see the littered bodies between the last trenches," King Secandor pointed. "Who is this with you?"

"My name is Argenit. I am one of the leaders of the nomadic clans."

"I have twenty thousand men with me. Most are trained hunters and archers," Tobin finished for him.

"This nearly doubles our forces, but still we have precious little ground to give. Have them release any arrows they have at the enemy horde. They are quite susceptible to fire. Do not to hit the trenches with any arrows until I give the command."

With nearly forty thousand troops under his command, the odds were reduced to a three to one balance. It was better, but still severely lopsided. The eve of that night saw the fifth trench blazing. There was only one trench left before they would have to leave the field. The army was tired. They had to move the ballistae even further back, as they had done each night previously. This would be the last time they were moved before being set ablaze as well. They could take no chance of the enemy figuring out how to use this weapon against them.

It was midnight. The fifth trench was still burning. There was a small repose between the fighting. King Secandor was delivered the message he had been waiting for. It was from Kelduun.

On our way to you

Watch for my sign to the north

You will know us by the sign of water driven by fire

Take no chances with this enemy

You will do well to shoot your own men before they turn into fiends

Cryptic as always, the King thought.

"I hope we do not have to retreat before we get this sign," he said aloud.

The rest of the night was sleepless. Vernon could not put Kelduun's note to good thought. He did not say anything about retreating. He made it sound as though it would be easy to sacrifice his men and send them forward. But this was war, and drastic measures must be taken to ensure this victory. Maybe that was what the sorcerer wanted the King to think about.

He paced in his tent until he saw the band of light to the east. It was the dawn of the sixth day. The last of their fortifications would be spent today. Tomorrow's fighting would be costly for the free peoples of the lands.

** ** ** ** **

The power of the dragons was immeasurable. The speed at which they flew was unknown before this very morning. Ashlyn had to hold on with everything she had to keep a grip as the wind continually struggled to free her of her mount.

It only took a day to reach the island of Trecania. The vast forested area below was so large that it almost seemed as if they had reached the mainland. They landed, thinking that the dragons would need to be rested. Each was surprised when they dismounted and found the dragons not even so much as breathing heavily.

"We will camp and proceed at dawn," Kelduun said.

"How much longer do you think it will take to get there?" Merion asked him.

"I think it will take another day. But it depends much on where the battle is. If they have maintained their defenses, they should still be closer to the border of Gildesh and Strayos," Kelduun answered.

"Between the mountains," Merion said.

"We will be flying over Gildesh," Dur said.

"I hope there is something left to save," Tiras said with him.

"Cities can be rebuilt. When we save Strayos, we save ourselves," Panalt said.

"Before we leave this island, there is something we must do. It will swing the tide in our favor, so to speak," Kelduun said to them. "Rest now, and I will wake you in the morning."

They mounted their dragons again in the morning. Kelduun instructed them what to do as they did so. Coming around to the very southwestern tip of the island, they found it to be a sheer wall of stone. The cliff was nearly vertical, standing six hundred feet tall.

The group took their mounts and guided the dragons to encircle the peak of it. Giving some area between them, they each had their dragons blow the ultra hot flame toward the rock. Slowly the stone heated and then began to smoke. The rock turned a slight orange color, then red, under the heat. As the rock heated further, the mountain actually began to liquefy under the immense heat. The melting rock was under the unbearable pressure of gravity pulling at its weight, and a great shard broke free, plummeting into the sea.

The splash rose almost to the height that they were flying at. The result was a great wave, reaching forty feet high. It sped quickly to the south, west, and east. The shock wave was blindingly fast. Before they could guide their team of dragons to turn toward Gildesh, the wave was at the horizon.

** ** ** ** **

It started as a low rumble. The tide shrunk back hundreds of feet, exposing the glistening sand underneath. Plant life was left tangled on the ground, instead of gently floating in the current. Even some fish were caught by surprise and were flopping on the drying sea bed.

There was no one left in Gildesh to witness it. The tsunami came, fast and devastating. Not losing much of its momentum, it remained at over thirty feet as it washed over everything along the coast. Covering ground from the bulge near Brondin, it engulfed the entire coastline of Gildesh. The mighty forest of Albinion stood against it, but anything not securely rooted down was washed inland.

The force of the water's battery crashed upon the avalanche at the border of Caldorn. The immovable obstacle that turned away the monster's army was dashed and shattered. If not for this barrier, Caldorn would have suffered as Gildesh did.

The water rushed so far inland that it got diverted by the Vitirral Mountain range. It was still rapid in velocity as it struck the rear line of the enemy horde. Great numbers of the attackers were decimated and still the water came on. The tsunami wiped out as many of the fiends in mere minutes as the entire defensive strategy of Strayos did in the past five days. When King Secandor looked out over the field he could see the waters blasting toward the enemy's rear. Above the wave, flames licked and curled, their black soot blooming upward. He remembered Kelduun's message, 'Watch for my sign of water driven by fire'. The King ordered a massive retreat of his forces. The water ultimately slowed and settled near the second trench.

King Secandor retook his stance overlooking the field and watched as the wave of death continued into a new phase. There were five dragons bearing down over the enemy's ranks, breathing fire throughout the region. Nothing could withstand the inferno created by this attack. It was a systematic sterilization of the area.

His men stood in awe. Neither running, nor preparing to fight, they watched the dragons as they took no mercy on the monsters before them. When the carnage was complete, the dragons turned toward them. Each swooped down and landed inside of the sixth trench. Again the soldiers were dumbfounded as men jumped off of each mount and bade the dragons to be still.

Panalt's group then stood together. As Panalt held up his arm in salute, King Secandor gave the word. A cry of victory rose up throughout each line of men.

XV

"Have we done it?" Dur looked at Panalt.

"I think it is finished!" Tiras replied. "There are no enemies left on the field. We have beaten them."

Ashlyn raced to King Secandor and asked him to escort her to see her mother. He sent a scout with her to find the Queen. She was waiting at the rear of the camp. Embracing each other, there were tears in their eyes.

"It is because of you that we saved Strayos," King Secandor said to the group. "How did you accomplish this?" he said, pointing to the dragons.

"It was a feat requiring all of our wits and skills," Panalt answered him.

"When you flew over, how much destruction did you see in Gildesh?" King Secandor asked.

Panalt hung his head slightly.

"No doubt, it was a wasteland after the monsters had their way with the land. But then the tsunami took its toll, as well. It will be a long time before anything can call that land a home," Panalt said to him.

"There is but one more thing to accomplish," Kelduun said, changing the conversation's direction. "Evil still lurks in the mountains. The warlock is still in his fortress at the Fountain."

They turned to him, having temporarily forgotten the source of all that had transpired.

"What needs to be done?" the King asked.

"We must take him down. If he lives, he will spread the disease again," Kelduun answered.

"We nomads will do our part. We will travel over the Valley and lay siege to the plateau. We will be the new keepers of the Fountain," Argenit said in anger.

"I do not know if the Fountain can even be saved. But the evil master must be vanquished. If your men wish to help, then do as you said and come across the Valley of Whent. We may need you to help contain anything we come across," Kelduun replied to him. "A different approach may be the true answer here. Panalt?"

Reading his mind, Panalt strode to his dragon.

"I can fly there faster than any force on the ground!"

"I am with you, brother!" said Dur.

"And I too, brother!" Tiras said.

"You have me at your side, My Lord," Tobin bowed, taking up his old role as advisor to the royalty of Gildesh.

"Tobin, it is good to have you, and we need you. After all this time and after so much loss, you are the family we have left," Panalt said unto him.

"You will need this!"

Tobin drew the talisman sword from his back and presented it to Kelduun. The blade was alive and pulsed as he did so.

"I cannot wield it. It may kill me to do so. I can feel the power within it from here," Kelduun said warily.

Panalt took it in his hand and noted the electrical vibe surrounding it. This blade would be deadly to anything magical.

"We will rise and conquer!" Panalt said to his new team.

He looked for Ashlyn in the crowd of soldiers. She was just making her way back to the front lines with her mother in tow. Panalt and Ashlyn came together in an embrace. He whispered in her ear.

"We will be together again."

She nodded, a tear dripped from her left eye.

"Stay with your mother. I will come for you."

They separated, and she drew back to the crowd. Merion stepped forward.

"I have been with you this long. I will come with you and offer what help I can."

Panalt grasped his outstretched hand, and they shook in agreement. The new team was set. Kelduun would again ride with Panalt. Dur, Tiras, Tobin and Merion would each have their own steed. Before they departed, Ashlyn whistled to settle her dragon. Then she went to Tobin and taught him the call to master it.

The team mounted and readied for flight. Panalt warned Tobin of the immense force the dragons could create and bade him to hold on tightly. They took the shortest route from their origin to the Fountain and flew over the Valley of Whent.

As in other parts of the lands, it was being destroyed by the dark magic emanating from the Fountain. The ground seemed blackened. There were funnels of wind dipping toward the earth. The tornadoes were many, and they reached down to the earth like probing fingers. The riders had to dodge between the twisters. The closer they got to the Fountain, the worse the tornadoes were in ferocity and the number present. It was as if the winds knew they were against them.

When the group finally came west enough to visualize the Western Vitirral Mountains, they could see the black billowing smog. The cloud cover was as dense as a volcano's eruption; the very air was noxious. Lightning bolts were jousting in every direction. The area around the base of the plateau was equally turbulent. There was an immense sand storm engulfing the entire western end of the Valley. The earth here had seen the last of its aura pulled from it, and the decayed plains were whipping into a frenzy. The sand created a wall, advancing to the east.

Had the party been on foot, the Valley would have been impassible. Even riding through the clouds had its dangers, but the dragons' strength and swiftness kept them out of harm's way.

As they approached the plateau, they could see the massive fortress. Spreading out to cover the Fountain, it encased the waterfall on the mountainside. The giant was standing there, waiting for them. The dragons sped downward and spewed flames upon him. He remained motionless, allowing the fires to engulf him. He was still standing when they finished their attack, impervious to the heat. Smoke was rising from his shoulders. The black cloak he wore was shifting independent of his arms' movement; the cowl drew back, exposing his face. The red eyes were filled with anger.

The dragons landed, and the men dismounted. The dragons stayed behind the riders.

"Did you think fire could take me?" the warlock's voice was powerfully strong as it echoed along the walls of the precipice. "I control the very earth you stand upon!"

The dark conjurer outstretched his arms. Cracks spread from his position and crept to the attacking party. They widened into fissures, and lava from deep inside the earth welled up, giving the plateau a veined appearance.

The twins and Merion each readied their bows and shot. The arrows found their mark in the warlock's chest, causing him to take a step backward. He remained on his feet looking down at the damage done and smirked. He broke each shaft at its entry point, and the skin scarred quickly over the wounds.

"Mortal weapons will not harm him!" Kelduun shouted, witnessing the warlock's action.

Kelduun lifted both of his hands high in the air. At each of his fingertips grew a long white light. In a split second, the light morphed into arrows of his own, driven by magic. Kelduun brought his left hand down and flung the arrows in the direction of the necromancer.

This got a reaction from their adversary. Clearly knowing the danger of the light arrows, the warlock jumped back. He was bobbing and ducking until they each plunged into the earth and disappeared. When he was finished, he looked at Kelduun with menace. There were still more arrows to dodge.

The cloak that the giant wore now moved again. This time, it revealed his full body. Not a cloak at all, it separated and unfurled into enormous, sinewy wings. The veins could be seen through their translucent covering. His bluish skin was accented by previous wounds and scars, opening and closing. The warlock leapt into the air. Kelduun released his other hand, and the arrows shot into the air. The demon dove, then hovered. He again outstretched his arms, and the fissures creeping toward the party widened further. The lava burst upward in walls and separated the party.

The fiery walls were spilling down and caught Dur before he could retreat. The lava seared his face and left side of his body. Tiras jumped to save him, but the damage was already done. Panalt went to them. Dur was already slipping toward unconsciousness, the shock overwhelming him. The sword in Panalt's hand was pulsating. He grasped it and concentrated. As he raised the sword, it flashed and lit up. His energy was being focused into it. White magic began to form a barrier around the men.

"I will watch over him," Tiras said to his older brother. "Go!"

Panalt now understood a little more about what the blade could do. He knew there was unbridled magic in the sword; it could be made to enhance the powers of its owner.

Kelduun conjured new light arrows and was beginning to release them. Again the beast dodged, but one of the arrows pierced a huge hole in the right wing, and another seared its leg. The pale blue devil tumbled slightly before regaining control of the wing. In the end, he was forced to the ground.

Once there, the wing began to remake itself. It was healing before their eyes. The warlock could use his own energy to heal himself, but the amount of energy it took kept him grounded a little while longer. Panalt took his chance and rushed to him.

Seeing Panalt dashing to the warlock, Kelduun lit new arrows and shot them into the ground surrounding the two in a ring. The demon was hemmed in by the magical light arrows and now was in a duel with Panalt and his white blade.

The warlock attacked with his clawed hands. Panalt blocked with the sword. He had no other defense. The powerful blow staggered Panalt, but he did not release his grip on the sword. As Panalt looked at his opponent, he noted the burn on the evil master's hand where he struck out. The monster could be injured with this blade.

Panalt feigned a jab motion with the sword. The warlock was eager to avoid the attack and moved too quickly, before realizing he had been fooled. Panalt now had an opening and took it. He spun quickly severing one of the wings, close to the base.

Smoke poured out of the wound, and the necromancer whirled about. He was forced to choose upon using more energy to heal himself or fight on the ground. Panalt struck again, this time in a downward swinging motion. The warlock caught the sword between his hands and held it tight. The blade was melting through the skin of its hands, and the beast let it go.

The dark conjurer thrust his arms down and opened a chasm directly in front of Panalt. Lava rushed up, but was blocked by another field created by the sword. The demon had no recourse. His magic was failing him in the face of the wielder of the white blade.

Panalt swung again, slicing the midsection of the warlock. His enemy was brought to his knees by this. Again, black smoke belched from the wound. The warlock closed this laceration with his energy and stood tall again. The white arrows were beginning to fade. Soon he would not be confined in this area.

Kelduun was studying all that was occurring. He yelled out to Tobin and Merion.

"The Fountain! He can heal himself because of the Fountain!"

Tobin and Merion ran hard to their dragons. They were each still waiting at the edge of the plateau. Tobin nodded to Merion, and they took to the sky. The warlock was distracted by Panalt's attack.

The dragons descended on the hall which was built over the Fountain and landed on its rooftop. Their weight was enough to buckle the buttresses and collapse the structure. The broken rooftop had the appearance of a newly hatched egg. The walls stood erect and the jewel was in the center. The Fountain was exposed; its black waters were swirling, causing a cyclone in the center of it.

"Crush it!" Tobin yelled.

His dragon obeyed him and pounced onto the lip of it. The weight caused the entire front portion of the bowl to give way. The inky waters gushed out, spreading across the floor. When Tobin looked toward Panalt on the plateau, nothing seemed to change. The warlock was still fighting back.

"It is still flowing," Merion said to him.

Tobin turned back to him, and Merion pointed skyward.

"The source must be up there. This is only a basin. The Fountain must spring from the top."

They quickly flew to the summit. The black tower wrapped around the stone sides of the waterfall. There were no window holes along its ascent. The crown was easier to destroy than the hall below.

It was much smaller, and the thatching was not thick. There were no beams reinforcing the steeple.

Again the dragons made short work of the turret's rooftop. They peered inside and found the source. There were cut stones surrounding the orifice and another set of stones channeling the water down into the waterfall.

"How do we destroy it?" Tobin asked.

"I have seen the power before. We can do it again. The dragons are here for a reason," Merion answered him.

Merion's dragon separated itself from the tower and Tobin's followed. Their fiery breath was directed onto the orifice. Tobin watched as the water evaporated as quickly as it welled up from the earth. Then the stones began to glow, and the entire area heated to a scorching, bright white. The stones, which were cut to perfectly fit around the orifice, fell away and left the ground bare to the immense heat. The uppermost layers of dirt were blown away.

The water was still evaporating; next they came to solid stone. With a strong burst, the dragons let even more fire pour down on the source. When they finally stopped, the ground was fused closed. The flow of the waters was stopped. The Fountain was no more.

On the plateau, the ring of light arrows faded and disappeared. The necromancer was free to escape the ring of magic holding him hostage with his attacker slicing at him. Distancing himself a small margin, he stopped and tried to regenerate his slashed wing.

Nothing happened. The smoke had stopped coming out of the wound. He turned to cast his eyes at the smashed hall. The Fountain's basin was shattered. His eyes ran up the tower to the peak. The crown had been decapitated. Dragons were circling it. He lingered only a moment before the white blade surged out of his chest.

Panalt was behind him and drove the blade deep. It entered between the wings and ripped through to the other side.

The conjurer spat out black blood from his maw; the wound gaped open as Panalt drew the blade back.

"Finish him!" Tiras hollered at his brother.

The warlock slipped to his knees. Panalt swung again, taking the head off of its perch. The red eyes blinked as the head rolled a short distance away.

The ground began to tremble. The lava shrunk back, and the fissures began to close. The warlock's body remained upright. Smoke again was billowing from the severed neck. The smoke was issuing in a column directly into the heavens. It continued to mix with the ever present smog.

And then, it reversed. The smoke and the smog began to be drawn into the body. The wound was the portal; all that was toxic was being sucked inward. It took several moments, but the sky regained its color as the sweeping blackness was retrieved into the warlock's body. In the next instant, a blinding flash erupted from the body, and it was gone.

The group was left on the plateau staring at the carnage the dragons caused to the hall over the Fountain's basin.

After a moment, Tobin and Merion returned, and everyone was gathered around Dur. He was moaning and in obvious pain.

"The Fountain is gone now, brother. You'll have to heal up the old fashioned way," Tiras said to him.

"Can you do anything for him?" Panalt asked Kelduun.

"I can take his pain away, but he will need to heal," the sorcerer replied.

"We won't look like each other any longer," Tiras said sadly.

"But you are alive, and that is worth being thankful for. Your father would have been proud of each of you on this day," Tobin said to them. "And yours, as well," he said to Merion. "It is time we head home to embrace the family we have left."

Kelduun knelt down beside Dur and placed his hands on him. Gradually, Dur came around and was able to sit up. The sun was shining. It had been a full year since its rays fell upon the Western Vitirral Mountains. They rested then and watched the sun dip below the horizon, casting its red and purple hues over the peaks. The land was free again.

EPILOGUE

They flew to Strayos. The journey was longer than anticipated. Dur was not able to fly for very long before needing rest.

Out on the field before the city, the group dismounted from the dragons. The combined armies had made their way to Crute. Panalt spoke to his battle companion. "You are free, my friend. Go to your home in the north. I thank you for your service."

The dragon rose up as if waking from a deep sleep. It let out a long blast of fire into the air. Then it leapt up and circled the army on the ground. With another belch of fire, it turned north and flew off, neither turning around, nor wavering in its direction. The others bade their dragons to follow, releasing them of their duties.

They turned toward the gathered crowd of soldiers and saw that the sea of men parted, giving way to the front gate of the city before them. When they entered the city, the men were regarded as heroes. People were lining the streets, cheering. The scene was the same when they got to the circular walls around the castle of Crute. Everyone was waving and shouting praises.

"I have never been happier to be in another man's city," Tobin said, turning to them.

"You may stay in Crute as long as you wish," Merion replied. "I am sure my father will agree. We will have a banquet tonight that will be the talk for ages!"

"There is one thing I need to do before that," Panalt said to them.

He left and found Ashlyn in the crowd. She embraced him and kissed him strongly.

"How long will you stay in Crute?" he asked her.

"We have been given an invitation to stay as long as we wish," she replied.

"We have been extended the same."

"How long will you stay, Panalt?"

"Not long, I have business to attend to."

"Oh? What is it you need to do?" she asked him.

"I am going to rebuild Albinion and restore Gildesh."

"You'll do it on your own?"

He turned away slightly, but was smiling when he looked at her again.

"Myself and another…Will you be my Queen?"

ACKNOWLEDGMENTS

Writing this book was, for a long time, just a dream, or rather, one might say a collection thereof. Mostly everything you have just read has come from the depths of my innermost sub-consciousness. It laid dormant for quite a while before gaining enough power to compete with the myriad ideas in my mind. But once given some serious thought, that concept would take on its own persona, carving a niche in my mind that would not be readily dismissed. This step in the writing process was made possible by Lynn Simon. Without her, my mind would never have allowed the dream to flourish; and thus, this story would have remained locked tightly away.

I must then come to the simple matter of merely writing a book and then the subsequently major endeavor of publishing a book. In this, Allan McDougall was the cornerstone. As one of my very first readers, he surprised me when he conveyed that my ideas were good enough for an actual publication. One must get to know me a little to know that I did not believe him straightaway.

There were other primary test readers including Lynn Simon and John DiTommaso. I gave a copy of this to my mother, Deborah A. Salvatore, for a test of scrutiny. Lastly, my wife, Natalie Salvatore gave it a go-through to see just what I had been up to in my spare time. Their recommendations have shaped this book by enabling me rethink, clarify, and expand my manuscript.

Several other influencing factors were at work, such was quick opinions here and there about successfully overcoming the dreaded writer's block. As my co-workers, Amanda Averell and Brian C. Jones had nearly no choice but to hear some off-the-wall ideas. To any other contributors, know that I deeply valued anything you may have helped me with.

There would not be a book in your hands if it was not for my publishing team. D&GG Advertising's consultants Troy Grossi and Dawn Flenner, along with Allan McDougall with AM Publishing, have put many hours into honing this product. Their professionalism and dedication have surpassed my imaginings. It is because of their direction and creative input that I continued on the path. This has even allowed me to begin thinking of a sequel.

Lastly, I have one more thank you to give. That is to you, dear reader, for giving me the chance to entertain you, if only briefly.